Praise for *The Moon Tavern*

"What a wonderful read! The story made me laugh and swoon and made me hungry. Bravo!" —Beth Dooley, James Beard Award-winning author

"Like a trip to Croatia without the jet lag. This book is the perfect blend of local history and culture, paired with Ves's quest to connect with her roots and find herself. Add in a little romance, good food and wine, and boom! *The Moon Tavern* had me checking the expiration date on my passport." —Molly Mogren, writer and co-host of podcast, *Go Fork Yourself*

"A delicious hybrid—a historical novel, a contemporary romance, a travelogue, and celebration of food and wine! With humor and joie de vivre, Stephanie Hansen and Kurt Johnson bring to zesty life both the characters and setting, giving readers a book to savor, as well as the bonus recipes." —Lorna Landvik, bestselling author of *Angry Housewives Eating Bon Bons*

"In *The Moon Tavern*, food is an introduction to the past and helps untangle the story of departed family. It begins with the search for the perfect sandwich, and ends with the nourishment of wine and food made by someone who loves us. Pour yourself a glass of chilled Grk and step into the warm Croatian air. *The Moon Tavern* is like a good friend who throws a party I don't want to leave." —Patrice Johnson, author of *Land of 10,000 Plates: Stories and Recipes from*

Praise for Kurt Johnson's *The Barrens*

**Winner of the Minnesota Book Award
Goldie Awards for Best Debut Novel and Best Fiction
2022 Great Group Reads Selection**

"*The Barrens* grabbed me from the opening pages and never let go."   —Michael Punke, author of *The Revenant*

"A deeply compelling tale, told in vivid, elegant but concise prose, *The Barrens* carried me along, swiftly as the river at the heart of the story. Most highly recommended."
— Jeffrey Lent, author of *In the Fall*

"I've rarely come across a text so visual, and so tangible."
—Alex Messenger, author of *The Twenty-Ninth Day*

"*The Barrens* is a bravura work, propulsive in its storytelling, simultaneously economical and fulsome, and as restrained as it is brimming with unspoken wisdom."
—Peter Geye, Minnesota Book Award winner for *Wintering*

"A poignant and engaging thriller with a formidable lead character . . . A vibrant, tender novel of love, loss, stamina, and self-discovery."   —*Kirkus Reviews*

"Close encounters with migrating caribou, and a haunting, hallucinatory encounter with a white wolf lend magic to this survival tale."   —*Minneapolis Star Tribune*

Praise for Stephanie Hansen's *True North Cabin Cookbook*

"Everyone is seeking a simpler, more localized, and home-created lifestyle these days, and Stephanie Hansen's *True North Cabin Cookbook* delivers that by the barrel. You can smell the pine woods, hear the rain on the lake, feel the sun on your skin."   —Andrew Zimmern, award-winning TV host

"Stephanie Hansen has captured and elevated the Minnesota tradition of 'going to the lake' in her delicious recipes. This book is everything we love about being at the lake, without the mosquitoes."   — Zoë François, host of Zoë Bakes

"Thoroughly 'kitchen-cook friendly' in organization and presentation, *True North Cabin Cookbook* is an extraordinary and unreservedly recommended addition to personal, family, professional, and community library cookbook collections."
—*Midwest Book Review*

"The book is marked by personalized elements, too, as with Hansen noting that her efforts to gussy up the traditional Thanksgiving meal clashed with her family's requirements for store-bought stuffing mix, canned cranberry sauce, and frozen peas. Indeed, humorous stories and poignant accounts abound, as with a story about surviving breast cancer and memories of lost loved ones. . . . *Seasonal Recipes from a Cozy Kitchen* is a fun cookbook that oozes Minnesota charm."
—Rachel Jagareski, *Foreword Reviews*

ALSO BY STEPHANIE HANSEN

True North Cabin Cookbook Volume 1

True North Cabin Cookbook Volume 2

ALSO BY KURT JOHNSON

The Outlaw Shuffle

Las Vegas Turnaround

Rough Diamonds

The Barrens (with Ellie Johnson)

THE MOON TAVERN

A Culinary Love Story (with Recipes)

KURT JOHNSON
&
STEPHANIE HANSEN

Cover & Illustrations by Xee Reiter

First Published by Street Level Press

Copyright © 2026 Kurt Johnson &
Stephanie Hansen

All rights reserved.

This novel is entirely a work of fiction. The names, characters, and incidents portrayed in it are the work of the author's imagination. Any resemblance to actual persons, living or dead, events, or localities is entirely coincidental.

ISBN: 979-8-9900350-2-7

Street Level Press
www.StreetLevelPress.com

Acknowledgements

Thank you for reading this book. We both love writing, but more than that, we love having readers enjoy our writing. So, again, thanks.

Over our 30+ years of marriage, we've enjoyed traveling together, often in sailboats chartered at exotic locations. We've sailed the islands of the Croatian coast many times, and our favorite is always Lastovo with its sixteenth-century town, quaint taverns, and turquoise waters. But we love it all: Hvar, Korčula, Vis, Mljet, Split, Dubrovnik, and more. The people are always friendly and generous. This collaboration is really an ode to Croatian hospitality, food, and romantic settings.

We'd like to thank a few people who have helped with our journey. Dijana Jović set us straight on our use of the Croatian language and depictions of its culture. Then Stan Law guided us through the Croatian islands while on tour with friends. Stan was instrumental in helping us understand Croatian history, culture, and daily life—in his extremely entertaining way. Finally, it was the archaeologist Dinko Radić who, on our first trip to Croatia, after casually striking up a conversation at a pizzeria in Vis, gave us a personal tour of a Roman archaeological site along with his own dig in Vela Luka. He is the namesake of our handsome protagonist.

For Ellie and Kate

The fish must be fresh, the olive oil homemade, and the company good.

— Dalmatian Saying

Each lunch contained soup, a salad, two side dishes and a main meal. Baked fish and sliced potatoes along with fish soup, all slathered in olive oil, maybe pan-fried pork chops, with a sliced cabbage salad, and baked eggplant, or chicken, with chicken soup and a carrot and beet salad, and lots and lots of something called *blitva*.

— Cody McClain Brown, *Chasing a Croatian Girl*

PART ONE

Lastovo Island

The Perfect Sandwich

Where should I begin my story? I try to think back through the turning points, those pivotal events that set you on a new course through life. I could go back to when I was adopted by this polite American couple after my mother and father were killed in the Yugoslavian Wars. It's certainly important and becomes integral to what I'm about to relay, but starting there is like starting in the womb, and that's for sure going back too far. Meeting Reed? Yes, I could begin with seeing him for the first time in his preppy outfit as he began working at the same restaurant where I was Chef. Or maybe when I first caught him cheating. I won't start there either.

Central to my story is love and family, and I want to start in Croatia, where I first met this man, Dinko—I know, funny name. But I wouldn't know his name until much later. All I knew at the time was that he held my hair as I vomited over the side of the ferryboat during my voyage out to the small island of Lastovo. So, let me start with where I bought the food that fell into the white-capped waves of the Adriatic Sea.

That story starts in Split, right after I left the ruins of Diocletian's Palace. I'd spent that morning strolling through the third-century palace built by the Roman Emperor Diocletian for his retirement after a career of ruling the empire. This was no condo in Boca Raton, but a huge walled city of seven acres with barracks, stables, servants' quarters, the emperor's apartments, and temples. Much of my time inside was spent in the central peristyle—a square surrounded by Egyptian marble columns with a temple at one end where the emperor would sit to receive dignitaries. The square was lined with stone benches, and I found a seat among the other tourists. I ordered a cappuccino to take in the crumbling beauty of the place while, at the same time, spying on groups of mostly older couples trailing tour guides holding up their little follow-me flags.

I thought of those older couples. At that time in my life, it was hard for me to imagine so far into the future—married, retired to our Boca condo, kids in the rearview, and traveling with, I guessed, my soulmate. Hard to imagine because it would all need to start with a man I trusted, then a marriage. At one point, Reed had been my soulmate, or so I thought, and we'd talked about marriage. But he never offered the ring, and maybe, deep down, I had my doubts. What was real and what was imagined? For a time, I had this vision for my life, and then, poof, the vision turned out to be just a funhouse mirror.

From the Palace, I walked west toward the town docks. I had tickets for the Lastovo ferry leaving in two hours. Along the way, I planned to stop at the city market—the *pazar*—and buy something to eat on the ferry for that long four-hour trip.

Yes, that food, which would soon be fish food.

My passion had always been food—a chef, a restaurateur, and now a cookbook writer—and I wanted to purchase specific things. What I then had in mind was the perfect sandwich. My life might have taken a wrong turn, but I still had my passions.

The pazar was twice the size of the local farmers market back in Minneapolis, where I'd gone each day to buy fruits, vegetables, meats, breads, and cheeses for the restaurant Reed and I once owned. Vendors were set up at awning-covered tables arranged throughout the ancient cobblestone alleyways.

The perfect sandwich—a mystery to be solved by my own sleuthing. At a bakery stand, I checked out the selection of mostly sweet pastries. Under a small sign that said "Burek" were wedges of flaky pastry filled with a soft ricotta-like cheese. Then *krafna*, like American donuts without the hole. There was more, but I was searching for a baguette or a Mexican *bolillo*. In a basket simply marked "Roll" was precisely what I wanted—a crusty loaf the length of my forearm and as thin as my wrist. I paid a woman behind the table two euros and then asked if she spoke English, "*Znaš li engleski?*"

The woman said, "A little," pinching her fingers together so they almost touched. What was a little? In my experience, it meant that I'd proceed with my English—without using my clumsy translation app—whether she understood or not. I asked her, with the added help of wildly theatrical hand gestures, to cut the bread in half lengthwise.

At a charcuterie stand, a pig's hind leg was held in place by a vice-like contraption. I pointed and asked, "Prosciutto?"

The thirty-something man, muscled and handsome, with a taut abdomen covered by a stained white apron, said in English, "This is *drniški pršut*. Best quality." He smiled, a quick turn of the lips that I imagined to be a casual flirt. I was flattered.

I tried the pronunciation, "Pur-shoot." Then added, "Same as prosciutto?"

As though I were a child with a speech impediment, he said again, slower, "*Pršut*," then, "Same but different. Best quality from Drniš. They have been making it since fourteenth century. Salted, cold-smoked, and dried for twelve months. The wind is most important in Drniš. Cold and dry *bura* winds from the north. Warmer *jugo* winds from the south. In Italy, they do not smoke ham, and they do not have proper winds."

He sliced off a thumb-sized piece and offered it. And for a nanosecond, our hands touched. I ignored the skin-on-skin feeling and moved forward with my perfect sandwich mission. Like, really, I'd wait around, miss my ferry, and have a fling with this young vendor? Then, the thought did cross my mind—he was handsome, and his hands and body were butcher-strong. Then another image—his wife and two infants, and maybe a mother-in-law or cousin, all crammed together in one small apartment and waiting, while Jakov, or whatever his name was, had another fling in the back of his funky-smelling delivery van.

I put those conflicting images out of my mind and tasted the meat. The deep smoke and salt flavors reminded me of the Virginia-smoked ham I'd used in my now-closed restaurant. Back then, I would arrange thin slices of the ham inside a split, grilled biscuit along with a poached egg, and smother it all in a sage-infused hollandaise—my take on an Eggs Benedict.

I held up my fingers and pinched. "This much." I then ordered slices of a mild salami called *kulen*. The handsome butcher took my euros, handed me change, and then turned to flirt with the next customer. That woman was tall, beautiful, and, by the look of her handbag and chic outfit, wealthy. For a stupid second, I felt jilted—once again.

At a produce stand, I bought a single lemon and small bunches of basil and arugula. Another stand sold julienned roasted red peppers packed in a jar with olive oil.

Then, cheese. What I wanted was a soft cheese. I asked for brie.

A woman in her mid-thirties, my age, said in English, "No brie. *Basa*."

"*Basa?*"

The woman's hair was wrapped in a headscarf with an attractive pattern of daffodils against a field of sky blue. She wore no makeup, but with her high cheekbones, narrow nose, and full lips, I could tell she was quite stunning. The woman smiled and responded, "From Lika. Best for charcuterie or sandwich." She offered a sample served on one of those doctor "say-ahh" sticks.

I took a bite. Creamier than brie, spreadable, almost like cream cheese. Perfect, I thought, and nodded my head, yes. I purchased a small six-ounce container.

The last thing I bought was a bottle of local white wine called *Pošip*, made from grapes grown on the island of Hvar, which I'd soon pass on the ferryboat trip to Lastovo.

The perfect sandwich. The recipe was so simple, and one I'd never put in my cookbook. I'd never considered including a sandwich. It seemed beneath me in a way, like plain potato chips on a restaurant's menu. But right at that moment, all I wanted was simplicity—a sleepy Croatian village, a simple stone cottage, and time to learn about my past and possibly figure out my future.

The facts of my past were skimpy. I was adopted when I was five. I believed I was born in Dubrovnik. I had no birth certificate but knew my birth name was Vesna Ivelja. That last name was common on the island of Lastovo. Like any adopted kid, I'd scoured the Internet for information. In an obscure online town census, I found the name and address of a Marta Ivelja. The name seemed familiar, as though I'd heard it as a child. "Marta." Maybe my grandmother—or maybe just imagined.

On Airbnb, I'd rented a small stone house sweetly named The Oleander Cottage. It was all marketing, of course, and I knew it was no Roman palace. The photos showed a bedroom with a single bed, a living area with a fireplace, a rough-cut dining table surrounded by four chairs, and a small kitchen with the kind of narrow cooking range I'd had in an apartment rented after finally leaving my adopted home. The oleander bushes overran the place. But it was simple, and I looked forward to my stay there, whether or not I found any lost relatives.

Or figured out what to do with my life.

I carried what I'd bought from the market in a nylon, lemon-colored satchel that hung from my shoulder. At the docks, I gave an attendant the ticket for my checked backpack. The contents included all I'd left Minneapolis with—just a few clothes, a MacBook, and my toiletries. Half an hour later, the ferry pulled up—a two-story structure atop twin hulls.

Immediately, people crowded around the gangplank being lowered from the back. I didn't feel there was any reason to hurry; they wouldn't sell more tickets than seats. It was like boarding an aircraft—the queue of frantic people thinking the plane might leave without them. I'd always been one of the last to board, head down and walking through the aisle of onlookers like a shy debutante.

When the line of people thinned, I stood up and crossed the gangplank onto the ferry. What I hadn't considered was the difference between a plane and what I was then boarding—there were no assigned seats. Every seat on the convenient first level of the ferry had been taken. I walked the steel steps to a small outdoor deck where a gaggle of passengers stood smoking. Inside the second level were a few seats still vacant, and I took an aisle seat in a row of three. Next to me was a young girl—I thought ten or so—her chestnut-brown hair tied up in pigtails. Next to the girl was, I assumed, her father, who sat watching out the window.

I would eventually find out that this was Dinko, and the girl beside him was Mia, his daughter.

Neither looked up as I put my backpack on the rack above and settled in with my satchel of food for the tedious four-hour ride.

The big diesel engines came to life, creating an almost deafening roar as the boat left the dock, spun around, and headed into the Adriatic Sea. Once at speed, the engines throttled back, and the sound diminished. I could barely see outside but watched as Diocletian's Palace became a speck against the city of Split. Then, all I could see was blue sky, clear of any clouds.

I saw land half an hour later and left my seat to stand on the rear deck among the smokers. I knew the island was called Brač, and that much of Croatia's extra-virgin olive oil came from its groves. I'd tasted the local award-winning variety called *Oblica*—a small bottle that sold in the United States for around fifty dollars. Tastes trigger memories, and somehow the oil's flavor reminded me of simple, earthy escargot with butter, bitter garlic, and lots of Italian parsley.

As soon as the boat passed the island, the sea swells increased, and the ferry lunged up to meet each one. The movement pushed me back and forth, and I held on to whatever I could. Most of the smokers, likely veterans of sea travel with their long-established sea legs, seemed to think nothing of it and kept up their cancerous puffing.

I wobble-walked back inside to take my bolted-to-the-floor seat.

The young girl looked up at me as I sat down. I noticed her eyes then, a surprising and rare emerald green. She asked, "Are you American?"

"Yes, how did you know?" I hadn't spoken with her before and wasn't draped in an American flag or sporting a forearm tattoo that read "Made in the USA."

The girl looked down, now shy. "I like to guess. But your T-shirt—it says, 'Trampled by Turtles.' I was wondering what kind of turtles could trample. Big turtles, I guess, like the ones on the Galapagos Islands. Then I wondered why anyone would wear a T-shirt of big Galapagos turtles that would go on a rampage and hurt someone. But I just Googled it on my phone. A band from someplace called Duluth in the United States. No one outside of America would have heard of such a band—I don't think. So, I guessed American."

"You're very smart. I'm guessing you're from Croatia?"

The girl looked up. "How did you know?"

I joked, "Only girls from Croatia wear their hair like that. In America, we call them pigtails." Ironically, as a child I also wore pigtails.

"That cannot be so. I saw a photo of Selena Gomez in what you call pigtails. Selena is no pig, and I don't think she has tails."

That was funny. "It's just what the hair fashion is called. Anyway, you look cute. And I think you're from Croatia because I've heard that few tourists go to Lastovo, so I thought you must live there."

"Yes, I live there."

"And your English is so good."

"Many here speak English. English is taught in school, and plenty of English television, so we all learn."

I looked up at the father. He was watching us, smiling, and enjoying the exchange. He said, *"Game of Thrones, Seinfeld, American Idol."*

"Top Chef?"

"Beat Bobby Flay."

I laughed, then asked the two of them, "Would you like some of my sandwich—the perfect sandwich? I have way more than I can eat."

"Yes!" the little girl said. Then, "Peanut butter?"

"Not peanut butter. You watch."

The seatback in front pulled down into a table, and I proceeded to lift out all of my market-foraged ingredients. I started with the meats, laying the *pršut* and *kulen* along the bottom of the long roll. I carefully placed basil and arugula leaves over the meats. I spread the soft cheese on the top half. Over the cheese, I laid the roasted peppers. Finally, I pulled out the lemon. I realized then that I had no knife to cut it. A sandwich with olive oil but no acid would not do. I held the lemon up like a fragile egg. I looked around stupidly, as though maybe a flight—or, I guessed, ferry—attendant might be of service.

Then a knife miraculously appeared. The father held one out with the blade extended. He asked, "Is this what you are looking for?"

"Thank you."

The man switched hands with the handle now offered. I took it. I noticed his smile then—his teeth crammed together like teens at a rock concert. But it was the smile that caught my attention, lips pulled tight into a grin that almost spread ear to ear.

I cut the lemon and squeezed a teaspoon of juice along the length of the green basil and arugula. What else was needed? The seasoning, of course—something else I'd forgotten. I looked over at the father and asked, "Would you also have salt and pepper?"

Now, a playful, quizzical look came to his face as he gazed up toward the ceiling. "Well, let us see." He patted both breast pockets of his white cotton shirt, then the pockets of his pants. He shook his head, no. Then he said, "Just maybe," and pulled a knapsack from beneath the seat. From a side pocket, he lifted out two plastic shakers of salt and pepper. He said, "Aha!" and then handed the black and white shakers across. And I thought, *What kind of man carries around salt and pepper shakers?* The answer came to me instantly, *The kind who loves food.*

I seasoned the sandwich, then clapped the two halves together. I cut it in thirds and passed two helpings over to the girl and her father. Finally, I pulled the Croatian Pošip wine from my satchel. I looked closely and curiously at the foil-wrapped neck and imprisoned cork. Before I could ask, the man was back into his knapsack, now producing a corkscrew. He held out his hand for the bottle, went through the process of twisting and pulling, then handed it back. Before I could ask again, the man produced two plastic glasses and passed one over. He reached in once more and pulled out an orange soda for his daughter. Then, finally, the man produced a bag labeled

"*Čipi Čips.*" A photo on the front showed potato chips with ridges, like Ruffles.

I sarcastically asked, "Do you also have chip dip?"

The man smiled, reached into his knapsack, made a big show of searching around, and said, "Unfortunately, we will have to make do without your American chip dip."

I poured wine for both of us. Then, before eating, the girl pulled her perfect sandwich apart and began carefully picking out the marinated roasted peppers. She said, "Not to my liking."

To that, I opened mine and said, "More for me!" The girl dutifully placed her peppers on my sandwich.

Half an hour later, we'd finished, and the bottle of wine was almost empty.

The ferry passed the island of Hvar and turned west. The swells in the open water now came at us from an angle. The boat moved up and down and sideways, all at the same time, shaking passengers like a mixed cocktail.

The random, jarring movement suddenly made my stomach uneasy.

Then I felt it in my chest and the back of my throat—a feeling I was not unfamiliar with. Nausea.

The father, once quiet and reserved but now a little loose with the lubricant of wine, peppered me with questions. "Where are you from?"

"Minneapolis," I answered, knowing that few outside of the United States—and many inside—had no clue what or where it was.

That inevitable question came: "Where is this Minneapolis located?"

"In the state of Minnesota, near Chicago. Close to the Canadian border."

Then the next inevitable question: "Is it cold there?"

I was starting to sweat profusely but managed to answer, "It snows in the winter. The lakes freeze." I wanted to say something jokey, like, we huddle in igloos and hunt polar bears, but all I could think of was the nausea now ballooning just below my trachea.

The girl chimed in, "I have never seen snow but would like to make a snowman."

To that, I nodded but said nothing.

Then the father again, "What do you do in this Minneapolis?"

The movement of the boat was still there, and my nausea became all-encompassing. I was ready to puke. I forced out an answer. "I write cookbooks." Then I asked, "What is it that you do?" I hoped he'd talk about himself and leave me in my nausea and silence.

"I make wine on the island of Lastovo."

The young girl said, "It is good wine, though I am not allowed to drink it until I am eighteen."

Unfortunately, the man turned the conversation back toward me. "What is your specialty?"

An hour ago, I'd been pleasantly thinking about olive oil and escargot. Now, all I could think of was the gross, slimy snails cooked inside their shells.

I forgot what he'd asked. I turned toward the man and was only able to reply, "I'm sorry. Can we please stop talking?"

He looked at me, sad eyes unblinking, and his ear-to-ear smile now turned into a tight grimace. I could tell he was confused, but all I could think about was keeping the perfect sandwich I'd just eaten from coming back up.

Before he could say anything, I added again, "I'm sorry."

The man turned away and looked out the window. He

then turned back and said, "I am sorry to be so inquisitive. It is not my nature."

The little girl interrupted, "*Tata*, can't you see that the woman is seasick?"

I felt my stomach turning and then the first minor spasms. In an almost out-of-body experience, I felt my jaw drop, and my mouth open on its own, but nothing came out.

I heard the man say, "*Ajme!*" which I took to mean, Oh no!

He stood, crossed over our knees, and stepped into the aisle. He grabbed me by my shoulders and lifted. I bent to the pressure of the man's hands and allowed him to move me toward the door that led to the outside deck. I could smell the stale cigarette smoke, now mixed with the gut-churning odor of rotting fish. I knew it would be seconds before the perfect sandwich made its comeback.

Then I was at the railing.

I leaned forward. As my head hung over the edge, the man pulled back the curtains of hair from each side of my face. I watched as the perfect sandwich—now just greasy bits— descended toward the white-capped sea. My eyes watered, and I felt my face swell from the uncontrollable exertion. More came up, and I closed my eyes as my stomach exhausted itself. I continued to lean against the railing, and the man continued to hold my hair.

He finally asked, "Are you okay?"

I couldn't talk just then; I could barely think. I looked up at the horizon and could see an island in the distance— Korčula, I guessed. At the far end was a walled medieval city similar to Dubrovnik. I knew we were, thankfully, getting close to Lastovo. Without turning around, I finally answered, "Yes, better."

He let go of my hair, and a few strands stuck to my wet chin. From somewhere, the man produced a white napkin, and I wiped away the detritus.

Then, from beneath, a hand was raised with a plastic cup—the same cup that had contained wine seemingly hours before. The thought of wine made my nausea return. It was the girl who said, "Water. Drink."

I took the water, rinsed my mouth, and spat. I took another sip and swallowed. The cool water was comforting and refreshing.

I turned around. "Thank you," I said to both the girl and her father—her *tata*.

The man smiled, maybe wanting to laugh. "Many people get seasick on the ferry. It is not uncommon. Nothing to be ashamed of."

I was ashamed, if that was the word. Maybe more embarrassed. Vomiting is such a personal, humiliating thing, like urinating—something you want to do in private and above a toilet. Then, I knew my face looked red and swollen, my eyes bulging like a frog's. I just wanted to be alone, but there was no place to be alone. And now I felt vulnerable. I didn't answer the man and just nodded my head.

"We should stay out here. It is better to be outside where you can see the water and anticipate the rolling of the swells."

I felt better. And, most likely because I'd emptied my stomach, the nausea dissipated.

The daughter went back inside, but the father stayed beside me. He kept silent, maybe remembering when I'd told him to stop talking. I felt guilty for that comment and now asked him a question, "You live in Lastovo?"

"Yes, my daughter Mia, my aunt, and I. We live just outside the village of Pasadur. Pasadur is the place where the ferry will stop. Are you just visiting?"

I looked closer at his face. His wavy dark hair was brushed to the side, revealing a forehead clear of any worry lines. Then, a beard with a week's growth, and a pronounced and curved nose I could only describe as Roman. His complexion was dark, Mediterranean. The effect felt comforting—like confidence mixed with compassion. But then, maybe it was just my seasickness talking.

Regardless, I believe you can tell a lot simply by exploring a person's face, and be deceived if you instead listen too long to their forced and witty banter. I liked this man's face. I responded, "Visiting for two weeks. I rented a place near Lastovo—the old town."

"The small stone house near the junkyard?"

Now I remembered that in the background of one photo was a collection of rusted-out autos. "I think so. How did you know?"

"Did Sara rent that to you? She is crafty. The house is one of the few on the island that is rented to tourists. It is very primitive."

I was stuck on the word "crafty." "Crafty? Like, she is good at knitting or knows how to make clay pottery?"

"No, like a witch. Crafty like a witch." He smiled at his little joke.

Then, just as I wanted to ask more questions about Sara and the cottage, the ferry's horn made three loud bursts, and in the distance was the dock at Pasadur.

He said, "We should now go back and get our things." While walking away, he added, "The island is very small. We will meet again."

The passengers were all standing, collecting their bags and luggage, then crowding the aisles. The father and his daughter were already near the stairs when I pulled my backpack from the overhead rack and joined the rest.

Then I was at the dockside quay waiting for Sara, the witch, to bring me to the primitive stone house, which I now imagined had an outhouse toilet and a pump handle instead of a faucet.

I sat down on a low stone wall, my backpack resting on the ground. The crowd of passengers had dissipated into waiting cars, shops, or taverns. The daughter and her father were nowhere to be seen.

He'd said we'd meet again, but at that time, I still didn't know his name.

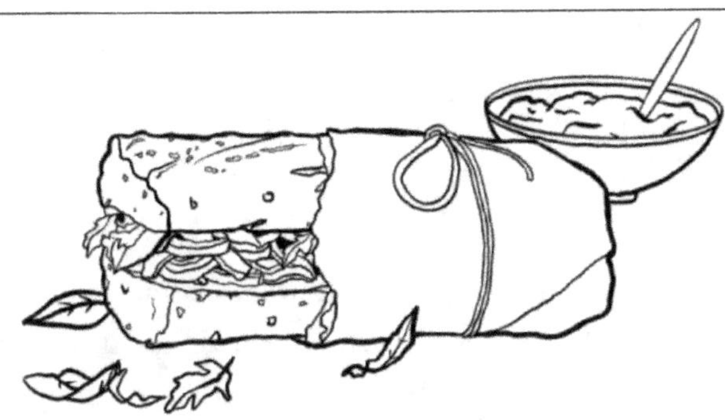

Roasted Red Pepper Sandwich with Feta Spread

Of course, there's much debate about the perfect sandwich. In France, the *jambon-beurre* is a simple baguette with just butter and ham. Mia likes peanut butter and jelly on soft white bread. This favorite sandwich recipe is very Mediterranean.

Serves 4

Feta Spread

8 ounces crumbled feta

⅔ cup full-fat Greek yogurt

1 lemon, zested

2 tablespoons extra-virgin olive oil

1 garlic clove, minced or grated

1 tablespoon honey

The Sandwich

2 baguettes, cut lengthwise

4 red bell peppers (or use jarred)

12 fresh basil leaves

Kosher salt

Freshly ground black pepper

2 cups arugula

For the Feta Spread

In a food processor fitted with the blade attachment, combine the feta, Greek yogurt, lemon zest, garlic, and honey. Pulse to combine. With the machine running, drizzle in olive oil until you reach your desired consistency.

For the Red Peppers

Preheat oven to 450°F.

Roast the peppers directly on the oven rack for 30-35 minutes, turning occasionally until they are charred on all sides.

Remove the bell peppers from the oven, place them in a paper bag, and fold the bag to seal it. Let the peppers steam for five minutes. Remove from the bag and rub the blackened skins off the peppers.

Tear open the peppers and discard the seeds and stems.

To Assemble the Sandwich

Spread the baguette halves with feta spread. Lay the basil leaves on top of the feta spread and top with the roasted red pepper halves. Pile on the arugula and place the baguette halves together. Season with kosher salt and fresh black pepper. Cut the baguettes in half and wrap in waxed paper or parchment.

An Improvised Frittata

Pasadur lay at the waist of two hills covered in silvery-green pine and cedar. The concrete town quay stretched along the seaside, broken only by an arched stone bridge over a channel leading from one bay of azure-blue water to another in the distance. Sailboats tethered to moorings bobbed in the oncoming waves. Other boats were more firmly docked, their sterns against the quay with narrow planks bridging the gap. Houses, shops, and restaurants faced a cobblestone promenade. All were constructed of hand-laid stone or white stucco and roofed with clay terracotta tiles. I'd seen photos, but the feeling of being there was overwhelming.

Then relief with the thought of finally getting off the rolling Adriatic.

The man and his daughter were gone, and now, what I remembered of him was that, while I'd been leaning over the deck rail and vomiting into the sea, he'd gently held my hair.

I'd always grown it long but mostly kept it tied up in a sloppy ballerina bun while working in a restaurant kitchen. When I wasn't in a kitchen or in a catatonic slumber, I liked it down and wild—maybe for the feeling of freedom that I wasn't tied to the stove. He'd held it back, and then there was that touch of his wrist against the skin of my neck that seemed personal, physical, even if it was just to keep my hair from getting soiled. All that skin-on-skin sensitivity—first the butcher in the market and now this guy. I knew it was all hormones whispering, trying to slowly awaken something inside me. But honestly, I couldn't care less what they had to say or how loud they said it.

I looked around for the witch, Sara, who'd said she'd meet me when the ferry arrived. No one nearby looked like a crafty, peaked-hat-wearing, broom-riding witch. Then, strangely, I saw a car driving way too fast, screaming down the two-lane road that paralleled the quay. The car was the color of a Halloween pumpkin. The driver was a woman with almost-matching copper hair that fluttered behind like a battle flag. She suddenly leaned on the horn, blasting a man crossing the cobblestones. He jumped out of the way, raising his forearm and fist in what I took to be the local equivalent of "the finger." Closer, the pumpkin-orange car was a BMW convertible, and at the wheel was a red-headed woman wearing Ray-Ban aviators. The BMW braked hard directly in front of me, sending out an ear-piercing sound of skidding rubber.

The woman said in English, "Sorry, I am late."

"You must be Sara. I'm Vesna, or you can call me Ves."

Then, abruptly, "Okay, get in."

No civilized salutation. No Croatian two-kiss greeting. Just, "Get in."

I threw my pack into the back seat of the convertible and

stepped in. Then, before I could completely close the passenger door, the woman drove off just as fast as she'd arrived.

Up close, Sara was no witch. Her curly hair was long and full, with a sheen that gave its copper color a campfire glow. She wore a sleeveless white dress that showed off her freckled, toned arms. Her gloss-orange fingernail polish matched her lipstick, which matched her hair and sports car.

When Sara spoke in her loud and Slavic-punctuated English, she took her eyes completely off the road. "That is all your possessions for two weeks? A backpack? You are like a hippie?"

"What do you mean, hippie?" I didn't know whether to be offended or amused.

"You know, hippie. Hitchhike around with strangers, smoke the marijuana, sleep with many men, and maybe women too."

Okay, I felt mildly offended. "I'm a cookbook writer and chef. I didn't hitchhike, and I don't do drugs. And I don't sleep around with men, women, or anything in between."

"Hey, hey, did not mean to make offense. Just asking, you know. Trying to make American conversation."

I calmed myself. "What do you do?"

"You know, some this, some that. I am only lawyer on the island. But there is not much need for lawyer here. Then, real estate agent. You want to buy a house here?"

The woman paused, then quickly added, "No, no, you do not want to live in this place. No good restaurants, no nightclubs, no beach clubs. You get bored. In two weeks, you will be so bored you maybe think of beating your head with a sharp rock. Nothing to do here. Maybe you like Hvar. Plenty party, party, party in Hvar."

"You're not much of a salesperson for a real estate agent."

"Hah! Tell people one thing, they think the opposite. See, you are already thinking that you like boring, that you buy house from me. No?"

Strangely, I'd been thinking just that. "I like boring. I want quiet."

"Divorced? Is this why you are here alone?"

The woman was a busybody. The man on the ferry had been right, *crafty*. I said just that, "You're a busybody."

"What is wrong with my body?" Sara's hands left the wheel for a brief, scary moment and touched her hips. "This is certainly not busy."

"Busybody. It means intrusive, like asking unwanted questions."

"Man trouble for certain. Bad breakup. Or death? You are a widow? So young."

"No, not a widow." The woman was beating me down. "Breakup. But I'm here to find my grandmother. I was born in Croatia but put up for adoption after my parents died during the war. My last name is Ivelja. There's a Marta Ivelja living on the island. Have you heard of her?"

"No. I did not grow up on the island, so there are very many people I do not know. Your story is sad, but it is not so uncommon. I myself had to live in another country during the war. Maybe you find her, buy a house in Lastovo, and live, as you say, happily ever after."

I looked over at the woman's hands. No wedding ring. "What about you? Divorced? Separated? Widowed?"

She threw her head back and laughed, a cackle that went on for seconds. Then, just ahead, a goat wandered onto the road, and Sara braked hard, turning at the same time and just narrowly missing the animal. The incident had no visible effect on her at all. She then answered my question, "Lesbian."

The goat was still on the road, now behind us, carefree and without a clue. "Lesbian in Lastovo?"

"Yes, I know. Only one other lesbian on island, and she is a hag. How can that be?" A pause. "You leave your boyfriend because you like other women?"

"No, I'm sorry."

"No need for apology. Once a month, I go to Hvar. Plenty of sex activity in Hvar. It is enough for now."

I definitely wanted to change the subject. "Where is this place, The Oleander Cottage?"

"Middle of nowhere. You have car? You will need car. None of your Uber here. Just Miša and his taxi, and he is lazy."

We moved through the hills, and the convertible charged through each twisty turn, the tires squealing against the hot pavement. I tested the seatbelt with a quick yank and then held on with both hands—one on the door handle and the other on the seat bottom. I did not answer Sara's question. In fact, I'd forgotten what was asked.

Sara didn't wait for an answer. "The owner of this house you are renting—and I will tell you it is for sale—has a good car that he will rent you. Cheap. Twenty euros per day. For the two weeks, two hundred eighty euros."

I didn't respond—I was too frightened.

"Okay, for you, for the whole two weeks, I talk him down to two hundred fifty euros. And this car, it is also for sale."

I probably did need a car. "Fine," I squeaked out.

Then Sara had her phone out, looking down at the number dialed, and then holding it to her ear. She now drove erratically with just one hand, talking loudly in Croatian—Cro.

I knew snippets of the language. As a small child, I spoke Cro but lost it along with everything else. What I did understand, among a few other words, was, *"Da, da, da."* Yes, yes, yes.

Sara hung up and said, "You are set. You pay him two hundred fifty euros, no more."

Both of Sara's hands were now on the steering wheel, and the BMW descended into a valley with the road pinched between rows and rows of trellised grapevines, their leaves bright green, their small flowers dotted with specks of white, like powdered sugar on a tea cake. I knew that by the end of the hot summer, the vines would be covered with lush, pastel green or purple fruit. A winery was off in the distance, a stone building the size of a barn back home. Next to it was a two-story stone house not much smaller. Both buildings had the ubiquitous terracotta roofs. We passed a sign, "Radić Winery." Beneath that, in English, "NOT OPEN TO THE PUBLIC."

Without being asked, Sara offered, "Famous Lastovo vineyard. Radić makes both white Grk and red Plavac Mali. *Plavo* means blue and *mali* means small. Little blue grapes. Wine like zinfandel but stronger with the alcohol. Very hard to grow. *Grk* means Greek, but Grk grapes are only grown in Croatia, so I do not know why we are insulted by that name. The sign is also insulting. Dinko Radić, owner, is snobbish and does not enjoy tourists. Should write on sign, 'No Trespassing, Intruders Will Be Shot!'" She said this with a straight face, but I laughed.

The road now hugged the steep coastline, and below, I could see glimpses of the numerous inlets with their sparkling azure waters. Farther out was deeper sea the color of green bottle glass. The island of Korčula was just a shadow on the horizon. We reached a pass between the hills, and below, I took in the ancient old town of Lastovo, built over five hundred years ago. I'd seen photos of the Venetian-style homes and churches, one built seemingly on top of the other. I also knew the buildings were mostly abandoned, with many of the homes now in ruins.

Sara barely slowed as the road narrowed and cut through the old town toward the valley below. Minutes later, she stopped at the small cottage I recognized from the photos online, the overgrown oleander bushes now in bloom with soft pink flowers. Next to it was a small vegetable garden, and across the road rose the junkyard of rusting cars that the father on the ferry had mentioned.

Close to the cottage—something missing in the online gallery of photos—was clearly an outhouse. I wasn't necessarily put off by them. I'd spent many years vacationing in northern Minnesota on an island with one. But I guessed it was just unexpected. You rent a cottage for a vacation and typically assume indoor plumbing.

An old man near the front door of The Oleander Cottage leaned against a shovel. Next to him was a battered two-door car that appeared to be a Volkswagen Rabbit. My adoptive father once owned a Rabbit, but that was twenty-five years ago. The man wore a misshapen chocolate-brown fedora, pushed back from his deeply lined forehead. His uncovered ears stuck out like pot handles. The old man began quickly speaking in Cro, and to me, it sounded like a fistful of hard consonants stuck in his throat—nothing like the lyrical sound of Italian or the elegance of French. He was apparently trying to describe the vehicle, which, on closer inspection, turned out to be a Yugo, a brand I'd never heard of.

Sara translated in a way that suited her. "He says it has

been a good car that belonged in his family forty years and it is reliable, which is not true. This car was made by communists and Serbs. Is a cheap piece of garbage, but okay for Lastovo since no Autobahn here. He says fuel gauge does not work, but is full of gas and will go hundred miles before needs to be filled. He says also speedometer does not work, so odometer not working either."

Sara then turned to the man. I guessed—or hoped—she was asking how I would know when a hundred miles were up.

The old man spoke rapidly to Sara, his short arms now off the shovel and gesticulating like some traffic cop. The shovel tipped to the ground.

Sara said, "He does not believe you could drive a hundred miles in this car in two weeks. I think is correct. He says, for safety, fill it up in one week, then fill it up before you leave. He would like you to return car with full tank."

I looked at him, smiled, then nodded my head. "*Da, da.*"

The old man nodded back, then said something again to Sara.

"He says that he would like his money now. Two hundred fifty euros." She then introduced us by first pointing at me. "Vesna," then to the man, "Stjepan."

I had my wallet in a fanny pack—my travel purse. I reached in, counted out the euros, and handed the paper money to Stjepan. He said, "*Hvala vam,*" then picked up his shovel and began walking toward the nearby vegetable garden.

I remembered *hvala vam*. Thank you.

Sara led me through The Oleander Cottage. A heavy wooden door with hand-hammered hinges led to a central sitting room with a fireplace large enough to cook in. It was also likely the only source of heat during the cold winter months, since the cottage had no apparent heating or air-conditioning system. The bedroom was small, with a full-sized bed and two windows—one facing the hills, while the other opened to the garden where I could now see Stjepan turning over dirt and bending down to pull out weeds. The bedspread was a quilt of colorful fabrics, and next to the bed stood a vase with stalks of oleander blooms.

In the kitchen, Sara showed me how to flip a switch to fill the roof cistern when the water pressure dropped. She said, "Stop the well pump when water comes off roof." She added, as though anticipating my thoughts, "This is typical Croatian custom. We put water tank on roof and well in the ground."

Sara opened the fridge and showed me greens from the garden, milk, and cheese. On the counter lay a fresh loaf of bread and a bowl of eggs. In the cupboard were assorted spices and a Pepsi bottle labeled "Olive Oil." On the small kitchen table stood a bottle of red wine with the label "Plavac Mali" and beneath it "Radić Winery."

She said, "I provided food for you to get started. No charge for this service, but please put excellent review on website. This is not just for me, but also Stjepan, the owner."

Then I wondered if this was the old man's home, and where he was living now. Did he just rent me his only car? I guessed I felt uncomfortable, like taking food from a hungry child.

I asked, "Where will Stjepan sleep if I'm living in his house?"

Sara sat at the kitchen table and then pulled out a pack of cigarettes from her purse. She offered me one, which I declined, but she lit up herself—right in my rented house, no doubt another typical Croatian custom. She inhaled enough smoke to flavor a rack of ribs, then spoke. "Stjepan lives across road. You can see his house past the pile of garbage automobiles. He thinks they are worth money, but he is crazy. Many people here think he is crazy lunatic. Stjepan never married and was close to his sister. They grew up in this cottage. His sister lived here alone, and Stjepan built his own cottage across road. His sister did not marry also. So, you understand what the ignorant people in Lastovo would think. I am not so sure. You are enlightened American. No? You understand. The way people live their lives can be different, and people should mind their own…" She stopped there, not sure how to finish.

"Business."

"Yes, business. Mind their own business. I am lesbian and do not care what others say, but I want them to mind their own business. So, I was saying, Stjepan lives across road and sister lived here. Sister—her name was Anja—worked the garden with Stjepan. That was their interest. Now Stjepan works the garden alone. I know, sad."

Sara inhaled another gust from her cigarette, then added, "If he is around too much and is nuisance, you just need to say in Croatian, *otiđi*. This means, go away."

I wasn't ever going to say *otiđi*.

Sara's story of Stjepan and Anja seemed unfinished. "So, what happened to the sister?"

"Dead. Before that, Stjepan built her a new bathroom with a bathtub. You will see. Anja was getting from the bathtub and slipped. Her head hit the new porcelain sink and she died. Stjepan found her the next day. Stjepan—he blames himself. Thinks making the indoor plumbing was a curse. I do not think this is correct. We are not backward people. We all have indoor plumbing now. Death was simple accident and now this cottage is for sale. Let me show you the bathroom."

Sara stood and extinguished her cigarette by holding the

smoldering end under running water, then threw the butt out the open window. *A little rude*, I thought. She led the way to the cursed bathroom.

And there it was: a flush toilet, a basin, and a bathtub. Through a small window, I could see Stjepan in the distance, still working the garden and pulling weeds.

Sara said, "The pipes beneath the cottage are old and fragile. Please do not flush anything down the toilet but your dumpings and small pieces of toilet paper." She used the word "dumpings," which, as far as I knew, was not in the English dictionary. She added with a straight face, "Be careful when you step from the bathtub."

"I will."

"Anything you need, you call."

There I was, alone in The Oleander Cottage where the owner had recently died in the bathroom, no doubt from a cranial hemorrhage. As soon as Sara left, Stjepan also left the garden, possibly because she'd said to him on her way out, *"Otiđi."*

It had been a long day, and I was tired from the exhausting trip, the strain of losing my perfect sandwich to the Adriatic waves, and the nail-biting drive with Sara. I put away the few clothes I'd brought and then settled in with a cup of tea.

I sat outside in the cooling late afternoon beneath an arbor of the wandering oleander and thought about the past I'd been told. I was born in Dubrovnik two years before the Yugoslav Wars broke out, or, as they called it here, the Croatian War of Independence. My parents died during the war—my mother in the bombing of Dubrovnik in December 1991, and my father somewhere in Croatia as a soldier fighting for independence. My mother's name was Ivana, but my father's name was unknown. That was what I'd been told by the nuns in the orphanage.

But there had to be more to my past. My mother likely had siblings. She certainly had parents and in-laws. Marta Ivelja might be my father's mother, but I had no other pieces of information. The name Marta rang familiar, but mind and memory play tricks. I might have so desperately wanted her to be my grandmother that I'd ultimately come to believe it.

What did blood mean? If I eventually found my distant relatives, what would that be like? How would that feel? I had a friend in high school who tracked down her birth parents in China. Her adoptive parents paid for the overseas flight, and she was reunited. But it didn't go well. The birth parents had given her up because, at the time, the one-child policy was law, and they wanted a son. They did get their special son, but now this other girl wanted back in. When I talked to her about it, she felt her presence reminded them of the abandonment and associated guilt. The trip hadn't gone as expected. But blood had to mean something—the genetic component that could determine destiny. I wanted that, whatever *that* looked like. Desperately. And I wanted to be connected by blood to a family who cared.

I finished my tea and then realized I was famished, with nothing left churning in my stomach.

I had the ingredients for an improvised frittata. On the counter stood a small earthenware bowl filled with half a dozen eggs. The eggs were a light brown—fresh—and I cracked four into a larger bowl. The milk in the refrigerator was in a glass pitcher covered by a square of cloth, no doubt right from the cow (or sheep or goat) and unhomogenized. I scooped the thick, sweet cream from the top. I whisked the cream and eggs together with salt and pepper. I chopped Swiss chard from the refrigerator into half-inch strips, but needed something savory for flavor—an onion, a shallot, or some garlic. I walked out to the garden in search. Among the greens, pea vines, lettuces, and other vegetables, I found the mature fronds of leeks. Perfect. I unearthed just one—I'd settle up somehow with Stjepan the next time I saw him. Herbs grew in a pot close to the cottage, and I pinched off a few stems of thyme.

After washing off the fresh dirt, I chopped the white meat of the leek and combined it with the Swiss chard. I found a frying pan and sautéed the leeks and chard in olive oil, along with the thyme sprigs. I added the whisked eggs and cream. The mixture then went into the small oven for fifteen minutes. In that time, I opened the bottle of wine from the vineyard we'd passed earlier and poured some into a jelly jar. The red Plavac Mali smelled lush with a deep, earthy aroma. Then the flavor—full-bodied with the slight fruit taste of figs and plums—reminded me of a fine Bordeaux. Radić was one good winemaker, and though I would've preferred a white with a frittata, this would do just fine.

I ate alone at the small outside table. The sun hadn't set, but hung just below the surrounding hills, casting a fading light.

In that moment, I imagined myself as an infant—my mother, father, and perhaps a grandmother, all gathered around a similar table, enjoying a simple meal of a frittata and deciding on chores for the following day. My mother would need to tend the garden and then go to the market, while my father would have plans to set out before sunrise in a small dory to handline for grouper and sea bass. My grandmother would be caring for me and helping prepare the meals. Or perhaps it wouldn't be the next day's chores they were discussing. Maybe they'd be dwelling on the latest news from mainland Yugoslavia, wondering how the war would soon change their lives.

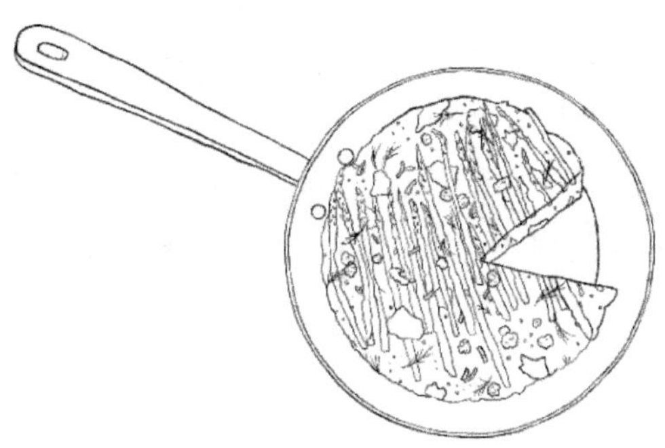

Swiss Chard and Leek Frittata

As Vesna has shown, a frittata is a great dish to improvise with. As long as you have eggs and some veggies on hand, it's a meal.

Serves 6

8-10 leaves of Swiss chard
Coarse salt
Freshly ground black pepper
12 large eggs
2 leeks, thinly sliced
3 tablespoons chopped fresh dill
2 tablespoons extra-virgin olive oil
4 tablespoons goat cheese crumbles (half of a 4-ounce log)
Preheat the oven to 400°F.

On a baking sheet, toss the leeks with 1 tablespoon of olive oil. Roast in the oven for 10 minutes.

In a sauté pan over medium heat, add 1 tablespoon of olive oil and the Swiss chard. Sauté until the leaves are wilted. Set aside.

In a mixing bowl, whisk the eggs. Add the sliced leeks. Stir to combine.

Use butter or spray oil to grease a 10-inch cast-iron skillet or deep earthenware pie dish.

Pour the egg mixture into a skillet or pie dish. Dot with goat cheese crumbles.

Bake for 15 minutes, or until set. Sprinkle with fresh dill.

Serve warm or at room temperature.

Grilled Anchovies and Blitva

I woke late in the morning to the sound of something alive in the yard. I stayed quiet. I heard footsteps right outside the window, possibly a peeping Tom. The stone cottage was out in the middle of nowhere, and I essentially knew no one. The front and back doors seemed a hundred years old, with locks to match. I couldn't remember if I'd even set the locks. Probably not. I lay nearly naked under the bedcovers, afraid to move. I waited and listened.

The footsteps moved around the yard, soft on the dirt and grass. Then something struck the earth. I heard steel scrape a rock. Another strike and another clink. In an instant, I understood. Someone was working in the garden. I sat up in bed with the sheets held tight to my chest. I peeked through the loose curtains. I knew before I saw him—the old man, Stjepan, from the previous day.

I left the bed and quickly slipped on one of the two light dresses I'd brought. I stepped into my well-worn Birkenstocks and walked to the garden. The man was using a four-tined rake to weed between the rows of vegetables. I walked with heavy footsteps along the stone pathway, trying to subtly announce my presence. As I neared the garden, the man did not look up.

I said loudly, "*Dobro jutro.*" Of the few Croatian phrases I remembered or had learned before the trip, three were *dobro jutro*, good morning; *dobar dan*, good day; and *dobra večer*, good evening.

Stjepan turned—his deeply lined face covered in a growth of gray beard, the battered fedora giving shade to his pot-handle ears. He smiled. In his Croatian accent, he repeated, "*Dobro jutro.*"

That was it for my Cro vocabulary, so I stumbled along in English like any other rude American, hoping or assuming they understood. "I'm sorry to disturb you." I said this, knowing it was him who'd disturbed me. I realized that Stjepan owned the property, but as with other rentals, the owner wasn't supposed to hover.

It didn't matter. The man just smiled and nodded. He had no idea what the rude American was saying.

We stood looking at each other. I remembered then that I'd pulled a leek from his garden the previous evening, and now tried to apologize. I spoke slowly and loudly, the dumb American thinking Stjepan might better comprehend. "I... took... a... leek," and pointed at the row of leeks. Knowing the alternate meaning of what I'd just said, I added, "For... my... supper." I repeated, "Supper," then pointed toward my mouth.

How idiotic.

I added, "Sorry." It could have gone either way—sorry for the leek, or sorry for the use of a language he didn't understand, no matter how slowly and loudly I spoke the words.

Stjepan continued to smile and nod. He said, *"Poriluk."* Then, more slowly, "P-o-r-i-l-u-k."

I repeated, *"Poriluk,"* then, "Leek."

He repeated, "Leek," and then leaned over to unearth a stalk. He brushed off the dirt surrounding the root whiskers. He said again, "Leek." Seemingly, a breakthrough in language and cultures.

I smiled. *"Poriluk."*

He quickly unearthed three more, then stood and held them out.

I realized then that Stjepan had thought I was asking for leeks, not understanding that I was sorry for taking one in the first place. I considered refusing his offer but realized that doing so would lead to more uncomfortable miscommunication.

I smiled and took the vegetables offered. "Thank you," then *"Hvala vam."*

I felt like such an idiot.

The car was parked in the gravel driveway—a Yugo with encrusted rust, and paint faded and discolored as though dipped in acid. I opened the driver's door, the rusted metal hinges making an ear-splitting squeal. I'd been given the keys— three of them—and tried two before finding one that fit the ignition on the steering column. The starter motor turned, and the engine sputtered to life. A cloud of smoke lifted from the car's rear and settled over the driveway like fog. I owned a hybrid Subaru back in Minneapolis that hummed like an electric fan and got over forty miles to the gallon. This car was a relic in comparison and not what you'd call environmentally friendly. But then, the nearest Hertz location was likely in Belgrade.

I reached down to shift the car into drive. But there was no Drive, or Reverse, or Neutral. What I hadn't noticed was that the car was a manual. And like most Americans my age, I'd never learned how to drive a stick.

I stopped the engine and stepped out. I had no alternative but to get further instructions from the old man who did not know English.

The process took half the morning. I'd had a boyfriend in high school who owned a Volkswagen with a stick shift. A nice boy who, despite my refusals, really wanted me to learn. So, I knew the gist. The clutch was the third thingy on the floor that you needed to depress to shift gears, and I knew the basic movement of the shifter back and forth to get from first gear to fourth, or fifth, or reverse, or wherever.

Stjepan sat in the driver's seat. I sat next to him as he spoke his language and went through the motions: push in the clutch, push the shifter forward into first, step on the gas, and let out the clutch. He showed me the four gear locations: *prva, druga, treća, četvrta*. He showed me how to wrench the shifter over and down to get the car moving in reverse. With me beside him, he demonstrated driving up and down the road, pushing in the clutch and shifting gears. He knew enough English to point in my direction and say, "You."

It was my turn.

The shifter was loose, like a big spoon in a pot of chili, but I found first gear. I let out the clutch. The engine instantly sputtered and stalled. Stjepan sat next to me, exasperated, making emphatic Cro noises and gesticulating wildly with his hands.

It took me a moment to understand that I needed to let out the clutch more slowly and lay in more acceleration. The engine stalled five more times before I really stepped on the gas. Then the car lurched forward so suddenly that my hands and feet came off the controls. The car took two halting jerks forward and then stopped. Stjepan was now speechless.

It took me another uncomfortable hour. Stjepan tried to remain calm and patient, but I could tell he was ready to give up. Then I made it down the road to the next intersection, put the clutch in, braked, turned around, and drove back. Stjepan, nervously clutching the underside of the passenger seat, smiled and said, "*Dobro.*" Good.

But then he was done. He opened the passenger door and stepped out. My lesson was presumably finished. I guessed I knew enough now to learn the rest on my own, even though I'd never shifted the car out of first gear and never into reverse.

I turned the engine off and stepped out. Stjepan stood in the road with an awkward, closed-lip smile. I said, "*Hvala,*" thanks, to which he just lifted a hand—I guessed his way of saying *no problem.*

It then occurred to me that he might be the same age as my real or imagined grandmother. He was old enough to have survived the thirty-five years of Tito's communism and the War of Independence. He must have seen so much and likely knew everyone on the island. I had Marta Ivelja's information on my phone.

I asked him, "Marta Ivelja?" I showed him the spelling along with the address.

He looked at the screen and nodded. "*Da.*"

I used the translation app on my phone. I typed in, *Is she still alive?*

Stjepan looked at the translation and then dug into a shirt pocket for a pair of readers. He looked again with the glasses balanced on the tip of his nose. "*Da.*"

I pointed to the address, and to that, he said again, "*Da.*"

The address was easily found on my phone's map, but the location didn't show a nearby street. It was up in the old town I'd driven through the day before with Sara. No doubt, the house or the apartment was located on one of the narrow alleyways we'd passed, built back at a time when roads were designed for pedestrians and donkey carts, but not Yugos.

My grandmother's presence now felt more real—a living person with a known address. Scary real, and I wanted more than anything to see if the connection of blood was also real.

I released the clutch, stepped on the accelerator, and drove off in the direction of the old town. The engine began to whine, and I knew I needed to shift into second gear. I pushed in the clutch and shifted, pleasantly finding second almost immediately. I found third before reaching a stop sign. I then had to start over.

The shifting began to feel more comfortable, and I felt accomplished, like when I first successfully made a billowing soufflé. But, like with all soufflés, that accomplished feeling eventually deflated, crumpled when the road started to narrow, turn, and steeply climb. If the car stalled on the incline, I knew I'd never get it going again. I'd be stuck until some kind of help arrived or be forced to coast erratically in reverse to the bottom.

Luckily, the road flattened at a turn with just enough room

for me to pull off and park. And just enough room to turn around without having to shift the car into the untried reverse gear.

I took off walking. The directions on my cell phone showed that the address was only two kilometers away.

On both sides of the road lay fields of larger gardens, some green with more leeks and early lettuces ready to harvest. I passed other stone cottages like mine, but few people were outside. One woman in the distance hung laundry, and her white bedsheets billowed in the gentle wind.

Then, a small cemetery. I decided to walk through and read the names on the headstones. Almost all were made of chiseled soft limestone, and much of the writing had blurred or disintegrated over time due to wind and rain. I could make out some dates, some going back over five hundred years. I did find an Ivelja—Andrijana, 1723 to 1758. She was my age when lowered into the ground, thirty-five. In my daydreamy mind, I imagined she left behind a saddened and burdened husband who still needed to work in the fields each day, and children who were then forced to fend for themselves. Or, like with me, find a new family and start a new life. I'd never wanted kids for that reason—someone who might be left behind. Around the Ivelja headstone, I looked for the graves of a child or a husband. None. They'd left or never existed, and it was hard to say if Andrijana was a blood relative.

Further down the road, I approached a school. Kids played on a soccer field outside a two-story building with rows of windows open to the comfortable May breeze. Opposite the soccer field were tennis courts, almost brand-new, with brightly painted white lines against a field of green. A young girl in a white pleated skirt volleyed with an older man who shouted instructions. I saw the chestnut-brown pigtails next—

the girl who'd been on the ferry. What was her name? I remembered—Mia.

I tried to slip by without being recognized and potentially pushed into reliving the embarrassing scene from the day before. No such luck. Mia saw me and waved. She said something in Cro to the man and then ran through a gate to buoyantly greet me. "Lady from the ferry! Trampled by Turtles!"

She was cute, all right—white skirt, white tennis shirt with a swish logo, pigtails, and those emerald green eyes that now beamed like search lights.

"How are you, Mia?" I asked.

She grabbed my hand. "Good. Are you here for a long time?"

"Two weeks."

"My father thinks you are very beautiful. I think so, too."

I remembered the man as he held my hair while I vomited over the railing. Loose strands of hair had stuck to the slime encircling my mouth and chin. I wondered how the man could seriously think I was beautiful, but I responded, "Thank you very much."

"Perhaps we will see you soon. My father, I am sure, would like to meet you again."

"Perhaps. I hope so." And if so, I would be reminded all over again of that particular embarrassment.

Then the man on the tennis court, presumably her coach, yelled something I couldn't understand.

Mia quickly said, "Goodbye," and ran off.

And still, I didn't know her father's name.

The map took me off the main road, and now I walked up through the maze of fifteenth and sixteenth-century buildings. The narrow cobblestone streets were worn shiny from years of use. They led past small homes, each sharing a wall with its neighbor. All were constructed of warm-gray stones the size of cinder blocks, hand-mortared and patched in places. Many of the terracotta roofs were original, with lichen and moss sprouting from the old clay. Atop most stood the conical, "witches' hat" chimneys unique to Lastovo. Other roofs had collapsed into their abandoned supporting structures. Inside those, I could see broken chairs, shards of old pottery, rotting wood, and rusting bed frames. Skittish feral cats roamed among the alleys and ruins, looking on as I walked, seemingly anticipating a scrap of food or a threatening kick. People once lived in these homes—maybe my people. Now, mostly cats and ghosts.

I found signs of life—homes rebuilt among the wreckage with brightly painted front doors and balconies lined with potted plants. Signs of construction—wheelbarrows, cement mixers, and wood concrete forms. "For Sale" and "For Rent" signs. I could see there was an effort to rebuild and repopulate, but renovations were going slowly.

I was getting closer to the address of Marta Ivelja.

Then, cold feet. What if she *were* my grandmother? What if she weren't? What would I say after she opened the door to this mysterious visitor? What would she think? If she were my grandmother, would she embrace her long-lost relative, or shun me like some unwanted ghost from the past? If she weren't, she'd certainly shut the door on the presumptuous tourist. I would've traveled thousands of miles to chase a shadow. Somehow, I'd never considered any of those scenarios. It was always about finding her or anyone who might have knowledge of my past.

I became anxious—that feeling which could render me immobile, scared to make any decisions, and certainly hesitant to just go and knock on a stranger's door. I knew I was simply panicked by what might or might not be real. What I needed was time to calmly think it through, time to let my anxiety pass.

I wandered into a small courtyard. Mismatched tables and chairs were set up under an ancient tree with its canopy of limbs and leaves. A wood-carved sign read "Konoba Lastovo." Beneath it was another lit-up sign that read "OTVORENO." Then another in English, "OPEN." It seemed a convenient place to let my anxiety fade and allow me the time to think and plan what I'd do or say. It was nearly noon. I hadn't eaten since the night before and realized I was famished. I sat down in the shade of the tree. I was the only customer.

A young woman approached my table—twenty-something with long, sun-faded brown hair held back with a yellow ribbon. "*Dobar dan.*"

I repeated, "*Dobar dan.*"

My accent was a dead giveaway, and the young woman switched to English. "Are you here for lunch?"

"*Da*, yes."

She dropped a laminated one-sheet menu on the table, written in both Cro and English. The menu was one I'd seen at a tavern in Split—the exact same photos of fish, meats, pastries, and beverages. I didn't think a mass-produced menu was a good sign of fresh food. So, I asked, "What's fresh?"

The woman didn't need to think. "Grilled anchovies. We have *blitva*, pickled turnips, salad greens. That is fresh."

I ordered, "Anchovies. And what is *blitva*?"

The woman looked at me curiously as though she'd been

asked to describe a simple carrot. "*Blitva*—Swiss chard and potatoes."

"Anchovies and *blitva*. And a beer, please." A beer would definitely help with my anxiety.

The server was back minutes later with a cold half-liter bottle of beer called Pan and a small glass. While I drank, an older man wearing an apron over a white T-shirt came out with a bundle of sticks. He looked at me, smiled, nodded, and then walked to a brick barbecue grill like the one I'd seen behind The Oleander Cottage. The man set out a crumpled sheet of newspaper and then a crosshatch of sticks. He lit the paper to start the fire. The smoke billowed up through the barbecue's roof and chimney. He laid on more sticks.

The fire quickly burned to embers, and the man was back out with skewered anchovies slathered with olive oil and rock salt. He placed a small grate over the bricks that bordered the embers, then set the fish on top. The man stood over the flames, occasionally looking toward me, his only customer. He turned the fish. The grilled anchovies then made their way back into the kitchen. Moments later, they were back out, served by the young woman on a plate with the *blitva*.

So simple and so delicious. I could imagine the same meal made decades or centuries before—nothing had changed—potatoes, greens, fish, salt, and olive oil. I slid a single grilled anchovy off the charred skewer, which was little more than a whittled cutting from an olive tree. The delicate white meat slipped off the fine bones. The fish flavor was mild and delicious, with a slight taste of the harvested olives pressed to make the oil. The *blitva* was just as described—Swiss chard and potatoes, with the bitterness of the chard complementing the earthiness of the potatoes. Maybe my mother and father had sat with my grandmother at this very same table, eating the same dish.

My mother and father. My grandmother.

If Marta Ivelja were really her, wouldn't she want to be reunited? Yes.

I took my time finishing my beer and paying the check. I procrastinated as long as my conscience would allow. But I did feel better, more relaxed, and more determined. I instinctively knew not to overthink it. Words would inexorably come from my mouth, and there'd be an exchange of language neither understood. But somehow, I would know if what I imagined was, in fact, real.

I stood up and moved on to that inescapable knock on the door.

Pasta Puttanesca

My favorite version of an anchovy dish, when only canned fillets are available, is pasta puttanesca (sadly translated as whores' pasta). A luscious Plavac Mali pairs well with this pungent, salty pasta!

Serves 4

16 ounces linguine
⅓ cup extra-virgin olive oil
3 cloves garlic, minced or grated
2 cups crushed tomatoes
6 anchovy fillets, chopped
6-ounce can tomato paste
4 tablespoons capers
½ cup Kalamata olives, pitted and coarsely chopped
1 teaspoon crushed red pepper flakes
2 tablespoons finely chopped fresh parsley
Parmesan cheese, for garnish

Bring a large pot of lightly salted water to a boil. Cook the linguine in boiling water for 8 to 10 minutes, or until al dente.

Heat the olive oil in a skillet over low heat. Cook the garlic for 1 minute before adding the crushed tomatoes. Cook for 5 minutes. Stir in the anchovies, tomato paste, capers, olives, and red pepper flakes. Cook for 10 minutes, stirring occasionally until the sauce thickens.

Toss the pasta with the sauce, garnish with parsley and parmesan, and serve.

The Dutch Baby

Memories would eventually come flooding back, but at that time, what did I know?

I was three when the bombs dropped on Dubrovnik in December of 1991. I had no memory of the explosion. My first memory was when I woke up in the hospital weeks later with burns on my back, still raw and excruciatingly painful.

I thought I had a real memory of my mother where I touched her hair, the same caramel-blonde color as mine, and that it ran long behind her back. We shared the same button nose and full lips. I clung to the memory, but it could easily have been a manifestation of my vibrant dream life. No photos followed me to the orphanage.

I did remember where my mother worked—a bakery— and that she took me with her to sit in a back corner while she made bread and pastries. The place smelled of flour and yeast. Even now, I can't go into a bakery without experiencing that sense memory. When that happens, it doesn't trigger anxiety or anger. Just the opposite—I can loiter in a bakery for hours, eating a pastry, drinking coffee, and just feel the presence of my mother. It's as close as I can get.

I'd been with her at the bakery when the blast came.

I had no memories of my father, but in dreams, he had dark, straight hair and a thick mustache. He appeared gentle, protective, and would take me by the hand to show me things in the forest: mushrooms, snails, rabbits, berries, and, in a few dreams, a wolf. The wolf often watched us from a distance, its eyes piercing, ears forward, and lips in a snarl with spiked teeth. It was there as a threat but never pounced. And, while I held my father's hand, I felt calm. But in another dream, I was with him in the forest, the wolf again baring its teeth, and then instantly, the hand vanished, and I was left alone. I woke up terrified. The man in the dreams—my father, I believed— never changed. Always the dark hair and mustache, my hand nestled in his.

I somehow knew that the wolf was the embodiment of the war.

Memory is a tricky thing. Were the dreams of my father a manifestation of a real person? Did I possibly once know him? Did my mother really have the same hair color and the same nose? But memory could come down to blood proof. I had the burn scars on my back—scalloped pink skin that itched in the dry winter months. I'd always been embarrassed by the scars, afraid to take showers at school or, later, undress in front of a boyfriend. The scars were real and held the memory of the blast.

I remembered snippets from after I was released from the hospital. My mother and father were not there, presumably dead, and I sat on a bus with other children, frightened because there was no one I knew. I remembered sleeping on a cot in a room with other cots.

I moved from one orphanage to another as the war progressed.

I remembered one woman who was particularly nice to me, but we didn't speak the same language. For a time, I assumed she spoke English. I remembered that the woman taught me how to make a pancake in a skillet: eggs, flour, milk, sugar, and nutmeg, whipped together in a bowl and poured into a hot, buttered skillet, then shoved into the oven where it puffed up like a soufflé. Maybe twenty girls were in the dormitory, and we made five skillet-sized pancakes. Once out of the oven, they were dusted with powdered sugar and smothered with maple syrup. It was a happy moment when we all sat at long tables and devoured the special treat. Since that time, I'd learned that the pancake was called a Dutch Baby. And maybe the woman wasn't English but from the Netherlands.

I was one of the first to be adopted from an orphanage in Zagreb. A woman arrived, and the girls lined up to be inspected. I wore my hair in pigtails, just like the girl Mia. That was another memory; I always wanted my hair in pigtails. The other girls called me Kika, which in Cro means pigtail. When my future adoptive mother came to the orphanage, I was introduced that way. I was probably picked because I was a little girl, still impressionable, but not a baby in diapers.

I guess I looked cute.

I assume, by the way they lined us up to be inspected, that others were not chosen and were eventually left to languish in a series of orphanages and group homes.

I still feel bad for those unchosen who were mostly older and no longer cute. I can only guess what sort of lives they eventually led.

For many years in America, in Minneapolis, my parents called me Kika. My adoptive parents were kind and generous but with strict religious morals that hung between us like a glass wall. They did, though, provide whatever I needed, and I felt lucky. I *was* lucky.

Geography and appearance are destiny for so many people.

At the age of four, I could only speak Cro. But by the age of ten, I'd lost most of that language, and it only came back in snippets. Thank you, *hvala vam*. How are you, *kako ste*? My name is Kika, *zovem se Kika*. I remembered what Stjepan had said that morning when I'd stalled the Yugo: "*Polako, polako!*" It came to me soon afterward, "Slowly, slowly."

I was no longer Kika.

The streets weren't marked by obvious signs, and I followed the directions on my phone as best I could through a labyrinth of alleyways that crisscrossed the hills on which the old town of Lastovo was built six hundred years before. For a time, I wandered aimlessly. Then I noticed the street names chiseled in stone and embedded into the corners of the homes that bordered the crossroads. I retraced my steps and found the alleyway marked "Pušćet." It was a short walk to find the enameled plaque, 4.

I stood outside and looked around for any sign or detail that might tell me something. An old grape press was on a side terrace, rusted and now used as a planter, with shoots of lavender showing off their fragile purple flowers. Stuck in the planter was a rusted garden whirligig—a red rooster with propeller wings that would twirl in the wind. Next to the press was a small meshed-steel table surrounded by a single matching chair. The double doors to the house had once been white, but the paint had peeled, revealing the weathered gray wood beneath. I looked up. On the terracotta roof stood an old-school TV antenna, and from the roof gutters, I could see traces of flourishing weeds. It seemed like the home of an old woman who lived by herself.

I knocked on the door.

I waited and then knocked again.

From inside, I heard a voice, then footsteps. The door cracked open, and a woman looked out. *"Dobar dan."*

"Dobar dan." Then, *"Engleski?"*

The woman opened the door the width of her shoulders. She shook her head no. Behind her, the room was dark. I could hear the television in the distance playing a Croatian program with the volume turned up. Behind the babble of TV, I could just hear a bawk, bawk, bawk. It struck me that somewhere through these doors lived a walking, squawking chicken.

I stood there, stunned. The woman opened the door wider and looked at me, waiting to see what I would do or say next. Was this my grandmother? The woman was stooped, thin, and smaller than me. Her white hair was brushed across her brow, cut short just below the ears, and mostly covered with a dark headscarf. Her face was deeply lined, with small eyes that peeked through crowded lids. The woman wore no makeup, and her lips turned downward into a scowl, likely wondering if I was just another lost tourist. But there was something else, just a twist of her lips that showed bewilderment. I'd seen that same expression in the mirror.

She was moving to close the door when I said, "Marta

Ivelja?"

"*Da.*"

I pointed at myself. "Vesna Ivelja."

The woman stared up at me, looking to find the recognition in the lips and eyes. It was there, and I could see that she knew. My grandmother let out a wounded, mournful sound, and then her face twisted into one of complete sorrow, tears now bursting from her eyes.

I was crying. And then joyously laughing. The woman nearly collapsed, and I moved to embrace her, my hands around her shoulders, and hers tight around my waist. We held each other until a sound from inside—the bawk of the chicken—snapped us from our strange reunion. I then took her arm, led her into the house, and guided her to a stuffed chair in front of the television. I turned it off.

I pulled a chair close, sat, and held my grandmother's hands. She looked at me and then lifted her fingers to touch the contours of my face, searching and trying to understand.

I watched her expression. I had hoped, I guessed, for pure joyfulness, but really, I had no idea what to expect. A lost grandchild had returned home. Then the questions: *How had this happened? How had she found me?* What I thought I saw on the woman's face was bewilderment.

I could only imagine what had happened. The woman's daughter had died, the grandchild lost to the chaos of war, and then the years of mourning.

I leaned forward and held the woman, and again she began to cry. She cried for minutes, her eyes closed and her body limp in my arms.

Slowly, she regained composure. Her body stiffened and I loosened my embrace. Her hands moved to wipe away tears.

I sat back in the chair, and for the next awkward minute,

while we looked at each other, there was near silence.

No instruction manual came with confronting lost relatives.

She then stood and said, "*Skuhat ću čaj.*" I knew the word "*čaj*," tea.

My grandmother moved to the back kitchen, and I listened as she filled the kettle and lit the stove. Again, I heard the clucking of a chicken, but none appeared. It wasn't uncommon then for city-dwellers to have a chicken coop, and I was sure it was very common in Croatia. But the sound seemed to be emanating from inside the kitchen.

Marta, my grandmother, came back with two mugs of hot tea.

We settled down and composed ourselves.

There was so much to learn. But then the language barrier was hard to overcome.

From a closet, Marta pulled out a shoebox and started rummaging through a pile of photos. One was of a woman who looked like me, and Marta said, "*Mama,*" and pointed in my direction. My mother, Ivana. She appeared just how I'd remembered, with the same caramel-blonde hair and button nose. I hadn't imagined it. She wore a summer dress with a pattern of swirling fish on a field of turquoise. Marta pulled out another photo, one that needed no explanation—my mother holding me just after I was born.

I asked, "*Tata?*" My father.

Marta shook her head. She said slowly, "*Rat,*" then, "*Vojnik.*"

I didn't know what those words meant, so I looked them up on my phone. War, soldier. Then I translated, What was his name? "*Kako se zvao?*"

"Josip."

My grandmother added, *"On je mrtav."* She looked at me sympathetically with a sad smile, the small eyes behind her heavy lids expressing what I had already known or assumed. I didn't need the phone for translation. Both of my parents were dead. What was known—my father had been in the war, no doubt in the military during the War of Independence. And I learned something else. Marta Ivelja was my mother's mother. My parents had not been married.

For now, I avoided discussing that piece of information. Of course, Marta had to know what I now knew, but it was a fact that neither of us wanted to broach just then.

We went through the box: my grandmother and grandfather, more photos of my mother, and what looked like a restaurant with all three standing out front. My mother and grandfather wore aprons. Marta pointed and said, "Konoba Mjesec."

I guessed this was our family tavern. The irony that my biological family had owned a restaurant and I was a chef would not sink in until much later.

No other children were in the photos, and I assumed I was an only child.

Other questions twisted through my mind. I wanted to know if my grandmother had other children, if I had uncles, aunts, and cousins. I wanted to know if other relatives were still alive. I wanted to know who I was. So many overwhelming questions, but I didn't know how to ask. And translating on the cell phone seemed clumsy, rife with errors, and prone to misunderstandings.

Then I could see that my grandmother was beginning to tire.

I lifted my phone and typed a message. *There is so much I want to know, but it is getting late and I should leave.*

I showed the translation to Marta, and she nodded.

I typed again. I wanted to meet when we could sit down for a long meal, and I could hear my family's stories. I wanted to get Marta to The Oleander Cottage where I could prepare the meal. I knew I'd need someone to translate—maybe Sara. I wrote, *I will pick you up for supper tomorrow. I will have someone to translate. Ok?*

Marta read the translation, looked up with a smile, and nodded. "*Da.*"

I set my mug of tea on a side table and stood to leave.

It was then that the chicken, which had made the noises when Marta first opened the door, came rushing in from the back of the house. It was no chicken, but a rooster with auburn feathers, red comb, and menacing beak. I hadn't a clue how it was kept in the kitchen or why it just then decided to attack. The rooster charged, wings spread, screeching. I instinctively held out my hands to shield whatever the creature intended to do.

But before it reached me, Marta stepped in front and scooped the bird up to her chest.

She said, "*Žao mi je,*" which I assumed was some sort of apology.

I smiled and let out a short laugh.

Then, at the door, she held him up toward me.

I gave the now more docile creature a cautious pet.

My grandmother nodded at the rooster and said, "*General Gotovina. Goto.*" Presumably, the rooster's name was General Gotovina or simply Goto. Now we were friends.

It all seemed so bizarre.

The Dutch Baby

This old family recipe can be made even more perfect by adding fresh blueberries or strawberries right before serving, along with warm maple syrup and whipped cream.

Serves 2-4

2 large eggs
½ cup whole milk
½ cup sifted all-purpose flour
1 pinch ground nutmeg
1 pinch cinnamon
1 pinch kosher salt
2 tablespoons unsalted butter
2 tablespoons powdered sugar, for dusting

Place a 10-inch cast-iron skillet into the oven and preheat to 475°F.

Whisk the eggs in a bowl until frothy, for about 5 minutes. Whisk in milk, then gradually add flour, nutmeg, cinnamon, and salt.

Remove the skillet from the oven and reduce the heat to 425°F. Place the butter into the hot skillet and swirl to coat the bottom and sides.

Pour the batter into the skillet and return it to the oven.

Bake until puffed and lightly browned, about 10 minutes. Remove from the oven and immediately sift powdered sugar over the top.

Serve immediately while the pancake is still puffy!

Garden Salad with Mustard Aioli

What would it have been like if Ivana and Josip had lived? After leaving my grandmother's home, I walked through the narrow cobblestone alleys and the ruins of the ancient town, trying to imagine it. The war years would've been difficult with the summer residents unable to return. But at the age of three or four, I wouldn't have known the difference. And the islanders would've sustained themselves with home-grown produce, offshore fishing, olives, and grapes. I'd be happy with close friends and a family who loved me. Gradually, the summer residents would have returned—the Croatians from inland first, and then tourists from Europe and elsewhere. My family owned a tavern, and it would've been karmically perfect to grow up and work in that kitchen. Then, I'd have a family of my own, meeting someone on the island—a grape or olive grower, fisherman, or carpenter—someone who worked with his hands and was close to the earthly things that surrounded us. I wouldn't have carried the stigma of my parents' deaths, the abandonment to orphanages, or the adoption by strangers. The thought wouldn't have even crossed my mind. I'd have children, maybe even a sweet daughter like Mia. The child would be Mia's age by now, the two growing up together as besties. I could envision lively family lunches under a trellis of grapevines—everyone—my husband, our kids, my mother and father, Marta, and even close friends. We'd live among the ghostly ruins and turn them into a playground of our own. It would've been a good life.

At the bottom of the sloped valley, I retrieved my rented Yugo, turned around on the narrow road without having to find reverse, and then drove cautiously back to the stone cottage. The old man, Stjepan, had gone, but on the stoop of the front door, he'd very kindly left a wicker basket filled with more leeks, spring peas, lettuces, and radishes. I brought the produce inside and set it next to the kitchen sink to be washed later.

I called Sara to see if she'd be willing to come over for dinner the next day and do the translating.

Her response was blunt: "Going on morning ferry to Hvar for to get sex activity." Her English was good enough, but she hadn't quite learned the subtleties of the language.

I responded, "Good luck. Hope you have good activity," and then laughed.

I still needed someone to translate. But I also needed to buy food for myself and for dinner the next day. I decided to drive to a supermarket that my phone's map showed was near the ferry dock in Pasadur. I got back in the Yugo, started the engine, depressed the clutch, shifted into first gear, gently accelerated, and then let out the clutch slowly. The car bucked twice at the low engine speed. I gave the car a little more gas and it took off. I was getting the hang of it.

I crossed the hills that Sara had negotiated at frightening speed. I didn't stop on the climbs because I couldn't fathom how anyone navigated the simultaneous use of the clutch, accelerator, *and* brakes all at the same time. On the other side, going downhill, I mostly coasted. Then I was in the middle of a vineyard with its rows of spiderweb vines.

The Yugo's engine began to sputter. Then it stopped.

I waited a few seconds, superstitiously crossed my fingers, and then turned the ignition. The car miraculously started and idled. I put it into gear and released the clutch. I made it past a few more rows of grapevines before the engine again sputtered and stopped. Then, it wouldn't restart, even with both fingers crossed.

On my phone, I searched for the closest auto mechanic. The only one I could find was on the island of Korčula, in a town called Blato. Funny name, Blato. There was likely a mechanic on Lastovo, known to the locals, who didn't need to advertise on Google. Maybe it was Stjepan, with his collection of rusted cars. But even if he had a phone, I didn't know the number.

I left the crappy old car on the side of the road and began walking. Someone would pick me up or help get the Yugo started. For the next twenty minutes, no one passed. Then, I was at the sign that said "Radić Winery, NOT OPEN TO THE PUBLIC." I decided that, in my almost dire situation, I was not the public. I walked down the long driveway to the vineyard.

I passed another sign that read in English, "NO TRESPASSING," and wondered who would come all this way from wherever—all the way across the Adriatic, past the beautiful islands near Split and Dubrovnik, just to push through and get a glimpse of this place.

A tractor drove out from the stone barn. A man sat at the wheel wearing overalls and a baseball cap. Maybe the owner. He saw me and turned the tractor in my direction. He stopped, blocking my way down the gravel road. He yelled over the tractor's pulsing engine, "*Stani, stani!*" Then, assuming I didn't know Croatian or get the gist of what he was saying, the man said in English, "Stop, stop," whisking his hand as though shooing away a buzzing fly.

I shielded my eyes from the sun and yelled back, "I need help." Then the word for help came to me: "*Pomoć!*"

He ignored my Croatian plea and repeated, "Stop," continuing with the shooing motion. The man would clearly not help.

But then I heard another voice, barely audible over the sound of the tractor. "Turtle! Turtle!"

I looked beyond the tractor and saw the young girl in pigtails running toward me—Mia.

I waved.

She came nearer and now spoke to the man on the tractor. He smiled at her, then looked back at me, still smiling. He held up his hands and tilted his head in that universal gesture of "Oh well. How was I supposed to know?"

I responded with the same gesture right before Mia took my hand.

Past the tractor, I asked, "Is this your home?"

"Yes, this is our vineyard—Tata and me. Come, you will see and meet him." Then, "How did you find us? How did you get to our house?"

"My car broke down. I walked here for help."

"Tata will help."

Mia held my hand and led the way through the winery.

Past the barn was a tennis court, bright and new like the one at the school. Neon-yellow practice balls were strewn everywhere within the surrounding fence. We passed through the opening in a high cedar hedge. Behind it was a stone house—not really a house or a cottage, but a mansion, a château or villa, magnificent with two stories, terraces, and a terracotta roof. Double hand-carved wood doors opened to a foyer with a claw-footed round table. On top was a vase filled with fragrant lilacs. Still holding Mia's hand, I used my other hand to touch the flowers and move closer to get the whole fragrance. The smell made me think of spring in Minnesota, and the lilac blooms I'd pick from the side of a nearby road to fill restaurant bud vases.

Mia pulled me away. "Tata is in his study."

We walked through a large kitchen. I recognized the French Lacanche range and a commercial Sub-Zero refrigerator. A marble countertop on a center island was as large as a grand piano. This was a kitchen one could really cook in.

Mia kept pulling, and I kept following.

Behind a closed door was the study lined with dark wood and books. The father sat at a desk in a high-back leather chair but didn't turn around. He said, "Mia, *što je?*"

"Trampled by Turtles!"

The father turned and looked up. I remembered the wavy hair brushed across his forehead, the dark eyebrows that framed his gentle eyes, and the pronounced Roman nose. I recognized the smile that crossed his face. An attractive man. Then, I remembered the touch of his hand that held my hair as I vomited over the side of the boat. He was kind to help me, but the incident was still so fresh in my mind and incredibly embarrassing.

He said, "Yes, you!"

"Yes, me." *The one you watched become seasick.*

"What brings you to our house?"

I now had to ask him for another kindness. "My car broke down on the road near here. I'm wondering if you could help. Maybe there's a mechanic you know of?"

The man stood. "Let's see what is wrong."

"No, that's okay. You've already helped me enough."

"Holding your hair while you were... *povraćala?*"

I laughed. "In English, we say vomit, puke, throw up, hurl, bark, wretch, upchuck, heave, or toss your cookies."

"Toss your cookies? I like that. In Croatian, we sometimes say, *grliti školjku,* which means to hug the toilet bowl, or *izrigati dušu,* to spit your soul out."

"Tata, stop!"

We all laughed. Then the father said, "Come, let's go have a look. I will drive us to where you are broken down."

We'd never exchanged names on the ferry, and now I wanted that omission to end. I held out my hand and introduced myself using my legal, adoptive name. "I'm Vesna Thompson. Everyone calls me Ves."

He took my hand. "I am Dinko Radić." We locked eyes as we touched, his smile showing the white, crowded teeth. And somehow, they were cute, like a dimple or Cindy Crawford's mole.

I was the one to turn away.

The first thing Dinko said as he pulled up to the broken-down car in his Range Rover was, "A Yugo. Communist piece of garbage. Why would you rent such a car?"

I didn't need him to criticize my judgment. I just needed him to help me fix it or find a mechanic. I dodged the question. "It was running just fine. Then it sputtered and stopped."

"I'm surprised it ever started. Did you run out of gas?"

I looked at him now as though he'd insinuated that I was just stupid. "The gas tank is full. I picked up the car only yesterday."

"Okay, let me see." Dinko opened the creaky car door and sat in the driver's seat. He looked around, possibly shocked at the sparse and shabby interior. I'd left the key in the ignition, and he turned it, pumping the accelerator at the same time. The engine started, then sputtered and died. He turned the key again, and the engine cranked uselessly. He looked at the dashboard. "The fuel gauge is on empty."

Exasperated, I needed to explain. "The man who owns the car said the tank was full, but that the gauge didn't work. None of the gauges work."

Dinko didn't look up when he said, "Not surprising." He popped the hood using a lever under the dashboard, then stepped out of the car. He lifted the hood. Looking over his shoulder, all I could see was a spare tire above an engine not much larger than a lawnmower's. And who puts a spare tire in the engine compartment? Dinko just laughed and closed the hood.

Mia was at his side. "Tata, why don't you call Mika? He can fix it."

"Yes, call Mika, please." When he looked at me, I gave my best fake smile.

"Let me check something else." Dinko walked around the car and then lay on the asphalt, looking beneath. He banged on something with his fist. He banged again. "That hollow sound? There is no gas in the tank." He banged again to make his point clear. He stood and added, "I'll go get a gas can from our barn."

I fumed. Stjepan had said the car was full of gas, and I wanted to believe him. I wanted to say something to Dinko, tell him he was wrong. But then maybe he wasn't. And if the tank was empty, I'd look like such a fool. First seasickness, and now this. I crossed my arms and kept silent.

I stayed with Mia while Dinko drove back for the gas. I said, "I'm sorry about all this."

"That's okay. It's good for Tata to have visitors. He sits in his study all day working or is out in the vineyard working. Always working. He never goes out, and he never dates. I think this is good for him."

I hadn't seen a woman other than Mia at the farm, but I assumed a mother was around somewhere. I was wrong. He was either divorced or a widower, or like my own biological father, never married in the first place. I didn't want to pry and did not follow up with a question for Mia. I just said, "He seems like a good father."

Then Mia was out with it. "My mother is Russian, an artist. She left when I was just a baby. An artist's life does not include raising a child. I understand that motherhood is not for everyone, but I wish we could meet and talk."

"I'm sorry." That was a lot of information, and it took me a moment to process. What kind of woman leaves her child? Being an artist was no excuse, and I wondered if this was just the story handed out to a little girl who might not be able to comprehend the *real* story. My own life seemed complicated like that, and maybe I wished everything could be a lie.

But lies have a way of unraveling.

The Range Rover pulled up, and Dinko stepped out with

a red gas can. He emptied the can into the Yugo and then sat back in the driver's seat. I heard him pump the accelerator. He turned the ignition, and the car came to life. He looked up at me and smiled. Smug.

He said, "You'll need to drive directly to the gas station near the ferry dock. It is only ten kilometers away, so you can get there easily. If you have any problems, call." Dinko stepped away from the car and then handed me an old-school business card. I looked at it briefly—his name, the name of the vineyard, and a phone number, all embossed in black on creamy matte cardstock. I slipped the card into my pocket.

"Thank you." I said it sincerely. How was I to know the gas tank was empty? I'd trusted the old man, Stjepan. But then he might not have known either. Possibly, he'd rented the Yugo out to someone who never filled it up before bringing it back.

I got into the running car and shut the door. I rolled down the window. "Again, thank you."

Then Mia said, "Why don't you come for supper tomorrow?"

Dinko looked aghast. "I'm sure the lady has vacation plans."

Mia looked at me. "Do you have plans? Can you change them for us?"

My plan was to have supper with Marta. But my plan also included a translator who could ask the hundreds of questions swirling through my mind. Sara was off to get her "sex activity," and I knew no one else on the island. And I owed the man not only for fixing my car but also for holding my hair.

"Can you both come to my place for supper? I will cook." I didn't add that I was looking for one more favor.

And before Dinko could make up an excuse for not

coming, Mia said, "Of course!"

Dinko asked, "The rental house near the junkyard?"

"That's the one."

I was back at the cottage after gassing up the Yugo and buying enough groceries to last the next few days.

For that night's supper, I had a loaf of crusty bread, the greens Stjepan had given me, an assortment of Croatian cheeses, and a hard salami called *Baranjski kulen* from Baranja, a region near the Hungarian border. The leaves of the salad greens were hardy and would hold up well with an aioli-type dressing I loved, made from olive oil, lemon, egg yolks, garlic, and mustard.

I ate my supper outside in the cooling night air and could hear the cicadas chirping—a comforting sound, like the rustle of leaves or the lapping of waves. I drank what was left of the Radić Plavac Mali. I now knew it was from Dinko's vineyard.

I thought about the man. For years, I'd worked in male-dominated kitchens where I was usually the only woman. I was spoken down to and ordered around. Mansplained. When I finally ran my own kitchen, that attitude was no longer accepted. When Dinko stepped in to help with the gas situation, it grated and reminded me of the early days of working in a kitchen. Then, to make it worse, he was right; the tank was completely empty. He'd done the right thing by ignoring what I thought and inspecting it himself.

He was handsome, that was for sure, with his wavy black hair, gentle eyes, and Cheshire cat smile. He'd worn a rumpled white linen shirt, unbuttoned at the top, with soft curls of the same black hair rising up like pea tendrils. I hadn't slept with Reed for almost a year, not since I'd caught him still seeing the woman he'd had an affair with. I hadn't had the desire to be with a man since. I knew, though, that the need for human touch existed deep inside me, waiting to be let out into the sunlight. And now I could imagine Dinko's touch and our bodies entwined.

Later, I went to sleep with that image, the two of us entwined like those pea tendrils.

Lemon Kale Salad with Parmesan and Crispy Prosciutto

This salad recipe is not the one Ves had that night at The Oleander Cottage, but it's very Croatian, nonetheless.

Serves 4

For the Salad
4 large eggs
6 slices prosciutto
1 bunch kale, ribs removed, sliced thinly
½ cup pine nuts, chopped
⅛ teaspoon red pepper flakes
¼ cup grated parmesan cheese
Freshly ground black pepper, to taste

For the Dressing

¼ cup fresh lemon juice

½ cup extra-virgin olive oil

2 tablespoons chopped fresh mint

2 green onions, thinly sliced

1 clove garlic, minced

1 teaspoon kosher salt

Preheat the oven to 400°F. Line a baking sheet with parchment paper.

Lay the prosciutto slices flat on the baking sheet and bake for 10 minutes, or until browned. When cool, break into shards.

Lower the eggs into the boiling water for 10 minutes. Cool for 10 minutes in a cold water bath. Peel the eggs and chop coarsely.

Make the dressing by blending all the ingredients.

To assemble the salad, add the kale to a large bowl. Drizzle with 2 tablespoons of the dressing, then lightly massage it into the kale with your hands. Add the pine nuts, red pepper flakes, parmesan, chopped egg, and prosciutto shards. Toss with ¼ of the dressing and season with salt to taste. Divide among 4 bowls and drizzle with a bit more dressing. Finish with black pepper.

Stewed Chicken with Biscuits

I woke with that familiar pang of guilt—I hadn't told Dinko about my grandmother. What had begun as a thank-you for helping me with my seasickness and then car troubles now seemed like a dodgy move to ask him for yet more help.

I had his cell phone number and, after much internal wordsmithing, did a quick text. *I have also invited my grandmother, who knows little English. Looking forward to seeing you and Mia.* The text did so much—springing the news that my grandmother would join us, and also implying I'd need his translation services. My pang of guilt was downgraded to an annoying itch.

He texted back almost immediately. *Looking forward to seeing you!* The itch now no more than a tickle.

Another text, this one from Reed. *Had a customer complaint about the peppercorn sauce on her steak au poivre. Said she never ordered the sauce??? How are you?* It was like Reed to butter me up with kitchen humor, though our relationship was anything but humorous.

We'd separated after his affair—sort of. I hadn't moved out; I just moved into the second bedroom of the condo we owned together. We remained courteous. I guess, like an unhappy, unfunny married couple.

Then, after we finally closed our restaurant, I had no place to hide each day. That was when I planned my trip to Croatia. I told him, "I need some time to think," which might have implied an opening in the otherwise closed door to our relationship. I knew the humor and the question, "How are you?" were meant to crack open that door just a little wider. I wanted none of it. I didn't answer Reed's text. Again, the guilt was now back to that familiar pang.

The stewed chicken I planned was a recipe in the new cookbook, which was now with my editor. The recipe needed an accompanying photo, and one from Lastovo would work just fine. I chopped carrots, celery, and leeks—my mirepoix— then sautéed the mixture in the local extra-virgin olive oil Sara had left for me. In a separate cast-iron skillet, I used the same oil to brown the chicken I'd earlier cut into quarters and dredged in flour. I removed the chicken and deglazed the skillet with white wine. I then made a roux with more olive oil and flour, afterward adding chicken stock until it made a half liter of luscious gravy. Finally, I returned the chicken to the skillet with the sautéed mirepoix. The covered skillet went into the oven to slow-cook for two hours. Right before picking up my grandmother, I'd add disks of biscuit dough on top, which would cook into a flaky, brown crust. I'd serve the easy one-pot meal with more of the greens Stjepan had harvested from the garden.

I planned my drive into the village, avoiding the steep, twisting alleyways and parking as close to my grandmother's house as possible. When I arrived in the late afternoon, she was sitting outside, waiting. Her hair was wrapped in the same dark scarf and tied beneath her chin. She wore a coffee-colored blouse and a long black peasant skirt that covered her shoes. Marta looked dressed for a funeral instead of an informal dinner party.

I remembered, *"Bog, kako si?"* Hi, how are you? I leaned forward and hugged the grandmother I'd only just met.

"Bog. Dobro." She hugged me back, a deep embrace that showed how much it must have meant to find a long-lost grandchild. Whatever reticence and mixed emotions she harbored from the day before were now in the past.

Marta sat nervously in the passenger seat as I drove inelegantly back down into the valley. When I pulled into the driveway of The Oleander Cottage, the Range Rover was already there, Dinko standing just to the side. I could see that his hair was neatly combed, the curls corralled and forced to comply. He wore loafers, brown linen pants, and a generous white linen shirt that draped from his broad shoulders. He looked up, smiled, and then lifted two bottles of wine in greeting. He put one of the bottles under his arm and opened the door for Marta.

I stepped away from the car and made an introduction as best I could, first pointing at Dinko. "Dinko Radić," then at my grandmother, "Marta Ivelja."

She looked at him curiously before he spoke up to demystify his presence. *"Tu sam za prevođenje."*

Marta smiled. "*Da. Hvala.*"

Dinko turned to me. "I told your grandmother I was here to translate."

I smiled and mimicked my grandmother. "*Hvala.*"

He was alone. I added, "Where is Mia?"

"There is school for her tomorrow, and she has homework. Her exams are only one week away. My aunt is watching her. Mia said to say, 'Hello, Turtle.'"

I laughed. "I forgot that young girls go to school."

"Then you don't have kids?"

"No kids." I wanted to add, "And not married," but it seemed a little forward. Then again, I was sure he'd noticed the absence of a ring—the one Reed had never offered.

We sat at the outside table I'd set earlier with a canary-yellow tablecloth and a vase of oleander blooms. Dinko had a bottle of his red Plavac Mali and another bottle of white wine, which I later found out was his prized white Grk. I pointed toward the white that would pair well with the chicken. He opened the bottle and filled the jelly glasses I'd set out. He held up his glass and toasted, "To life! *Živjeli!*"

Marta held up her glass and repeated, "*Živjeli!*"

Dinko helped bring out the food. Inside the kitchen, I thanked him for coming and apologized for my ulterior motive. I was candid: "I've just met my grandmother. I was adopted during the war after my parents were killed. I haven't been back since. I'm grateful that you can translate some questions. I would like to know about my birth family." I realized this was so much information all at once. I looked up to him imploringly. I knew I was putting him in an awkward position.

He was kind. "Of course."

We sat down, and I placed the biscuit-covered chicken

dish on the table. Marta looked at the large skillet, and I could tell she hadn't a clue what it was. I was sure Dinko had no idea either. But then I scooped in with a spoon and lifted out a mélange of chicken, vegetables, and gravy, all topped with a flaky biscuit. I placed a helping on Marta's plate. She took a long look and then picked at it with her fork. Finally, "*Vrlo uzbudljivo.*"

Dinko translated, "She says that it is very exciting."

I wasn't sure how to react to "exciting," so I waited until Marta took the first bite. She looked at me and smiled. Then, "*Ovo je ukusno!*"

I didn't need a translation, but Dinko did regardless: "She says, 'This is delicious!'"

He took a bite and repeated, "*Da, ovo je stvarno ukusno!*"

I was anxious to get to my family's history, and it was then that I asked her, "Tell me everything, and from the beginning."

Dinko translated as Marta spoke. She started from the beginning, "I was born..."

I interrupted occasionally, letting her story unfold slowly, knowing it might take many dinners to reach the end. I was in no hurry, and I wanted to know all of it—every detail that led to my mother's and father's births, then every detail of their deaths. To me, it felt like a mystery that would soon be revealed and brought to life. And I wanted it to come to life like a long Russian novel. Love, life, birth, death, joys, and tragedies, all interwoven like the flavors of a rich broth.

Okay, I understand you want to hear about your mother, Ivana, but I must start with what I know of our family first. It is important that I

tell you this background. Everything is always more complicated than it first appears. You must understand that a tomato starts from a seed.

I was born in 1948, right after the Second World War, right here in Lastovo. There were many more people on the island then. This old town was filled with families who lived here year-round. There were sixteen churches on this small island, and all were filled each Sunday. My parents were born here, and theirs also. I do not know how far the families go back, but some gravestones go back to the 1400s. Many of the other names in the cemetery are also our relatives. On my mother's side, the Caravellos can trace their family back to Venice in the year 1000. We are the oldest families on the island, and we have always lived in Lastovo. The house where I live has been in the family for many, many years, and when I die, it will be yours.

The Caravellos were olive growers and owned three hectares of groves with over six hundred trees. They exported their oil all over Europe and were a very wealthy family, one of the richest in Lastovo. Of course, it is no longer there. The communist Tito took the land when I was just ten years old, kicked everyone off, and built barracks for the soldiers. Lastovo became a secret army base that no one was allowed to speak of. Many people left the island during the 1950s and 1960s. Like the Caravellos, some were forced to leave.

My maiden name is Ćurin, and the Ćurins have worked in taverns for generations. Like today, the island swelled during the summer months. Wealthier people from Belgrade, Zagreb, and other inland towns moved here to escape the heat. My father, Filip Ćurin, owned the tavern on the town square. Unlike the Caravellos, he was not wealthy. In the summer months, he would work sixteen-hour days, serve coffee and breakfast in the morning, then beer and wine past suppertime. I remember, as a little girl, that the smell of food cooking was like the air I breathed.

Now, you might ask why the daughter of a wealthy olive oil merchant would marry such a man. I will tell you. He went to school with my mother, Maria, in the early grades. She was two years younger, but they all sat and studied together in the one-room church school. Then, once my mother turned ten, she was sent off to a boarding school in Belgrade. Maria did not see Filip again for three years, not until she was thirteen and he was fifteen. They met at the Lastovo Carnival when she was back for Lent and Easter. Both were in the Carnival parade dressed in our old costumes. Friendship was rekindled then, but it was not to last.

The following year, 1940, Hitler and the Germans invaded Yugoslavia, and they immediately installed a new fascist government in Croatia called the Ustaše. It did not take long because Nazi sympathizers were already among us. My grandfather, Marco Caravello, was a sympathizer and became an important member of the Ustaše.

Your great-grandfather, Filip, just sixteen, went off to fight with the resistance. Filip was very tall and handsome, like an American movie star. Tito, the communist, led a resistance war against the fascists and the Ustaše. Filip fought with Tito and did many brave missions among the islands. He would never talk about the war, but I knew from others that he had assassinated many of the Ustaše. But he protected my mother's father, Marco, from harm. After the war, in 1946, there were many acts of vengeance. If a family had been part of the Ustaše, they were brutally murdered. Even here in Lastovo, men were hanged in the town square, right in front of our family's tavern. But not Marco Caravello. He was spared because of Filip.

Now you see why the daughter of a wealthy olive oil merchant would marry such a man. My father had always felt love for my mother since seeing her at the Carnival. They barely knew each other, but Filip was sure she would be the one he would marry. He protected the family so that Maria would not be hurt. My father was handsome, and also a war hero and high-ranking soldier in the People's Liberation Army. They met again after the war at the very Carnival where, six years earlier, they had first seen each other. There is a dance during the Carnival, called the Kolo, where everyone holds hands in a circle. My father held my mother's hand, and they danced. Afterward, he proclaimed his love. She, too, had always felt that way.

My mother had the same hair color as you do, Vesna. The same face, eyes like almonds, and a small nose. She was very beautiful and very smart. She loved Filip, even though all he wanted was to stay in Lastovo and run the family tavern. He was a war hero and could have gone to Belgrade with Tito and been an important person, but that was not who he was. She wanted to stay in Lastovo as well, even though her father's business was finished, when, a few years later, Tito confiscated the land to build his barracks. My parents had a simple life and raised four children. I was the youngest and now the only one still alive.

Marta stopped there. The translation had taken time, and we'd nearly finished the two bottles of wine, our salads, and chicken stew. My grandmother looked exhausted, leaning over the table, looking off in the distance, up toward the town.

What had she witnessed? What ghosts lurked that I couldn't see? I knew some history—the World Wars, revolutions, and the Cold War. But now it felt real—my grandmother born into communism after the fascists were defeated and then living through the Croatian War of Independence, where she lost a daughter and a grandchild.

Then again, it wasn't so real. I'd lived a sheltered and entitled life in America.

Marta finally looked over at the two of us and spoke in measured words, careful to let Dinko's translation pace out. "That is it for tonight. Another time, more of the story."

I smiled and nodded. "*Hvala ti.*"

"*Mogu opet doći za dva dana.*" I can come again in two days.

We all agreed to have dinner again the following Thursday.

Dinko insisted on driving Marta home and also picking her up later. Great, since the thought of driving the Yugo at night was beyond daunting.

Before leaving, he said, "Those were difficult times. My own grandfather was in the resistance. He was tortured in a Ustaše prison." Dinko held both my hands and then leaned forward for a sympathetic hug. Somewhat stunned, I let my lifeless arms dangle like a rag doll.

I cleaned up and then checked my email. Minnesota was seven hours behind, and there'd be updates about my cookbook and maybe something from Reed. I sat down, opened my MacBook, and logged on to the slow Internet using my cell phone as a hotspot. The few emails flowed in gradually. One from my editor said that the cookbook was almost finished and going into print in a week, though she needed the photo of the stewed chicken with biscuits. The release date was set for the end of May.

Another email was from Reed. It said simply, *Miss you.* First, a text I had ignored, now this. Before I left for Croatia, he'd tried to mend fences, but I was in no mood. I wanted to respond with a cutting comment, *Don't miss you,* or, *I've met someone in Lastovo who just came over for dinner.* I knew those responses were childish, and Reed was trying. I emailed back, *Miss you, too.* Was I softening to him? I just didn't know.

In ten days, I'd be on a plane back to America and the stew that was my real life. I'd figure it out then.

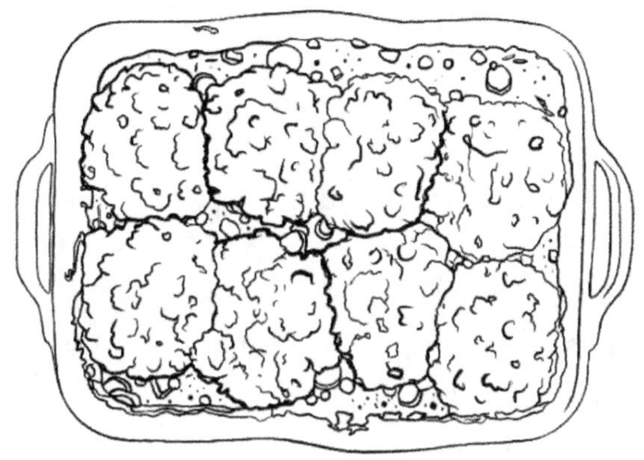

Chicken and Biscuits

Marta's initial skepticism about the stewed chicken dish is understandable—you just don't see heavy food with gravy on the Dalmatian Islands. This recipe is totally Midwest.

Serves 4-6

For the Stew
2 tablespoons extra-virgin olive oil
3 carrots, peeled and diced into rounds
2 cups sweet potato or butternut squash, peeled and diced into ½-inch squares
1 large onion, chopped into ½-inch dice
2 tablespoons salted butter
3 tablespoons all-purpose flour
1 tablespoon Better Than Bouillon Roasted Chicken Base or a dried bouillon cube
3 cups chicken broth

3 cups rotisserie chicken pulled off the bone, or poached chicken breasts
1 tablespoon fresh chopped rosemary
1 tablespoon fresh thyme
Kosher salt and freshly ground black pepper, to taste

For the Biscuit Dough
2 cups all-purpose flour
2 teaspoons baking powder
1 teaspoon granulated sugar
½ teaspoon baking soda
1 teaspoon kosher salt
8 tablespoons melted butter, cooled to room temperature
1 cup buttermilk, chilled

For the Stew
Preheat the oven to 400°F.

On a sheet pan, toss the carrots, sweet potato or butternut squash, and onions with the olive oil. Roast for 25 minutes, then set aside. Raise the oven temperature to 450°F.

Melt the butter in a Dutch oven over medium to high heat. Whisk in the flour, 1 tablespoon at a time, until a nutty base forms. Add Better Than Bouillon and chicken broth, ½ cup at a time, whisking to form a gravy.

When the gravy coats the back of a spoon, add the roasted vegetables, chicken, rosemary, and thyme. Season with salt and pepper to taste.   Reduce the heat to low and continue cooking the filling for 15 minutes. If it becomes too thick, add more broth.

Transfer the filling to a lightly greased 8 x 8-inch baking dish if your skillet isn't oven-safe.

For the Biscuits

Mix the flour, baking powder, sugar, baking soda, and salt in a bowl.

In a medium bowl, combine the butter and buttermilk.

Add the wet ingredients to the dry and combine with a kitchen spoon until a shaggy dough forms. Do not overmix.

Drop the biscuit dough on top of the filling with a ¼ cup scoop until the filling is completely covered.

Add the biscuits to the top and bake according to the biscuit recipe instructions, or until the biscuits are golden and set in the middle.

Brush the biscuits with butter and bake at 400° for 20 minutes.

Roasted Branzino

Two days later, Sara sped up to The Oleander Cottage in her BMW convertible. I was sitting serenely at the outside dining table with my coffee and a slice of toast with butter and blackberry jam. She braked hard, sending a cloud of dust in my direction, and I instinctively covered my coffee and food with a cotton napkin. From behind the wheel, Sara loudly sang out, "*Ćao!*"

I stood. Again, she wore the orange lipstick that almost matched her copper hair and burnt-orange car. I guessed, like in America, real estate agents and attorneys needed that personal branding—something to remember them by.

I was glad to see her. "You're back. Come join me."

Ten minutes later, I had another cup of coffee and another slice of toast and jam for Sara.

I asked, "So, how was your trip to Hvar? Did you get

lucky?"

Sara wore her thick hair back in a ponytail, Ray-Ban aviators up over her forehead, and a Hermès scarf tied around her neck with an intricate design of little motorcars. She had a look of surprise on her face as though, for the first time, she'd witnessed a rabbit plucked from a magician's hat. "I got lucky, all right, if that is the correct word."

"What happened?"

"Well, I visited my regular place. It is right in town of Hvar, steps up from Hvarska Pjaca where all tourists sit, drink their beer, Aperol spritz, and stare at each other. You would like this place, I think. It is called Kokošinjac. Translated, it means henhouse. So, I was in Kokošinjac, sitting at the bar, wearing very tight dress, and hair all sexy down around my shoulders. I am also wearing my sunglasses inside like an average closet lesbian cheating on her ignorant husband. It says to anyone interested, *One-night stand, please.* Not much later, this very attractive girl, maybe only twenty years of age, sits down beside me. She says, 'Buy me a drink?' Not, *Can I buy you a drink?* No, assumes I am the older woman who will take care of her."

"So, did you?"

"Of course. She ordered a martini, which is very American. She believes herself very sophisticated. All right, I think. This is okay. I ordered one also, though it is not of my liking. I much prefer the tourists' Aperol spritz. We talk, blah-blah-blah, and then she invites me to her apartment. I say, 'Yes.' She then drives me in her old Citroën to this building that is close by in the town of Milna. We get there, a nice building overlooking the sea. Then she says that we need to be quiet because she is living with her grandfather, and he will be asleep. Now, if I understood a grandfather would be involved,

I would have suggested we get a nice hotel room in Hvar. I know good place. But I am in Milna, and I am so desperate for the sex activity that I do not care. But when she opens the apartment door with key, the grandfather is awake and watching television.

"This is very interesting. The man was old, large, and bald. He is sitting in his underwear only, and around his neck is a tube delivering oxygen to the base of his nose like a scuba diver. At the sight of his granddaughter and her lesbian friend, he simply grunts like a pig. The girl says, "*Ej, Dida*," then introduces me. And like we have all known each other for a hundred years, we sit down and watch the television. He is watching *Yellowstone*. Very popular in Croatia with Kevin Costner and that very sexy Kelly Reilly.

"We stay for near an hour, waiting for grandfather to go to bed. But after one episode of *Yellowstone*, there is another, so he stays awake. Finally, the girl stands and says we are going back out. The grandfather again grunts like a pig, and we leave.

"The girl says she knows of a hotel nearby, and she drives us there. This place is a real piece of garbage. It looks like a boarding house for drunks and whores. The girl tells me to go buy the room, and I do because, you know, I am very horny— very desperate for sex activity."

I interrupted, "You don't have to say activity. It's just sex."

"What?"

I knew I shouldn't have corrected her English, but now it was out there. "Desperate for just sex. No activity."

Sara brushed my comments aside with a swipe of her hand. "Let me finish the story."

"Okay." I shut up.

The sun was rising above the house. Sara pulled down her sunglasses; I guessed the same ones she'd worn in Hvar to make her look like a cheating and closeted wife.

She continued, "I buy the room and the man gives me a key, and we go up the stairs to the room. It is very small with no toilet, only a sink in one corner. I am guessing the bathroom is down the hall and open to everyone. Thankfully, I did not have to go there. So, we had our sex, and believe me, it was good sex, the girl very well versed in the craft of oral manipulation."

She stopped there.

I had to admit, I was enthralled with her story. "And then?"

"And then nothing. She drove me back to Hvar where I purchased one more room for the night. This one clean and with a private toilet. The girl went back to her grandfather."

Sara paused to find a cigarette and light it. "But the bad thing is, bedbugs."

"Bedbugs?"

"Yes. I was very tired, and I go to sleep. In the morning, I had those little red marks from bedbug bites. I still itch." To prove her point, Sara then itched.

"I'm sorry."

"Well, I washed good at the Hvar hotel, and I have no more new bites. That is now the end of the story." Then she asked, "What is new with you?"

"I found my grandmother. We had dinner, and this man I met on the ferry, Dinko Radić, translated. You probably know he owns the winery we passed the other day."

"This is great news. And Dinko is very rich man, I think, and very available. He does not leave the winery often. His daughter's mother ran off. Very sad for him, I think."

"Yes, his daughter, Mia, told me that. What do you know about him?"

"He runs a well-known winery that he inherited from his father. He spent many years in Italy, in Capri and Rome. He was a party boy. I think you say, playboy. He made a girl pregnant, a Russian model. He brought her back to Lastovo where she had the child. Then she left. Now, his daughter needs a mother. And I think you need a daughter."

I wanted to laugh. What I needed was a grandmother. "I'm not interested in either."

"But you are now single and without children, no?"

"Yes, but that doesn't mean I want to jump from one bed into another."

Sara took a sip of her coffee and a drag on her cigarette. "Sometimes the bedbugs are worth the trouble."

I laughed and then changed the subject. "I am having another dinner tonight with Dinko and my grandmother. She is telling me the story of my family. Would you like to come?"

Sara thought for a moment. "No, I think I have had enough grandparents for one week."

I drove down a steep, winding road, and the village of Zaklopatica appeared as if in a dream—a turquoise cove protected by a small island covered in rock and pine. Three sailboats were anchored in the center of the cove, all with white hulls and blue canopies that mimicked the water. The boats were large enough for a small family to sleep, cook, swim, sail, and play in. Stone houses lined one side of the cove. In front was a concrete quay where a cluster of fishing boats, along with more sailboats, bobbed in the gentle swell. I parked near the village and walked along the quay to where Sara had said a woman sold fresh fish from a stall beneath her house.

I passed a man tying a wooden skiff up to a steel docking ring. I asked about a fishmonger using what I could translate with my Google app. *"Prodavač ribe?"*

The man looked to be in his sixties, bone-thin, with a face covered in gray stubble. He took off his stained baseball cap, ironically one with a Minnesota Twins logo. The man smoothed back his few remaining strands of hair. "Yes, fish market." He knew English. Then, "Wait, and I will take you there."

"Thank you."

The skiff looked ancient, with oars hand-carved and a tiller the size of a human leg attached to a rudder bound in forged iron. A small iron hook was screwed to the bow. I pointed to it and asked what its purpose was.

The man smiled, showing an almost completely toothless mouth. He held up a kerosene lantern and demonstrated how it hung from the hook. "At night, I go very close to the rocks. The *hobotnica*, the *polpo*..."

"Octopus."

"Yes, octopus. They are attracted to the light and come out from beneath the rocks. Then I get it with this." He held up a long trident spear. The man opened a cooler on the floor of the boat. Inside were six octopuses splayed out across crushed ice. "I am the best!"

He stepped from the boat, and I followed him with his cooler to one of the stone houses toward the end of the quay. The house itself was up a flight of stairs. Beneath it was a stall the size of an American one-car garage where the fish were sold. A stout woman came from behind a counter, a clean apron covering her light summer dress. She opened the fisherman's cooler and took out three, all the size of oven mitts, and said something to the man in Cro. It appeared they'd struck a bargain. The woman lifted the three slack octopuses with both hands and walked to an open-air cooler filled with more crushed ice. As far as I could see, the place had no refrigerator, just one noisy ice maker.

The woman looked at me and asked in English, "Yes, lady?"

"Fresh fish?"

She led me back to where the octopuses took up a corner of the cooler. I looked over the dozen or so fish arranged like roof tiles. A few I recognized—a large snapper, smaller panfish called sea bream, and branzino that I knew had a mild, sea bass-like meat. I asked for three of the branzino.

I spent the late afternoon preparing the meal. I roasted the branzino in the oven with olive oil, lemon, fennel, and thyme. With the oven in use, I also roasted turnips from the garden. With the turnips and branzino, I planned to serve a panzanella salad made with tomatoes, fresh basil from the planter right outside my door, and bread cut into cubes—all tossed in a lemon-olive oil vinaigrette.

Everything was completed and the table set by the time Dinko pulled into the driveway with Marta. His daughter, Mia, was with them, looking through the window of the back seat like some mutt with its nose against the glass. I waved, happy to see her.

I hugged my grandmother, and right away, she beelined for the kitchen and opened the oven door. *"Ukusna hrana!"* And, in the universal sign of great food, she kissed the tips of her fingers. Then she took my hand and led me through the back kitchen door. She pointed at the brick barbecue grill with a stone hearth the size of a breakfast table. I'd seen a similar barbecue in the town square where the man had roasted the anchovies.

Marta began speaking in Cro. Dinko was behind her to translate. "This is a traditional barbecue called *roštilj*. She says that in the summer months, you must cook here outside. You cook the fish over the coals or inside *peka*." Dinko searched around the fireplace and found a rusting bowl.

The grandmother pointed. "*Peka!*"

He explained, "There should be roasting pans somewhere inside your kitchen for *peka* or dome. You lay the branzino in the pan with vegetables, wine, and broth, then place the pan on *roštilj*. You cover the pan with *peka* and then cover *peka* with hot coals. You cook for a couple hours and it's done. This is very Croatian way to cook meats and fish."

Something new, and I could see that baking inside a house made of heat-absorbing stone during the hot summer months would become almost unbearable.

I could imagine its use, envisioning myself as a young girl living with my mother and father in a similar cottage, maybe with other siblings. We'd start the fire in the late afternoon, adding the olive cuttings that fed the playful flames. My father would slip the pan under the *peka* dome, and then we'd eat outside in the cool late evening. My grandmother would be there, along with the grandfather I never knew. This was what could be imagined, and I realized there were stories like that, which could only be imagined because they never happened.

I served the branzino while my grandmother continued with her story. I sat next to Mia, patiently listening as her father translated.

I will tell you now about your grandfather, my husband. I met him at a dance. I still worked with your great-grandfather and great-grandmother, Filip and Maria, in the tavern. Tito was the president of the Socialist Federal Republic of Yugoslavia, and he had turned Lastovo into a secret military base. The ferry service was very limited—you needed papers showing you were a resident to get in, then a special reason and a letter from our local governor to get out. No other Yugoslavs were allowed to go there unless they were part of the military. So, no summer tourists for the tavern. Many left the island and the old town, leaving it almost completely deserted. We had difficulty doing enough business to feed ourselves. But the soldiers who lived on the west side of the island came to eat and drink—the same soldiers who lived in the barracks built on the property once owned by your great-great-grandfather, Dante Caravello. Hundreds of olive trees were cut down to build those ugly barracks. But those barracks housed many of the young men my age. And even though we lived in communist times and abhorred the decadence of the West, we had dances.

The barracks had an auditorium, and the military had a band that could play both the heroic anthems of Yugoslavia but also the polka and your American music—we knew many songs from your Radio Liberty. I went with my friends to a dance held near Christmas time. We all dressed in the nice clothes we had, which were mostly folk costumes worn during Carnival—long white skirts, a blue shirt with red sleeve ribbons, and red scarves covering our heads. This was considered acceptable since it was not Western. At the auditorium, we lined up on one side of the room, the men on the other. The music would start, and the men would walk over and ask one of us to dance.

Your grandfather, Ivan, was a shy man, and it took him longer than the rest to find me. But he was a good dancer, and I thought he was very handsome. He had blond hair like yours and a small dimple on his chin. We danced all evening, never switching partners once, which

I think made his military brothers angry. At the end of the last song, he reached up to my headscarf and pulled it down to my shoulders. And then he brazenly kissed me. I can tell you, I was so embarrassed and humiliated that I just ran, leaving my scarf to fall behind. Of course, part of me was very excited. I was seventeen years old at the time, and I had never been kissed.

The next week, I could hardly concentrate on what I was doing at the tavern. He had told me his name, Ivan, and said he was born in a town near Split called Trogir, where his family were sailors who traveled between the islands and traded goods. They had helped smuggle spies and guns into Yugoslavia during the war. Both your great-grandfathers were war heroes. The Ivelja name comes from Ivan and Trogir. But I am getting distracted. I ran away from Ivan at the dance, embarrassed, but in truth, I wanted very much to see him again.

It took Ivan a month to find me. He had only a limited number of days he could be off the base. On those days, he went throughout Lastovo Island, from Pasadur to Skrivena Luka, Zaklopatica, and the old town, asking who might be missing the red scarf. No one knew that I had lost the scarf, so asking around was of little help. But then he came to the tavern to have an espresso. He had the scarf in his hand, and I recognized him immediately. This is a very Cinderella story.

My father, Filip, was there, and Ivan made an effort to be very polite. He asked my father if I could sit with him, and he said that I could. I took off my apron, and for an hour, we talked. In the army, he worked on radios, listening for the Western spies who could be on fishing boats or big battleships. He was a vodnik with three red stripes on his shoulders—very respectable. My father was impressed.

I was eighteen when we got married. His family was not allowed to come from Trogir since Lastovo was very top secret, but we had a traditional wedding in the old town church of St. Cosmas and Damian. Later, we traveled to Trogir where I met his parents.

The next year, I had a male child, Ivan Ivelja Jr., who died at birth. On the island, there was only one midwife to help with the birth and one clinic at the military base. No hospital to help with these difficult pregnancies. Two years after Ivan, I had your mother. I named her Ivana. It was a very terrible birth, and afterward, I could not have any more children. This was very sad for Ivan, but we had Ivana, and she was a lovely child. She did not cry too much and was never sick with ear infections or diseases. Maybe we were lucky to be so isolated on the island, because children were not so fortunate on the mainland. Many children died during those times from smallpox and other diseases.

This is what I want to tell you about Ivan. He was a soldier who was very strict, and he came from a devout Catholic family. Ivan was very involved with our church. Because he was a vodnik in the army, we were given seats in the second row. Later, Ivan became an acolyte, assisting the priest. He became a prominent member of the community and, because of this, was sensitive to what people said. I want to say here that your mother adored him, but more of that at another time.

Mia had been quiet throughout the supper but now sat up and asked a question. She spoke in Cro, talking to Marta. Dinko again translated, "If Vesna's mother's name is Ivelja, what was her father's name?"

Marta looked at the little girl, undoubtedly trying to decide how to respond. It was a question I also had—I only knew his first name was Josip. I'd assumed my parents had never married, but I was cautious about discussing this with Marta.

"Josip Dužević."

Mia, a pre-teen, wasn't shy about the issue and just came out and asked, "So, they were never married?"

The grandmother turned away when she answered, "*Ne.*"

Dinko looked into my eyes to comprehend what I was thinking. What could I think? I knew I was born out of wedlock. In America, that wouldn't have been a shock, but here in the more conservative and Catholic Croatia, it must have been a scandal. I had so many more questions but decided to wait. I could see that Marta was tired and probably ashamed.

Dinko touched my hand. He seemed to know what everyone was thinking and feeling. "I will take your grandmother home now. We can learn more tomorrow or the next day."

He translated for Marta, and she nodded her head in agreement.

Mia was clueless as to what had transpired. No doubt she watched American television, and an out-of-wedlock baby among all the scandals of reality TV was no more than a hair in the soup. I assumed she was more consumed with the idea of babies in general, like a new wife for her father and maybe a sister for her.

Mia said, "Maybe the next day." She looked over at her father. "Tomorrow, you should show Turtle the island. Take her to see the abandoned barracks and old military stuff." Then to me, "You are such a good cook. Maybe you can make a picnic lunch. Just for the two of you. I have school."

I was overwhelmed. I wanted to hear the rest of my grandmother's story, but I saw that the woman could only handle so much and could only tell her story one piece at a time. I'd waited my whole life; I could wait another two days. I had nothing to do in the meantime and did want to see more of the island, especially with someone who lived here. And the thought of being alone with Dinko for the day seemed exciting.

Dinko looked at his daughter, a scowl on his face. "Yes, you have school, and I have work to do."

Mia matched his stare. "Watch the grapes grow? They'll be there when you get back."

He looked at me. "If you have something else planned, I understand."

I smiled. "I have nothing else planned."

Seafood Soup

Branzino, if cooked in the *peka*, is like fish stew. A spicier version is Italian cioppino or French bouillabaisse. Here's a recipe that goes well with a home-baked baguette.

Serves 4

¼ cup extra-virgin olive oil
1 medium onion, diced small
4 cloves garlic, minced
½ cup white wine
1 (28-ounce) can San Marzano tomatoes
4 cups fish stock
1 tablespoon lemon zest
4 sprigs fresh thyme
12 ounces whitefish, such as black sea bass, monkfish, hake, haddock, halibut, striped sea bass

12 ounces shellfish, such as mussels, clams, scallops, and shrimp

½ cup chopped fresh basil

Kosher salt and pepper, to taste

Sauté the onion on low heat until translucent.

Add garlic and cook for one minute more.

Add the white wine. Cook for 5 minutes, until it reduces slightly.

Add tomatoes and raise the heat to medium-high. Simmer for 5 minutes.

Add the fish stock, lemon zest, and thyme. Simmer for 15 minutes.

Add the fish. Simmer for about 5 to 10 minutes, or until the fish is cooked through and easily flakes apart.

Add the shrimp, clams, scallops, and mussels. Simmer for 3 to 5 minutes, or until all the mussels and clam shells open and the shrimp is cooked through and no longer translucent.

Add salt and pepper to taste and garnish with chopped basil. Serve with fresh bread for sopping up the delicious broth.

Gazpacho Soup

The Land Rover pulled up earlier than expected. I was sitting outside, drinking coffee, trying to ignore the well-meaning emails from my editor who wanted updates on my acknowledgements and bio. I wanted to tell her to just copy both from my previous book but knew there needed to be changes. And I didn't want to acknowledge Reed like I'd done in the past. There were emails from the publicist who was lining up a scavenger hunt of places to do book signings, and then radio, TV, and podcast interviews. The list of what I was descending back into when I got home seemed exhausting.

I'd been ready for the day, getting up early and making a lunch of cold gazpacho soup with peeled and chopped cucumbers, chopped onions, Italian parsley, peeled and diced ripe tomatoes, extra-virgin olive oil, minced garlic, and seasoning. The kitchen had no gadgets for blending the ingredients, but I found an old-fashioned food mill with a hand crank that did the job perfectly. Who needs all those gadgets? If another cookbook ever came together, I'd prepare everything using tools that didn't come with a plug. I poured the soup into a liter canning jar. Then, for just a bit more acidity, I splashed on top the remnants of the white wine from the evening before. Along with the soup, I had a crusty loaf of bread and a sheep cheese from the island of Pag. Dinko would undoubtedly provide more wine.

Later, in the car, he asked, "I have a sailboat. It is a very nice day to tour the island by sea. Do you feel okay to do that?"

I remembered the first time we'd met, his hand against my neck, holding back the strands of my long hair. It was so embarrassing. But the thought of sailing around the island with this man seemed special and even romantic, though a romance was not really what I needed. "You don't think I'll get sick?"

"The wind is not blowing too strongly. We will be outside in the cockpit where you can see the shore at all times. I think before, it was that you were down below in the ferry, feeling the rocking motion. It is very common. Then, if you start to feel sick, we can quickly sail to the closest dock. But I think you will be okay."

It was what I wanted to hear. "Okay."

He drove out of the valley and up over the ridge to the village of Zaklopatica where I'd bought the branzino the day before. His boat was one of those tied to the quay. A narrow plank crossed the gap between the quay and the stern of the sailboat. Gold leaf lettering on the transom spelled out the boat's name, Zlata. Before I could ask, Dinko said, "My grandmother's name. This was originally my grandfather's boat. He bought it in very poor shape and restored it over the following three years."

Dinko held my hand as I stepped onto the plank. He let go, and like a gymnast on a balance beam, I stepped heel to toe until reaching the cockpit.

I'd expected something smaller, like the kind on lakes in Minneapolis—a rowboat with wings. Dinko's boat was the size of a city bus, with a cockpit that could hold a party of eight and a cabin that likely slept just as many. The hull was elegantly curved, with a glossy white paint that reflected the flashes of sunlight hitting the ripples of water. The cockpit and cabin were all varnished teak, and the hardware for pulling and cleating lines was polished stainless steel. The helm, with its wheel the width of my outstretched arms, was surrounded by modern electronic equipment. It was the kind of boat you could live on, and I suspect many did.

He explained, "It's a fourteen-meter Alden made in Hong Kong. It's been in our family for over fifty years and has seen much of the Mediterranean. It is very safe."

"And you're a good sailor?"

He smiled. "Very good."

While Dinko prepared the boat to leave the protected bay, I went down into the cabin to put away the lunch. It was more spacious than I'd expected, with a large dining table of polished teak, cushioned bench seats, a small galley kitchen, and an icebox that was already switched on and chilled. Behind the kitchen was a small bedroom with bright sheets and stuffed animals, no doubt Mia's room. Up front was a larger bedroom with no personal items. Dinko's room. Then, fastened to one wall of the dining area were old family photos.

One showed a young Dinko, with his unruly black hair and same ear-to-ear smile, standing beside two older men—I assumed his father and grandfather. Below that was a single color photo of Dinko posed with another woman, presumably the Russian model, Mia's mother. It showed her long brown hair, pouty lips, chiseled nose, and the stunning emerald eyes I'd also seen in Mia. She was model-beautiful. I wondered why she would leave the charmed life Dinko led—a man who owned a vineyard on a pristine, remote Mediterranean island. I wondered why the woman would choose to leave her child behind. I'd been left behind by my own mother, but it had not been a choice.

Dinko started the diesel engine, removed the plank, cast off dock lines, and motored forward, leaving the quay. We passed through a channel exiting the cove and entered the Adriatic. Dinko had me hold the steering wheel steady while he raised both the large mainsail and forward jib. Back at the wheel, he switched off the engine, and we moved under the gentle wind's power. Quiet, nothing but the whispering sound of the waves lapping against the hull. We followed the shoreline. An hour later, we saw the village of Pasadur on our left. The wind then carried us further west and away from the island.

I'd worked in restaurants for years, and a kitchen was a place where ideas, thoughts, questions, and even inquisitions moved around constantly. Often, if I thought it, I said it. And I did now. "I saw the photo of you and a woman. I assume she's Mia's mother. The same emerald eyes."

Dinko stood at the wheel, moving the boat to the will of the wind. He didn't look at me when he said, "Yes."

"What was her name?"

"Karina."

"Did you love her?"

"Perhaps, I'm not sure."

"But you had a child together."

And maybe because he knew I wouldn't relent with my questions, and also because there was no place to flee, he told the story.

"My father kept the vineyard together through the communist years. My mother and I kept it together during the war years. After the war, he was able to export his wine and make a lot of money. He eventually sent me abroad for college. I went to the American school in Athens. I was there for four years, only returning home for holidays and the summer months. Even though I was away for long stretches of time, I was very close to my mother and father. I wrote to each of them every week, and both responded.

"They'd never visited the school but planned to attend my graduation. They made a vacation of the trip and drove from Dubrovnik down the coast through Montenegro and Albania. In the Greek town of Ioannina, they were hit by a truck. They died. I tell you this only because it formed who I became."

As he spoke, he didn't look at me, but continued to stand behind the wheel and watch the waves. I could see his eyes glaze over in sadness. All I thought to say was, "I understand."

His head ticked to one side as though prodded by unknown fingers. "Afterward, I felt lost. I should have gone back to Lastovo to resume operating the vineyard, but at the time, I just couldn't. My mother and father were my whole life, and now there was nothing left for me. I inherited money that meant little at the time but allowed me to take my father's sailboat and explore the world and what I wanted in life—find myself. I left the vineyard to be run by managers."

Ahead was nothing but sea, ripples of water under an unbroken horizon. Dinko paused in his story, and I said nothing to break the silence.

He moved the steering wheel a few inches, adjusting to the wind, and then continued, "I ended up in Italy. I met people in Sicily and then Capri who were very wealthy. I lived on the boat but went to parties every night. I met many women. I met Karina. She was beautiful, of course, but also very determined to be successful. She had a modeling career but also wanted to be in movies and on television. Then, she became pregnant. I knew all that time that I was not finding myself, but drinking and partying to avoid myself. I knew my life was back on Lastovo. I convinced her to sail back with me and have the baby at the vineyard and home that was now mine. I wanted to share my life with her and our child. But she was not the type of person who could settle into the life of being a farmer's wife. She had left a farm back in Russia.

"Karina had Mia. A month later, she left. That is the story."

Dinko spun the wheel, and the boat turned back toward the island. He readjusted the billowing and flapping sails.

"What does Mia think?"

"This is very difficult. I try to say that Karina's leaving had nothing to do with her, that Karina left because she wanted to be a movie star, and sometimes a person's ambitions have to be larger than their family's—that they have to make sacrifices."

It wasn't something, as an adult, I would have ever thought or considered. And as a child, I would never have understood it. "I'm guessing that didn't help."

"I should have lied and said she was dead. And maybe she is. We have not heard from Karina in years. There is nothing on the Internet about her, and I expect the movie career never happened. I want Mia to move on, and sometimes I think she has. She wants me to move on."

"I'm guessing that's why she set us up for this tour?"

"Perhaps."

Dinko started the engine and lowered the sails when we neared a group of smaller islands just offshore from Lastovo.

We passed a spit of land surrounded by a shelf of rock, and Dinko handed me binoculars from a cubbyhole near the helm. He pointed out what appeared to be a man-made structure jutting from the land and floating above the water. I held up the binoculars and focused. Up close, I could see a tunnel of concrete large enough to drive a train through. Dinko explained it was one of two submarine pens on the island, built back when Lastovo was a secret military base.

We motored past, following the shore to a small inlet. He cut the engine and then stepped forward to the front of the sailboat. He dropped the anchor onto the sand seabed visible twenty feet below.

Abandoned buildings, like apartments, rose in the distance from the surrounding olive orchard. He said, "Those are the military barracks that were built on your great-grandfather's land." Rows of olive trees ascended to the top of a terraced hill. The surrounding vegetation was overgrown, seeming to choke the remaining trees. He added, "In different times, under different circumstances, I might have been working in the orchard for your family, tending to the olives."

"Could have been," I said. "Could have been that we grew up together, shared the same schoolhouse, hiked up into the hills each day, and swam in the Adriatic." I smiled at the thought. "Could have been that you came back from college one summer, and we spent the days at the beach reading novels, cooling off in the water, drinking wine pilfered from your vineyard, and making out." I laughed.

"What is this *making out?*" he asked.

"You know, kissing."

He gave me a wicked smile, then leaned over. "Like this?"

Dinko was sitting opposite me when the kiss happened, our knees almost touching. He leaned over and put two hands beside each of my thighs, bracing himself against the boat seat. He slowly lowered himself toward my lips. He gave me ample time to turn away or say no, but I didn't. I lifted my face toward him and let his lips touch mine.

How long had it been since I'd been passionately kissed? A year or longer, and now it felt so good that I wanted much more. His lips continued to mesh with mine.

Then his hands moved to lift my shirt.

My burn scars were beneath the shirt, there on my back. His motion triggered what had been a lifelong self-conscious stigma. The scars were still there from when I'd been an infant in Dubrovnik, when the bomb exploded in the bakery. They were dark, shiny-smooth but with a leathery feel. I'd rarely let a man see or touch them.

I'd developed a natural reaction of sorts and pushed Dinko back against the opposite bench, taking control.

I kissed him hard, pressing my tongue against his, my hands deep in his hair. I felt my body on fire, totally out of control, as though it had a mind of its own. I moved my hands to his pants and belt buckle. I undid his belt and then slid his pants down to the sailboat floor. I knelt above him on the bench, my knees on either side of his legs.

He'd started it, but I finished it.

We held each other for what seemed an eternity. It felt so good, and I rested with my mouth against his neck, my lips taking advantage of the taut flesh there.

I slowly stood and sat back against the opposite bench. I watched as Dinko pulled up his shorts and buckled his belt. He smiled but said nothing. Sex was so much better if nothing was said afterward, like trying to describe the taste of an excellent wine—sometimes the words fell flat, ruining the indescribable, sublime feeling.

It then occurred to me that I hadn't been nauseous while back on the water.

In fact, I was hungry for the gazpacho.

We continued around the island after lunch, the sails up and the boat tacking through the small channels and inlets. We passed Skrivena Luka Cove, where children swam from a planked dock into the bright azure waters. We rounded a point of land, Cape Struga, where a lighthouse above watched over the open sea to the west. We tacked through small islands to the south of Lastovo, deserted except for one beach with a few sailboats anchored offshore. I could easily imagine spending the night there, just the two of us drinking wine into the evening, thinking about the future, then going down below where we'd intertwine like eels. It was a beautiful thought but unlikely. In another week, I'd be going back to Minneapolis where obligations sat waiting to greet me—a cookbook release and an unresolved breakup with Reed.

I looked up toward Dinko, who stood at the wheel, watching the wind-pushed waves for any sign of submerged, hull-smashing rocks. "I'll be leaving soon, back to America."

"I understand." He kept his eyes on the water when he added, "We should be quiet about our day. Mia has so many expectations and fantasies. I do not want to have her hurt again."

The comment bothered me. What did he think? That I'd present myself to Mia as the new *mama*? That I'd fly off like her biological mother, Karina, and never talk to her again? I had a life back in Minneapolis, and I had no intentions of assuming one in Croatia.

What I said, though, was, "Why don't you allow anyone to visit your winery? Why the 'keep out' signs? What is it you really want to keep out?" I knew the answer—had known the answer—but I wanted to hear it from his lips.

He tilted his head nonchalantly as if the answer was easy and obvious. "I sell my wine to brokers all over the world. My wine is some of the best in Croatia. I don't need to do samplings or host weddings. I want to be there with my daughter and keep her safe. I don't want to speak with strangers or allow people in with their questions."

"I'm sorry that *I* have questions."

He looked at me, a distance in his eyes as though I were just one more person trying to push their way into his life. "I did not mean you. But questions can bring up things that are uncomfortable to discuss. Mia has illusions about her mother, who has never reached out to speak with her daughter. And now Karina is nowhere to be found, and perhaps she is dead. I don't know. But Mia does not need someone else to break her heart."

"She's almost a teenager. Before long, she'll be a woman. She'll want to leave the island and go to college like you did. Have you thought about that?"

"Mia will have the winery, and she will have our home. What more would anyone want? All that my education did was cast me adrift with the wrong sorts of people."

"Kids want to find out for themselves. They want to make their own mistakes."

"I've made enough mistakes for both of us."

It all made sense to me. Dinko had lost his parents at an early age. I knew how death could feel like abandonment. They died in a car crash, but I could imagine the thoughts that had gone through his head. Why did they drive when they could afford to fly? Was his father careless while he drove? Was his mother a distraction? Then, the guilt questions. Why did he even expect his parents to come? Why did he need to go off to school in the first place?

I knew. I had my own questions that lingered throughout my entire life. Why was I spared? What did my mother do at the expense of her own life to save mine? I could see why Dinko retreated behind the safe walls of his vineyard kingdom. But life has a way of knocking on the door—or breaking it down.

I asked him, "Don't you want love?"

Dinko looked up to the sky, maybe seeking answers there. He thought for a moment and then looked back at me. "Yes, very much. But as you say, you are off to America in a week. Love between us is impractical."

Impractical and unrealistic. He was right. "No commitments then." I knew it was true, but part of me wanted to cry.

The sailboat rounded the northeast corner of the island and into a headwind that stopped the boat cold. Dinko started the engine and dropped the sails. We said little else as he maneuvered the boat back into the cove at Zaklopatica and pulled up to the quay.

The subsequent drive to The Oleander Cottage was uncomfortable. When he finally came to a stop, I looked over at him as he stared ahead at the road, his hands on the wheel and shifter. I said, "I did have a wonderful time today."

There was a note of remorse in his voice when he replied, "It's been a very long time since I've had such a day."

"Will I see you again tomorrow evening?"

"Of course. I will again pick up your grandmother. And I am looking forward to your cooking."

"Bring Mia if you would like. I won't make it uncomfortable. But of course, she might."

A smile broke on his face. "I think it will be just the three of us."

Gazpacho Soup

Gazpacho is the perfect summer soup for a romantic picnic, especially when you can use vegetables and dill from your own garden. (Though, take a breath mint before kissing any dreamy men on a sailboat.)

Serves 6

6 fresh medium garden tomatoes, coarsely chopped
½ cup green bell pepper, coarsely chopped
½ cup red onion, coarsely chopped
1 cucumber, peeled and seeds removed, then cut into chunks
1 clove garlic
1 teaspoon chopped fresh dill
2 teaspoons kosher salt
2 teaspoons white wine vinegar
⅓ cup extra-virgin olive oil
Fresh dill sprigs, for garnish
Kosher salt and pepper, to taste

In a high-speed blender, blend for 1-2 minutes until smooth. Garnish with chopped fresh dill and season with salt and pepper to taste.

Octopus Peka

"Did you have the sex?" Sara sat across from me, sipping espresso. She wore a sleeveless cotton dress with a French provincial pattern of vines and berries. Her copper hair was elaborately shaped into a pile of natural, relaxed curls. And with her glaring orange lipstick, she looked ready for her day of lawyering or selling real estate. In comparison, dressed in my shorts, T-shirt, and Birkenstocks, I felt like a waif—which, technically, I was.

"That is none of your business."

"Does that mean in America the same as it does in Croatia?"

"What do you mean?"

"In Croatia, 'none of your business' means yes, but do not push me for details."

"In America, it means none of your business."

"So, now I am asking for details. I am not attracted to the

man, but he is very good-looking. I am sure you twisted the curls of his hair in your fingers. His lips tasted like his fine Plavac Mali. Where did your lips go next? For a man, oral sex is the best. This I have heard. Same for a woman. This I know."

The explicit talk made me blush and look away.

Then the thought of the previous day gave me that fluttering feeling. His hair, his lips, my fingers on his belt buckle. But I wouldn't discuss any details with Sara. And really, I'd never been the kiss-and-tell type—probably too self-conscious, too insecure.

The fact was, I hadn't had sex in over a year, and twice that since I'd experienced a true-to-life orgasm. And Dinko and I had parted on a rough note, neither wanting to get involved. We both knew I would be gone in a week. I'd come to Croatia to find blood relatives, and I'd done that. I'd also come to figure out my life, away from the demands of a restaurant and a relationship.

Reed was now texting me each day in his disarming and jokey way to ask how I was and when I'd be home. I responded as honestly and briefly as I could—yes, no, okay, soon. Home, just that word, had a mixed meaning. We owned a condo together, but had it ever been a home? I didn't think so. We'd worked long hours in the restaurant, and the condo was, for me, just a place to crash. Had I ever been in love with Reed? Yes, I had. But it turned into something less than that— friendship, maybe, or more of a business relationship. Now I was going home to Reed and the condo.

The Oleander Cottage felt more like home. A place of serenity, sanctuary, and family.

With that thought, I changed the subject. "I love this place."

"It is for sale. I can give you very good price. I can also

provide the necessary documents."

I knew I shouldn't have brought up the subject. I should've known Sara would turn into a selling shark. "No, I can't own property ten thousand miles from where I live."

"Why not? A day on plane, then ferry to get here. I thought all Americans have two houses—one for work, one for vacation."

"We're not all rich. I can't afford two houses, and I can't afford the flights."

"You consider this purchase. People on Lastovo are very nice, but they are also very small-minded. I need more people like you I can have conversation with. Here, and not Hvar. So, you think about it. Yes?"

There was nothing to think about. My book release was waiting for me back in Minneapolis, with a lineup of events.

The outside brick barbecue, the *roštilj*, was filled with moldy ash and molten chunks of aluminum I assumed were beer cans thrown into the cozy fire by inebriated tourists. I scooped the ash and garbage into a pail and dumped the contents into the trash bin. Beneath the oven was a stack of sticks and twigs, likely olive tree cuttings. Behind the *roštilj*, I pulled out the iron dome Dinko had found, the *peka*. The dome, about the size of a beach ball cut in half, was rusted but still intact. Welded around the top was a railing of sorts, and I figured it was mounted there to secure the hot coals.

I drove the Yugo back to Zaklopatica where I'd just been with Dinko the day before. I would see him again that night. The thought made me curiously anxious. I had nothing to be embarrassed about, and we'd parted amicably. But another feeling still resided. I guessed the best word for it was intimidation. He was rugged handsome, created brilliant wine, and I'd become, in a way, vulnerable to him. Sex for me had never been just about physical desire. There'd always been that piece that felt exposed, maybe because of my burn scars, but also the simple—maybe not so metaphorical—shedding of clothes, revealing one's bare-naked self. Ironically, the sex with Dinko had been mostly clothes on.

I parked the Yugo not far from the sailboat, which hadn't moved. I walked down the quay toward the fishmonger woman. I could see Dinko wasn't on the boat, the cabin hatch closed and padlocked. I avoided glancing at the spot where I sat the day before. It would've been like seeing the remnants of a crashed car and being reminded of the missed red light that brought it on.

I walked down the quay, past the fishermen tending their boats, and up to the stone house that sold fresh seafood. The woman stood at a wooden butcher's table wearing a white apron slightly stained from the gutted fish she was cleaning. She held a boning knife and looked up as I approached, right after she'd cut off the head of a ten-pound grouper.

She said, "*Dobar dan.*" Good day.

"*Dobar dan,*" I repeated.

The woman led the way toward the cooler of crushed ice and the fish that had just come off the boats. I chose two octopuses, likely speared by the old fisherman I'd met days before. The woman wrapped the *hobotnice* in newspaper and then placed them into a small plastic grocery bag.

I walked back to the Yugo, still keeping my eyes from examining the sailboat too closely.

Inside the car, I turned the ignition. But the engine would

not turn over and come to life. I tried again and listened as the starter motor made a horrible grinding sound. I waited a few seconds and then tried again. The same coffee-grinding sound. I tried once more. The engine wouldn't start, and now I felt stuck, sitting in the broken-down car across from Dinko's vintage sailboat.

The fishermen were now looking in my direction. I waited longer—two minutes, counting the seconds on my wristwatch. I turned the ignition again and heard the same grinding sound. Fuck. I wanted to cry or scream or take a hammer to the broken-down piece of shit Yugo. But I wouldn't do any of those things. I wouldn't give the piece-of-shit car, or the sailboat and specter of Dinko, the satisfaction. I leaned forward with my forehead against the steering wheel, exasperated. Then the horn embarrassingly blared.

The fishermen, four of them, stepped from their boats and came toward me, almost running. I rolled down my window in anticipation.

I heard, "*Što je bilo?*" which I took to mean, What's the matter?

I responded, "It won't start." Then, assuming they didn't know English, I turned the key and produced the grinding noise.

One pushed back a stained and frayed cap and said, "*Stjepanovo komunističko smeće.*" The obvious approximate translation, Stjepan's communist piece of junk.

The others shook their heads and repeated, "*Komunističko smeće.*"

The man with the frayed cap added in broken English, "You *Amerikanka* woman that rent house of *Stjepanova* dead sister?"

News traveled fast on the small island. I just smiled and

responded, *"Da."*

The man laughed. He then opened the door and motioned for me to get out. I did. He sat down behind the wheel and, in Cro, said something to the other three. Those three moved to the back of the car and began pushing. The car rolled down the quay, and I followed.

Abruptly, the man let out the clutch. The car jerked once and then coughed to life. The other fishermen yelled, *"Bravo, bravo!"*

The man left the Yugo running and stepped out.

I quickly smiled at each man, saying, *"Hvala, hvala."*

I drove off, putting all the embarrassment and mixed feelings behind me. But now I needed more groceries, and the chance that the car would start again seemed remote. My simple and obvious plan was to drive to the market in Pasadur and just leave the car running.

An hour later, I was back at The Oleander Cottage, chopping the carrots, potatoes, garlic, tomatoes, and onions for the *peka*. I placed the vegetables in the round pan my grandmother had pointed out two days before and then added white wine and olive oil. I put the two octopuses on top, which spread out like starfish. I started the fire in the late afternoon, and then, two hours before Dinko and Marta would arrive, I placed the pan beneath the *peka* dome and scooped the glowing embers above the welded ring. I documented my first *peka* with a photograph.

I poured myself a glass of the open white wine. I took the first sip and tasted the tartness and the subtle sweetness of apple. Delicious. Of course, it was a Radić Grk.

The Land Rover pulled up, and I was there to open the door for my grandmother. She slowly moved from the car, placing her feet on the gravel driveway, then making a concerted effort to stand. I held her arm as she stood. I gave Marta a hug, but unlike the day before, the hug felt mannequin-hollow.

I looked up at Dinko. "Is everything okay?"

He was dressed in a tight-fitting polo shirt. His hair was neatly combed, but he hadn't shaved. The look on his face, with the five o'clock shadow, seemed concerned. He shrugged his shoulders. "She appeared tired when I picked her up."

I unconsciously remembered a phrase in Cro and asked my grandmother, "*Jesi li dobro?*" Are you okay?

"*Dobro sam.*" I'm fine. Marta looked at me and smiled weakly. Her white hair was wrapped in the same dark scarf. Her eyes seemed vacant, tired.

"*Dođi,*" I said. Come. I took my grandmother by the hand and led her around the house to the back where the embers had burned down to ash around the *peka* dome.

Marta smiled, brighter now, and left my side. She shuffled up to the *roštilj*. I moved next to her and then used a long, wrought-iron rod with a spatula-shaped end to lift the *peka*. My grandmother looked beneath to see the splayed octopus atop a stewed medley of tomatoes and vegetables. She exclaimed, "*Prekrasno!*"

Dinko was behind and translated, "Beautiful." He added, "Just like my own *mama*."

We sat at the small outside table, and Dinko opened and poured the white Grk wine he'd brought. I was nervous around him, a feeling left over from the day before—guilt or embarrassment, or whatever. There could be no real relationship between us, but we'd had sailboat sex out in the open, in broad daylight. To get past the awkwardness, I desperately wanted my grandmother to continue telling our family's story. But Marta just sat there quietly, barely touching her wine.

I asked her questions, which Dinko translated. "What did my father do before he met my mother?"

"He worked in our tavern. At night, he played an instrument called the *tamburica*."

"Did he ask her out on a date?"

"I presume this."

"Did you or Ivan know they were dating?"

"No."

She replied with short, abrupt answers, and I could see that my questions made her uncomfortable.

I knew I was born in Dubrovnik out of wedlock. I assumed my mother and Josip had lived together and, possibly because of the war, had put off marriage. But of course, this assumption was through the lens of my American upbringing where many kids were born out of wedlock, and where some parents who lived together never married at all. In Croatia, in 1988, under Tito's socialism—when Eastern Europe was deeply skeptical of Western decadence—and in this very Catholic country, a baby born out of wedlock was a shameful scandal. And parents did not let their daughters date unchaperoned.

A baby out of wedlock might have meant that my mother was raped.

Marta was obviously reluctant to talk, and it could have been that the story she did or did not want to tell was uncomfortable and shocking.

I just said it. "Was my mother raped?"

Dinko paused, hesitant to translate, but I gave him a

forceful nod. The word in Cro was *silovana*.

Marta looked up, surprised and frightened. "*Ne, ne, ne.*"

"Then how did they meet? Why did my mother move to Dubrovnik? How was I conceived?"

"*U redu, ispričat ću vam priču.*" Okay, I will tell you the story.

Josip, your father, was a very nice boy. He had an uncle on the army base, and that is how he was able to come to Lastovo. Ivan knew the uncle and found Josip a job in the tavern with your mother. By that time, Filip, your great-grandfather, was not very well and would pass away soon after, and your great-grandmother, Maria, no longer worked in the tavern. I worked in the kitchen and did all the cooking. Ivana was the server, and Josip helped both of us and then washed the dishes. I only found out later why he was sent to Lastovo from Ston where he grew up. Both of his parents were sent to prison for black market activities. All I know is that Josip was a very nice boy and worked hard in the tavern.

Ivana was sixteen at the time. Josip was seventeen. He was always looking at her. Of course, your mother was beautiful and had many suitors from the army base. Ivan would not let her date any of them, and I know she was resentful.

This is what I want to tell you about your mother. She was always a good and obedient daughter. As a baby, she rarely cried, and as a toddler, she was very smart. She could count to one hundred when she was three. Ivan would read to her every night, and by the time she was sent to school at the age of five, she could read on her own. She did well in school. Ivan and I loved her immensely. We did not want her to ever leave us, and maybe that was why Ivan would not let her date. Maybe we should have. I do not know.

Of course, I knew there was something between them—all that looking at each other, smiling, and then whispering when they thought I could not hear. Josip also played the tamburica. Sometimes, after the customers were served dinner and he finished the dishes, he would play for the men who came around later to have a beer before we closed. He played very well, mostly old Croatian folk songs. Many of them were love songs. The men would sing along as they drank their beers. His playing was so excellent that he could drive some of them to tears. Of course, I knew he was playing for her.

I only caught them kissing once, and I said to Ivana that if her father found out, there would be the devil to pay. I know that did not stop them. Then, one night, Ivan did catch them. He came home late after the tavern had closed. I thought Ivana was in her room, but she had snuck out through her window to meet Josip. Ivan saw them kissing right in the town square. He was furious. The next day, Josip was gone, sent back to Ston by his uncle.

Ivana was very sad. As the months went by, she would not leave her room and would not work in the tavern with me. I talked to her, and all she would say was that her life was over. For me, it was such an overstatement. There were still plenty of young soldiers on the island—fishermen, winemakers, and farmers. The town had been emptied, but some people still lived here. Ivan would eventually let her date. I would tell her, "Other fish in the sea."

But then one day, I could see Ivana was with child.

I have told you about Ivan. He was a soldier, very strict, and a very important layperson in the church. He cared about what people would say. And an unmarried woman with a child on Lastovo was not a good thing. The woman was considered ruined. When Ivan found out, he was angry and embarrassed. He did not want Ivana in his house and arranged for her to leave the island. I could do nothing.

In Dubrovnik, there was a Catholic home for unwed mothers. Parents would send their daughters to the home, and when a child was born, the church would find another family to raise it. Then the mother could return to where she came from. That was the plan. But when she had her baby, Ivana did not want to give you up. She found a job at a bakery in Dubrovnik's Old Town. She found an apartment to live in. I would visit Ivana and you when I could.

This was 1988. Tito had died eight years before. Do not believe what most people say. Under Tito, there was communism, but we had food, we had peace, and we could watch American movies and go to church. After Tito, there was a revolving presidency—one day Serbian, one day Croatian, one day Slovenian. On and on. By 1990, there was no government. Then, the Serbian leader Milošević decided he was the next Tito, the next dictator. In 1991, Croatia declared independence. The following December, the Serbs were bombing Dubrovnik.

Your mother lived in the Old Town and continued to work at the bakery there. Each day, Ivana left you with a woman while she worked. Then the woman left Dubrovnik, as many others did. Ivana did not want to go back to Lastovo. Also, she had not done as Ivan had asked and was no longer welcome. I could do nothing. Ivana stayed at her work as the city was bombed. She baked and sold bread, but now you were in the bakery with her every day.

In November, the Serbs demanded surrender, but the Croatian forces refused. The Serbs said only the Old Town would be spared. Ivana thought she would be safe. She worked and lived in the Old Town. They lied. On December 6th, a bomb hit the bakery. What was not immediately destroyed was burned. I did not find out about her death until the following summer, when I could travel. I was told her daughter—you—had also died.

I had questions. "What happened to my father?"

Dinko translated, "Josip Duževič died in the battle at Slano, which was close to where he grew up in Ston." He added, "A neighbor of mine was also in that battle. The Armed Boat Squadron Dubrovnik attacked the Serbs but was repulsed. Many men died."

Dutch Oven Beef Stew

On the Dalmatian Islands, *peka* needs to be ordered by early afternoon. It takes hours to prepare, burning the wood down to embers that slowly cook the stew. Of course, we don't have the proper *roštilj* barbecue or the iron dome in America. Here is an alternate, fabulous beef stew.

Serves 8

2 pounds stew meat, cut into 1-inch cubes
1 tablespoon kosher salt
1 tablespoon ground black pepper
3 tablespoons extra-virgin olive oil
1 large onion, diced into 1-inch chunks
3 cloves garlic, minced or grated
8-ounce can tomato paste
3 tablespoons Wondra flour
4 cups beef, chicken, or vegetable broth (¼ cup reserved)
1 tablespoon Worcestershire sauce

1 tablespoon dried thyme
1 tablespoon dried rosemary
1 tablespoon smoked paprika
2 dried bay leaves
1½ pounds baby red potatoes, halved
1 pound baby carrots
2 cups sliced mushrooms of your choice
2 tablespoons chopped fresh parsley

Pat the meat dry with a paper towel and season it with salt and pepper.

In a large Dutch oven or stockpot, heat the olive oil over medium-high heat and, working in batches, brown the meat on all sides. Remove to a plate.

Add the onion to the pot and cook for three minutes. Add the garlic and cook for one minute more.

Add the ¼ cup of reserved broth and scrape the brown bits off the bottom of the pan.

Add the tomato paste and cook for one minute.

Add the beef back into the pot. Sprinkle the flour over the beef, then stir to combine.

Add the remaining broth, Worcestershire sauce, thyme, rosemary, paprika, and bay leaves. Simmer on medium-low heat, covered, for one hour.

Add the potatoes, carrots, and celery, and cook for 30 minutes, until the vegetables are fork-tender.

Remove the bay leaves and serve garnished with parsley.

Lobster Pasta

Stjepan lay under the Yugo muttering something in Cro. Earlier that morning, when I woke, he was already out in the garden planting young tomato seedlings for the summer season. I made him an espresso, and we sat at the patio table smiling and trying to communicate with our scant knowledge of each other's language. I didn't like to complain, at least not until some pleasantries were out of the way, so I waited until the espressos were finished before pointing at the Yugo. Using hand gestures and noises, I explained that the car wouldn't start. Stjepan nodded in understanding. He then stood, thanked me for the coffee, and then ambled over to the car. As I'd done the day before, he turned the key and listened to the starter motor make its grinding noise. He fetched tools from his house across the road and then crawled beneath the Yugo to begin his muttering.

I heard something drop and then what sounded like a

curse. Stjepan emerged moments later with the starter motor in hand. He said something I couldn't understand and then walked back across the road. I could only assume he'd return with a motor from one of the rusted heaps in his yard or, more likely, the old one somehow fixed.

I was still waiting outside two hours later when I saw Mia walking up the driveway, a backpack slung over her shoulder with a tennis racket handle protruding from the top. She waved and then ran the rest of the way. "Turtle, I was so hoping you were home."

"Mia, how nice to see you!" I returned the greeting but wondered what the young girl was doing at the cottage without her father, who hadn't seemed too keen on us having a relationship. I added in a light, upbeat voice, "What are you up to?"

Mia looked adorable in a yellow skirt and blue tank top, her hair up in pigtails. "I finished my tennis practice. I told Tata I was going to the beach afterward with my friend Nika, but she is not feeling well, so I asked Tata if it was okay that I come by to see if you would go instead. Please come."

"Your father said that it was okay to stop by my house?" Hard to imagine, but then, he'd do anything for his daughter. And if she asked permission to go to the beach with me, it would've been hard for him to refuse.

"Yes, and go swimming!" She looked at me with imploring eyes and a questioning smile.

"I have no car. It's broken."

"No, we will walk. It is not too far, and there is a path that goes right from the road and down to where we can swim and maybe have lunch. Saturdays, there is music at the restaurant, Konoba Plaža."

I couldn't say no to the girl and didn't have any plans for

the day. I'd been on this beautiful Mediterranean island for over a week and had only seen the swimming beaches from Dinko's sailboat. "Okay, let me change."

Mia took my hand as we walked. I'd changed into a one-piece bathing suit that I knew hid my scars, and then slipped on shorts and my Trampled by Turtles T-shirt.

Mia laughed when she saw the shirt.

Right away, she said, "Tata has been so happy since you've come to the island. For so long, he has been sad and moody, and I imagine he thinks back to my mother."

Dinko happy—I wondered how it had been. Mia's mother's name was Karina, and she'd left before Mia ever knew who she was. Dinko had been protective of his daughter for so long, but there must have been other women. I didn't dare ask his daughter. Instead, "Does he talk about her?"

"Yes, she was very pretty, and I've seen photographs. I think Tata was very much in love and was hurt when she left. He did not date after that and devoted himself to the winery. Our wine is famous now, and it is because of Tata's work. I am also sad that she left and has never spoken with me. I imagine she thinks about me but knows that she cannot be a part of our lives. Speaking with me would only make all of us more sad."

"My mother died when I was just a small child. I wish she were still alive so I could talk with her."

"What did your mother do?"

"Our family ran a restaurant. I think it was fate that I ended up a chef and restaurant owner."

"I want to be an actress and model like my mama. I look like her. Tata has said she was very successful. I think about that. If you want to be the best, you need to devote your whole life to what you want to do. Like Donna Vekić, best tennis player in Croatia, and one of the best in the world. She has a home in Monte Carlo but travels the world to play. And when she is not playing, she is running her business—her own perfume and clothing line. It takes everything, and Donna does not have time for men or children. My mother wanted to be the best, and I understand why she needed to leave. To pursue her dreams."

"Is that what you want, to pursue your dreams?"

"Yes, I want to be like Donna Vekić but also like my mother. I would like to be a model and actress, and maybe a professional tennis player. You are a famous cookbook author and chef. Didn't you have to be dedicated?"

Had I dropped everything to pursue my dreams? Had I done it at the expense of my relationships? I'd worked sixty-to eighty-hour weeks for years to get to where I was. You couldn't run a successful restaurant without being present almost every opening hour. Then, I wrote a cookbook on top of that. I'd given up a lot. But I also did it with Reed, and every night we'd go back to the condo and sleep in the same bed together—until we didn't. It was his choice to cheat. But was I actually present? Was I also somehow to blame? "I'm not sure. I would hope you could do both. Like Jay-Z and Beyoncé."

"Perhaps. Now follow me."

Mia departed from the road and followed a path that climbed into the hills. We passed blackberry bushes with fruit still green, ornamental cypress trees that punctuated the hillside, and then, further up, a dense pine forest. Mia was strong, an athlete, and plowed ahead in quick strides. I kept up as best I could. Running, or any athletics, had never been something I pursued, and now that lack of physical exertion had come home to roost. I could stay on my feet for twelve hours and cook in a sauna-hot kitchen, but not this.

Mia reached a ridge, stopped, and urged me on. "What I want to show you is right up here."

I reached the ridge, and below me, miles of Lastovo coastline opened up to the Adriatic Sea. I stood for a moment to take it all in. Shimmering blue water snaked along the rocky shores, then the green of lush pine and cedar.

Mia walked ahead. "This way."

We continued up from the ridge to the top of a hill. In the distance, I could just see a concrete building. Closer, the building was the size of my small restaurant kitchen and low-slung like a doghouse. A deep rectangular opening overlooked the ocean, and I instantly knew it was a wartime bunker. Mia disappeared through a side door, and I followed.

My eyes slowly adjusted to the darkness inside. On the concrete floor lay the remains of a small cannon, rusted in its arcing tracks. A cobweb stretched across the corner of the ceiling, and Mia said, "Watch out for black widow spiders." She pointed.

In the center of the web was a black spider with unmistakable red markings. "Mia, let's get out of here."

"It's okay. Stay near me. I need to show you more."

I stepped far away from the spiderweb and followed.

Against the back wall were the remains of a bunk bed—the rusted metal frame, springs, and a tufted mattress rotted and ripped. Then, above the mattress, Mia pointed to a faded painting. I stepped closer.

"It's the face of a woman. See?" Mia traced the edges of the hair, cheeks, and chin.

The paint had scarcely peeled, and the image was exquisite. Her upturned eyes were lined with dark mascara, her lips rose-pink, and her hair cut in a short bob that ended with the line of her jaw.

"Who do you think it is?" I asked.

"My mother, of course."

I did see that the eyes were emerald like Mia's—like her mother's.

But it couldn't be. The ruins of the bunker dated back to before the War of Independence and possibly all the way back to World War II. The image had been painted above the bed by the soldier who slept there—no doubt a girlfriend or wife back home. I thought of my own father in the war, banished from the island when my mother's father found out they were seeing each other. Did he spend time in a bunker like this? Did he think of Ivana with his child? And did he paint a picture of her above his bed? I responded honestly, "But of course it couldn't be."

"I know. But I like to think she has always been on the island."

It struck me that Mia saw her mother as a presence and not a person. And that the mother's presence could live on in anyone. I wanted to hug the young girl and embody that presence. But I was leaving, and now I understood what Dinko had at stake.

We walked down the path to a small inlet from the sea. On either side, turquoise water gave way to sloping eggshell stone. From above, the cove was like a dramatic crater made by a fallen meteor. I could see the stone tavern Mia had talked about. When we finally reached the water's edge, the shore was all jagged rocks, and the only way into the water was across a wooden dock. A few other sunbathers were there, and Mia and I took our place nearby, spreading towels beneath the hot Mediterranean sun. When the heat became overwhelming, we both jumped from the end of the dock into the refreshing salt water.

A family with a girl and a boy, both younger than Mia, showed up and practiced their dives. Mia joined them and taught the kids a game of funny walks. She spread her feet wide and duckwalked, screaming, "Quack, quack, quack," as she tripped and fell into the water. The kids laughed, then did their own walks. The boy did his, looking up and whistling absentmindedly, his hands behind his back. He feigned not seeing the dock's edge and suddenly tipped in. The girl then hopped like a bunny with her hands curled near her chest and bounded right off the dock. I joined in and did my best imitation of Charlie Chaplin, rocking back and forth as I walked, then doing an exaggerated surprise as the planks of the dock ran out. We all laughed at each funny walk. The children's parents and others looked on, also laughing and clapping at the sight.

Later, we dried off, dressed, and walked to the tavern. It was simple and rustic: a few stone walls supporting a terracotta roof, mismatched tables and chairs beneath, with views of the water, and a slate chalkboard with a menu in Croatian. A man close to my age and wearing an indigo-blue vest over a white apron welcomed Mia with a hug.

Mia said to me, "This is Karlo, one of the owners." To Karlo, she said something in Cro. I understood only my name and "America."

To me, in English, Karlo said, "Welcome, Vesna. I understand that you are famous cookbook writer from America."

I smiled and blushed. "Famous only to my friends."

"You are modest, but come. You should experience our lobster pasta. This dish is well known all over the islands."

He led the way and sat the two of us near a small stage set up with an amplifier and microphone. Then another man joined Karlo—this one an exact duplicate but dressed in a monogrammed apron the same shade of blue as his brother's vest. Mia introduced Arlo, Karlo's twin.

The two talked in Cro, and again all I heard was my name and "America." I guessed that I was, again, a famous cookbook writer.

Arlo turned to me and spoke in English, "Come, come. I will show you how our lobster pasta dish is made."

He led Mia and me back into the open-air kitchen, a terracotta roof the only protection from the elements. The thought of cooking in a kitchen like that was enchanting—the breeze coming off the sea, the smell of salt mixed with the smoke of the wood-fired *roštilj*, and the familiar clutter of knives, pots, pans, and dishes. So different from the cramped and windowless kitchens I'd been used to.

Arlo took his time, showing me first how to make the sauce. He started by sautéing shallots and diced tomatoes in local olive oil, then deglazed with Pošip white wine and added a splash of stock made from lobster shells. The brother reduced the stock, then added the thick double cream, rarely found in American stores. Finally, a pinch of tarragon and chunks of lobster meat. Fresh linguine was added, and the meat, sauce, and pasta were tossed in the sauté pan until mixed and coated. He said, "Now, back to your table."

The other brother, Karlo, served the steaming platter of pasta. We both dug in, scooping up the strands of delicate linguine and lobster with forks and spoons. Creamy, sumptuous sauce with the rich flavor of the stock and a hint of tarragon mixed with the delicate meat of the lobster. I thought I'd rarely eaten such a perfect pasta, and very rarely a dish I hadn't made myself.

Mia asked, "You like?"

"Love!"

Then the music started. A woman dressed in jeans and a white T-shirt took the stage and sat before the microphone, an instrument like a violin perched on her knee. Behind her was a man sitting with another instrument, more like a small-bodied guitar. Only a handful of people were in the *konoba*, but all looked up and clapped before they started.

Mia said, "Her name is Vanja, and she's the best *lijerica* player in all of Croatia. She is married to Chef Arlo and lives on the island but travels all over the world to perform. The man behind her plays the *tamburica*. They call him *Barba*. It means uncle. He is not from Lastovo but is also one of the best in Croatia. It is very special that they are playing here today."

I watched as the woman drew her bow slowly across the neck of the pear-shaped instrument. The sound it made was lonesome in a way, a dark and moody note that held us all captivated. She then looked out at the audience and stamped her foot three times loudly on the wooden floor before turning back to the *tamburica* player, Barba. The tempo jumped, and both moved furiously to elicit a wall of sound. Barba looked down at his instrument with a singular intensity. The sound it made was like a mandolin but softer, closer to that of a classical guitar. The woman, Vanja, seldom sang but made humming noises as she played. I thought the intricacies of their playing, the touch of each string, was ethereal, enchanting.

After a third song, Vanja looked over at our table and smiled. "*Mia, dođi na pozornicu, molim te.*"

Mia translated, "She wants me to come to the stage."

There was no hesitation; Mia leapt up to stand next to Vanja. It was apparent they'd performed together in the past.

Vanja looked at Mia and asked, "*O Marijana?*"

Mia nodded. "*Marijana.*"

Vanja and Barba played, and Mia sang. I'd never heard the song before, but it was beautiful, with the refrain, "*O Marijana. Slatka, mala Marijana.*" The translation came to me: "Sweet, little Marijana." The performance reminded me of a full mariachi band I'd once heard at La Plaza in Mexico City, but this song was performed by just the three of them.

Mia's voice was high-pitched and perfect, a young girl—cute, little—with an angelic voice. I held back tears and clenched my teeth to stop my lips from trembling. I'd never wanted to have a baby, never wanted to possibly subject a child to what I'd been through. But maybe I was missing something in life. A child who would grow up to laugh, play, and sing. A child who would someday have children of their own.

We walked back along the same path, Mia leading the way. We passed the side trail leading to the bunker but kept walking. I thought about the painting on the wall inside. Mia had said that the image of the woman was of her mother. If her mother were still around, she'd be proud. And that was what I said to Mia. "You sang so beautifully with Vanja. You could be a model, an actress, and a singer. Your mother would be so proud."

Mia stopped then and turned back to look at me. "That's if my mother actually had any interest in what I do."

I was stunned. "I'm sure wherever she is, she thinks about you and cares. I don't know the circumstances under which she left you. I can't imagine the circumstances, but I won't judge."

A tear fell from her eye. "I can't imagine either. What is she doing that's so important she can't have a relationship with her only daughter? But I do want to have a mother who truly loves me. I want to think she is out there in the world, glamorous and successful, still thinking of me. My fantasy is that one day, she will return, and we will be reunited. But I am not deranged or stupid. I searched the Internet for any sign of her. The name on my birth certificate says Karina Chernoff. There are Karina Chernoffs all over the world, but none are actresses or models, and none are the age of my mother. Only one mention that I could find, and that was from fifteen years ago, before she met Tata. She had a Facebook profile. She lived in London and was listed as an actress and model. Born in Moscow. The photo had a resemblance to me. There were only three posts, all from right after she created the profile. And then nothing. I showed Tata, and he said that the woman was her. I know if she were truly famous or even still trying to be famous, she would be everywhere on the Internet. But nothing, not even a death notice. She is just an idea of a mother, a ghost."

We'd stopped walking and now faced each other. "I'm sorry for you," I said. "I never really knew my birth mother. She died when I was just three. We were together in Dubrovnik when it was bombed by the Serbs. She died, and I lived. My father also died in the war. I was adopted and brought to America, but I was never close to my new parents. I know how you feel. But you have a loving father and a wonderful life here on Lastovo. And you are so smart and talented."

Mia wiped away the tears. "Why did you come to this place?"

"Just like you, I wanted to know. When my mother and father died, the Internet didn't exist. But I did find a Marta Ivelja online who turned out to be my grandmother. I'm just learning about who I am. I never knew my parents and never will, but I can know where they came from and who they might have been. Like you, I can use my imagination. I can be whatever I want, and I can have my parents become the people who I hoped they might be."

"But now you are leaving?"

"I have to go back. Right now, my life is there."

"But you will return?"

I thought about what Lastovo meant to me. The island was a gem—remote, beautiful, almost forgotten except for the few lucky ones who knew. I'd reconnected with my grandmother—my blood relative—and that wouldn't change. I wanted to stay a part of my grandmother's life and learn more about what that life might mean to me. I'd met a wonderful man named Dinko. We couldn't commit to each other, but something existed between us. We'd made love. I'd thought sex might never appeal to me again. Now, I wanted more.

Then, this wonderful young girl. I believed we could have a relationship of sorts. Mia didn't need another mother—probably too mature and too smart for that. But she might need a friend, someone older who could listen to her ideas and longings, and not preach or condemn. I would like that.

"Of course, I'll visit. And we can talk or text or email or DM or whatever they come up with next."

Mia took my hand, and we walked.

Near The Oleander Cottage, Mia said, "I have to leave now. I will go to say hi to my friend Nika, who was not feeling well earlier. I will call Tata to pick me up later."

"I can drive you if the car is fixed."

"No, not in that *komunističko smeće*."

We both laughed and then hugged. I watched as Mia took off down the road.

And then I noticed something. Mia was skipping.

Lobster Pasta with Cherry Tomatoes

The lobster pasta on Lastovo is something special. We usually have it at the Triton Restaurant in the cove of Zaklopatica, where it must be ordered in advance. Here's my version. This recipe is simplified by using store-bought frozen lobster tails, though feel free to use fresh ones.

Serves 2

2 medium lobster tails – 6-8 ounces total
2 tablespoons extra-virgin olive oil
1 medium yellow onion, diced
4 cloves garlic, minced or grated
½ cup dry white wine
¼ cup tomato paste
1 cup fresh tomatoes, pureed
1 cup cherry tomatoes, halved lengthwise
½ cup heavy cream
1 pound linguine pasta

2 teaspoons kosher salt

½ teaspoon ground black pepper

1 cup fresh basil leaves, chopped

Open lobster tails using kitchen shears. Cut through the shells lengthwise on the underside. Remove the meat and cube it into ¾-inch pieces.

Bring a large pot of salted water to a boil and cook the pasta until al dente. Drain and reserve a cup of pasta water just in case.

In a large skillet, heat olive oil over medium heat and sauté the onion until translucent and softened, about 5 minutes.

Add garlic and cherry tomatoes. Cook for 2 more minutes.

Add tomato paste, stirring for 2-3 minutes to coat the onion and garlic as they caramelize and turn deep red.

Add ½ cup of the dry white wine to deglaze the pan. Stir and reduce the liquid by ⅔.

Add the tomato puree and cook until the liquid is further reduced and starting to thicken.

Once reduced, add ½ cup of pasta water and the lobster meat. Cook until the liquids fully evaporate into the sauce mixture and the lobster meat is cooked, approximately 5 minutes.

Reduce the heat to low and stir in the heavy cream.

Add cooked pasta to the sauce. Stir or toss well to coat the pasta. Add salt and pepper to taste and garnish with chopped basil.

Buzara Mussels

I called Dinko the next day. I wanted to visit my grandmother one more time before leaving, and I wanted him to translate. I kept thinking there was more to the story of my mother and father. What happened after the explosion? What happened with Marta and Ivan? Of course, I could've asked Sara to translate, but I did want to see Dinko again. I was leaving in two days and probably wouldn't be back for months or a year. I knew he didn't want a woman in his life, and certainly not a part-time one who lived thousands of miles away. But something existed between us—a spark or a flickering flame, or just a smoldering fire. I asked, and he said that he would.

I called my grandmother, and with help from the translation app, set up a time to meet. My grandmother said, "*Ja ću napraviti ručak.*"

I said, "*Da,*" and only later, after translating her response on my phone, did I understand that Marta would be making lunch.

We met at her house near the old town square, Dinko in his Land Rover, and me in my beat-up Yugo with the fixed starter. Marta wore a black peasant skirt and another of her dark brown blouses. Her white hair, brushed back from her forehead and gathered in a tight bun, was covered by a dark gray scarf that tied beneath her chin. She held the pet rooster, Goto, beneath her arm. The rooster squawked at the two visitors, squirming and craning his neck against her hold. She calmly petted his feathers.

We exchanged pleasantries at a distance, and then Marta forced the rooster into what appeared to be a wire kennel for dogs.

It turned out that Marta lived just behind our family's old tavern, the *konoba*. She led us through the back door of the house and across an empty lot. I could see where a good-sized vegetable garden had once thrived within a border of cleared stones. Opposite stood the remains of a chicken coop, the wire fencing still intact, the wood coop itself now a pile of rotting boards. Dried-up weeds were everywhere, and Marta led us down a narrow path of crushed rock. We walked around to the front of the tavern, which faced the empty town square.

Dinko knew the place. He talked to Marta in Cro and then translated. "I remember this tavern from when I was a boy. Konoba Mjesec. We'd come here for *pečeni vepar*—roasted wild boar."

Marta smiled. "Yes, we were known for wild boar, also our *peka* and *brodet* stew with sardines, tomatoes, herbs, and wine from your father. We will eat our lunch here."

I knew the family once owned a restaurant but had no idea it still existed. The thought that it did was thrilling. I'd only seen photos and heard the stories, but now there was tangible proof.

Marta plunged a skeleton key into the hand-forged lock and then opened the centuries-old wood-paneled door. She switched on the lights, and we walked into the small dining room. I counted eight tables that could each accommodate two to twelve people. One table was set for the three of us.

I saw the sign then, "Konoba Mjesec," sitting against a wall. The letters were hand-carved and filled in with white paint. Next to the letters was the carved relief of a full moon shaped into a pleasing and satisfied face—tight-lipped smile, broad nose, closed eyes, and pencil-thin brows that tipped at the ends to almost meet the edges of the smile. Around the moon were carved stars filled in with gold paint. The sign hadn't hung since the tavern closed. I guessed over twenty years ago.

Dinko translated, "Moon Tavern."

We walked through and looked at the photos lining the walls. Some of the faces I'd seen in the box of old photos from the previous week. I recognized my mother in one, dressed in a skirt and apron. Again, the resemblance. Another black-and-white photo was of Marta when she was young, my grandfather next to her holding a platter of roasted boar and *blitva*. Then, even older photos. One showed a family in front of a two-story stone house with olive trees in the background.

I turned toward Marta and asked, "Caravello?"

"*Da.*"

She pointed to another photo, this one of a young man with my mother. Marta said, "Tata." My father. His light brown hair hung over his ears, a broad smile showing a row of smallish teeth beneath a wispy mustache. He looked like a child.

The kitchen was through an open vaulted doorway. Pots and pans hung from the ceiling above an expanse of four-inch-thick butcher block where Marta had been chopping garlic, peppers, and flat parsley. On one end of the kitchen stood a vented stone barbecue grill, a *roštilj*, big enough to roast a whole boar on a spit. Next to that was a six-burner stovetop with an oven the size of a steamer trunk. For me, it was hard to comprehend that this place had served the Lastovo community for hundreds of years.

I stood beside my grandmother as she cooked. The garlic and peppers were slowly sautéed in olive oil. She produced a basket of fresh mussels from a small cooler. White wine and chopped parsley were added to the pot, then the mussels. She covered the pot, lifted it from the stovetop, and placed it into the oven.

Twenty minutes later, the mussels were cooked, and we sat down to eat. My grandmother then talked about life after the war.

I did not know about Ivana's death until eight months after it happened. The Serbs continued to bomb Dubrovnik until the following summer. There was no way for me to get there, and no one in Dubrovnik to let me know. Ivan was still in the war, somewhere near Zagreb, and I was here all alone. The bombing ceased in July 1992, and I was finally able to travel.

The devastation was everywhere. The boat I took docked at the Komolac marina miles away. The ferry quay in town was completely destroyed. I took a taxi to Dubrovnik's Old Town past the rubble of destroyed buildings and apartments where people had lived. The driver pointed to the bluffs above and explained where the Serbs had stationed their big guns. He said the shelling was often nonstop and that there was nothing to be done except find shelter when they heard the guns. He dropped me at the Pile Gate. The Franciscan monastery just inside was still standing but had been hit and badly damaged. Just past that was the bakery where Ivana worked. Little was left, mostly blackened rubble. I asked someone nearby what had happened, and she said that the bakery was hit by a single shell that ignited the propane fuel tanks used to heat the modern ovens. All inside were killed.

I still hoped there was a chance Ivana survived.

The apartment where she lived was up the hill near the Buža gate, and I walked through the destruction to find her. The apartment was still standing, with people living there. I could smell the food they were cooking and see the laundry drying on the clotheslines. It was as if nothing had happened. But I know that life goes on, while misery continues. I know this.

Your mother lived with you on the second level. I walked up the stairs and down the hallway to the door. I knocked. A strange woman answered. I asked about Ivana and a small infant. The woman did not know and quickly closed the door on me. I knocked again, but she would not open the door.

I knocked on other doors. I finally found a man who knew of Ivana. He said she went to work very early in the mornings with her child. He knew she worked in the bakery. The day the Serbs started shelling the Old Town, he was finishing his morning meal. He heard the first shell and then ran to the basement where everyone in the building took shelter. The bombing that day only lasted an hour. He said Ivana never returned. He heard about the direct hit on the bakery and assumed she had died there with her child. That is what he told me.

I still had hope. I returned to the ruins of the bakery and spoke with the other shopkeepers in the area. All said the same. Direct hit, explosion, no one survived. I asked if any of them knew of a girl with her baby. Some said they did. The owner was a man named Kovačević, who they said had died in the explosion. I found the home of this Kovačević in the area of Ploče iza Grada. His widow was there, alone, with no business left to support her or their five children. I was very sad for her. It was this woman who confirmed that Ivana and her child had died, along with the woman's husband and one other shop girl. Then I asked about where the bodies were taken. This is when the woman became very sad and began to cry. She said there were no bodies to be buried. All had been consumed by the explosion and then fire. What was left could not be identified. That is all I knew.

I traveled back to Lastovo. I had to work and run the tavern, or I would have nothing to eat. I cooked and had one girl hired to serve the food. There were no more soldiers at the military base to buy my food, and many more people had left the island. If someone had a relative anywhere else in the world, that was where they went. It was not a good time. Eventually, the war ended, and then we were no longer Yugoslavs but Croats.

Ivan was in the military during the war and was not killed or injured. He came back to Lastovo a war hero, but the war was over, and the military had no use for him. We worked in the tavern together. For years, it was difficult, but eventually Croatian families returned for the summer. Then, the tourists. A few people who had left for family elsewhere came back. Just a few.

Ivan died in 2003 of a heart attack right here in the tavern in front of many people. I closed the tavern after that, and I have lived on a survivor's pension, a death pension.

My grandmother was close to tears. I tried to imagine what it was like, losing your daughter and granddaughter. And the not knowing. Going from house to house, looking for any information. Heartbreaking. I would never really know, and that was a good thing. I reached across the table and held my grandmother's hands. I just then remembered the words, "*Žao mi je, Baka.*" I'm sorry, Grandma.

Marta said it again, "*Smrt je sve što znam.*" Death is all I've known.

For minutes, no one spoke. The empty plates were before us, along with an empty bottle of Grk. Then I asked, "Did you ever know what happened to me?" Dinko translated.

"*Ne.*"

"Is there a grave for Ivana, a marker of some sort?"

"*Da.*"

"Where?"

The grandmother explained where it was, in the cemetery behind the Church of St. Mary.

Dinko said that he knew the place.

When it finally came to saying goodbye, I held my grandmother in my arms. The woman felt small, light as a feather, and frail. Since her husband died, she'd lived alone with no relatives to call and check on her. That could all change.

I had a real family now, and I wouldn't lose that.

I said, "I'll be back as soon as I can."

Outside in the afternoon sunlight, Dinko said to follow him in the Rover. He'd take me to the cemetery. I got behind the wheel of the Yugo and stayed close to his bumper. He drove down through the valley of the old town and then took a road that veered south. In the distance, I could see the steeple of a church rise above an olive grove. Closer, the cut-stone church was massive, with a cascade of roofs descending from a four-sided Venetian steeple, no doubt built in the sixteenth century. Each block of the cut stone was slightly different and expertly joined by mortar. No signs were outside, and once out of the car, I could see that the paint-blistered door was padlocked. No one had worshipped in the church for years.

Dinko stood next to me, and although we were in the presence of the church and cemetery, I couldn't stop thinking about him. His dark hair was brushed back, with stray curls falling to his eyes. His skin was deeply tanned, and his muscles defined—a man who worked side by side in the vineyard with his hired help. I remembered slipping off those pants only last week, his stomach muscles tight above the smooth pelvis. The thought made me shiver. I forced myself to think of something else. Anything.

I'd be leaving in the morning, and nothing with this man would last.

I said to him, "Thank you for being so kind and helping me with my grandmother."

"It was no problem. Thank you for spending the day with Mia. She said you talked with her about Karina, her mother. She came back—I don't know, satisfied."

"I was surprised that you allowed Mia to go with me."

"I have thought about what you said on the sailboat. She will want to find out things for herself. She will want to make her own mistakes. I can't be like the horse's bridle."

"She's a smart, beautiful, and talented young girl. I know you must be proud."

"Yes."

"I probably won't be back for months, maybe a year, but I would very much like to keep in touch with her. And you. I would like to see both of you again."

"Yes, I would also like to see you again."

He took my hand, and we walked the path around the church to the back. A stone wall surrounded a cemetery with an arched gate. The wrought-iron gate opened. Inside were gray stone crypts mixed with more modern marble slabs embedded in the earth. I read dates: 1652-1701; 1589-1630; 1923-1991. Some were so old, eroded by rain and wind, that the engravings were indecipherable. One crypt was marked with a skull-and-crossbones symbol. I asked Dinko what the symbol could mean.

"It is to remind us that we will all eventually die."

We walked on, holding hands. I felt my palms sweat and loosened my grip, our fingers then lightly touching. We kept walking, looking at each of the more recent markers for the name Ivelja.

We found the headstones in the very back, two small marble slabs resting above the bare ground and cut-back weeds. A vase was filled with fresh sprigs of pale violet lilacs.

One marker read simply, Ivana Ivelja 1971-1991, below an engraved cross. Next to that was another identical marker—mine—Vesna Ivelja 1988-1991. Instead of the cross was a chiseled resting lamb.

Dinko held my hand tighter as we both looked at the

infant's grave—my grave.

He said, "What does it feel like to die and be reborn?"

Garlic Mussels

Most of the mussels served on the Dalmatian Islands are harvested from oyster and mussel beds in the bay at Mali Ston. Once harvested, they are often kept fresh in pens sunk just off the docks at seaside konobas.

Serves 4

2 pounds mussels rinsed, scrubbed, and de-bearded
2 tablespoons unsalted butter
1 large shallot, minced
5 garlic cloves, minced
1 Thai bird's eye chili, finely minced
2 teaspoons fresh thyme, minced
1 cup white table wine
⅓ cup heavy cream
A handful of fresh Italian parsley, roughly minced

2 teaspoons sea salt, or 1 teaspoon kosher salt
Freshly cracked black pepper to taste
1 lemon, cut into wedges
Crusty bread, for sopping up the juices

Place a large, heavy-bottomed skillet over medium-high heat.

Add the butter and shallots, and sauté for about 3 minutes until translucent and soft. Then add the garlic, chili, and thyme, and sauté for another 30 seconds.

Add the mussels to the pan and pour in the wine. Stir, cover, and bring to a boil for about 3 minutes. The mussels are cooked when they open up. Once they have opened up, stir in the heavy cream and parsley. Stir to combine and bring to a low simmer.

Taste the broth and add a good pinch of salt and freshly cracked black pepper.

Now tip your mussels into ceramic serving bowls, squeeze lemon juice over them, and serve with the crusty bread.

PART TWO
True North Island

Beef Bourguignon

I'd been flying all day, chasing the sun west from Split through Amsterdam to Minneapolis. The course took us over Iceland and then Greenland. I looked down from my window seat, watching the world go by in blistering technicolor. The sky was crystal clear, and I could trace the steep slate-gray fjords and blue-white glaciers spilling into the Arctic Ocean. Dots of icebergs floated above a dark sea like chips off a stone carving. Entering Canada, the tundra spread out in a mottled carpet of mosses and shrubs among what looked like alleyway puddles after a downpour. In a few hours, I'd be walking through customs and reentering the world I'd left only two weeks before.

For whatever reason, I thought back to the spark that brought me into the world of food and cooking. It wasn't when I lived with my adoptive parents. My mother, Lisha, cooked large meals to feed seven hungry kids—big pots of spaghetti with store-bought sauce, Hamburger Helper, ham steak with macaroni and cheese, a pot of chili with saltines, fried chicken with mashed potatoes and gravy—that sort of thing. The food would be served in large bowls and platters and then doled out like fresh water to shipwreck survivors. Second helpings could be hoped for but rarely realized. I'd grown up hungry for food, and a real treat was a McDonald's Big Mac.

The spark didn't happen until I was living on my own and attending a community college in a Minneapolis suburb. I was never a great student, B's and C's, and it wasn't long before I got behind. I knew I needed help, and what the college offered was free tutoring services. I signed up.

Bryce was his name, and we met in the cafeteria right after breakfast. I'd expected a brilliant but nerdy kid who'd become impatient with my inability to quickly comprehend. The boy who showed up was anything but. Bryce was tall and lanky, with thick auburn hair swept behind his ears. He was patient. If I didn't understand an algebra problem, he'd have me go back over the explanation in the textbook. If that still didn't catch, he'd offer a similar, though easier, problem for me to solve. He also helped with history papers, going over my writing with a red pen and then having me complete another draft.

At first, it was hard to sit next to him and listen to his explanations. I'd see the outline of his chest beneath a T-shirt, his smile, or his clever eyes. Eventually, I moved into a more relaxed feeling around him, and I actually learned. By the end of the semester, I wasn't exactly getting straight A's, but I wasn't getting C's or D's either. More importantly, he showed me *how* to study and learn. If I didn't understand something, I knew how to go back through the materials and find what I needed.

Then we started dating. I'd never thought of myself as attractive, and I rarely went on dates in high school. I felt that much of my low self-esteem had to do with the burn scars on my back. I didn't want to date because that might lead to kissing and then sex. Eventually, those boys would want to undress me, and then they'd see the ugly scars. Thinking back on it now, maybe I purposely made myself unattractive—no makeup, baggy clothing, and lace-up Doc Martens. I wore those same clothes while being tutored by Bryce. I'd never owned lipstick or eyeliner. But that didn't stop him from asking me out.

And then, eventually, he saw my back, outlining the web of scars with his fingers. I cringed at first, thinking he might pull his shirt back on and run away. But Bryce didn't care. He said that imperfections made something rare and beautiful— an old postage stamp with the wrong color, the patina of aged copper, a small mole above a woman's lip, freckles, slightly gapped front teeth.

I met his family and began eating Sunday suppers with his parents, brother, and sister. I became close to his mother. She worked during the week as a graphic designer, but her passion and hobby was cooking. I started showing up early on Sundays to help out.

One Sunday, we cooked cassoulet. His mother explained that the dish was a French staple, prepared by working-class folks, and that the ingredients were more suggestions than dictates. The only stipulation was meat and beans. That Sunday, she started by rendering fat from pork belly and then browning inexpensive chicken thighs—instead of traditional duck. The thighs were removed and set aside. She added diced onions to the pan, which were then sautéed slowly. Aromatics like carrots, celery, a whole head of garlic, a bay leaf, and parsley came next, cooked in homemade chicken broth. The white beans, which had soaked in a salt brine overnight, were added. After an hour of simmering, the chicken thighs were returned to the pot, along with chunks of mild Italian sausage. Then, the whole mélange was poured into a shallow earthenware dish and placed in the oven. An hour later, what came out was a thick bean casserole with a dark crust. The family dug in with loaves of baguette.

That was the spark—cassoulet and the ability to make something so beautiful and delicious out of entirely raw ingredients. From there, I started watching cooking shows—Anthony Bourdain, *The Barefoot Contessa*, and old reruns of Julia Child. I began cooking for my college roommates. Then I took my first restaurant job as a prep cook at the French bistro Chez Colette. Now that I knew my Croatian family had worked at a tavern, a *konoba*, I wondered if it was somehow genetic.

Where was Bryce now? I had an Internet connection on the plane and Googled his name. I clicked on images and found a likeness. He had a Facebook page. It showed him living in Washington, D.C. and working for the State Department. Bryce had always been that smart.

He'd posted photos of his family: a beautiful wife, a young child, and a newborn. The wife could have been me, but after community college, he moved on to get a four-year degree at Georgetown University. The geography had been too overwhelming to keep us together, and we drifted in different directions.

I guessed that was how it worked, and I thought of Dinko as I moved further and further away from Lastovo.

Reed had said he'd pick me up at the terminal. I texted him when the plane landed, and he was there curbside when I exited the airport with my backpack. He immediately jumped out of his old Mercedes convertible and walked around to open the passenger door. It wasn't something I wanted, and Reed wasn't usually the type who opened car doors for passengers. I wouldn't have gone out with him if he were.

I knew he was looking for a hug and maybe a kiss. The tone of his texts somehow implied that he wanted to get back together. It wasn't something I was ready to do. I unslung the backpack from my shoulders and held it out like a shield.

"Great to have you back," he said, and took the backpack. I opened my own door and slid inside, while Reed opened the trunk and stowed the pack. Once in the driver's seat, he thankfully did not attempt an across-shifter kiss.

"Thanks for picking me up," was all I could say.

He put the car into gear and then snaked his way through traffic to exit the airport. "I missed you."

There it was again, the buttering up. I looked at him. Reed had always been handsome. I'd first seen him come down the stairs from the office of the restaurant where I was Chef. He'd been hired as the new manager. Reed wore khaki pants, a pressed white dress shirt, and brown loafers. Preppy, I thought. His blond hair was parted on one side, and he wore mock tortoiseshell glasses. At the time, I said to myself, *I could marry this guy.* A week later, I asked him out for coffee. I'd never been that forward with a guy.

Now, he was wearing the same khaki pants and white shirt. He'd had LASIK surgery and no longer wore the tortoiseshell glasses. His hair had grown out and hung straight to his pronounced jawline.

"Seems like you've been away for years." I wondered whether he meant physically or emotionally, but I chose to ignore the comment. He seemed to understand that I wouldn't bite on the remark and moved on. "Pretty amazing that you found your grandmother. What was *that* like?"

What was it like? I'd thought about my biological family for years. Growing up, I'd tried to search the Internet for any signs of who they might be and who would be left. I knew there had to be uncles, cousins, and grandparents still out there. I found thousands of Iveljas in Croatia. Finding one related to me was like finding a needle in a haystack, and I made no progress. Then, what would it be like to finally meet relatives? Joyous for sure. But they'd also be startled—all thought I was long gone, possibly dead. Years later, it was just a fluke that I found my grandmother, and then she *was* startled. But Marta was also joyous and wanted to bring me back into the fold. She wanted to pass on our family history. I knew I would stay close to her. I answered Reed's question vaguely but honestly. "Just weird."

"Like taking a DNA test and finding a long-lost brother."

Those stories had popped up in the press every year or so since genetic testing had become widespread. "Yes, like finding a long-lost brother."

"I'd like to find a long-lost partner."

That's how he'd always referred to me in social settings—my partner. He glanced over with his brilliant white teeth, smiling, no doubt suggesting that his comment was not meant to be antagonistic.

I wasn't buying any of his passive-aggressive nonsense. "Listen, I've been traveling for eighteen hours, and I'm really exhausted. So, what's going on?"

"It's just that I missed you."

"So, I'm guessing that you're done with what's-her-name."

"I haven't been seeing anyone else since we officially broke up."

Broke up, a kind way of saying I left him when I inadvertently read his emails and found out he'd still been seeing the same woman. We owned a two-bedroom condo together, and "broke up" meant I wasn't going to sleep with him anymore. I moved into the second bedroom that doubled as an office. I slept on a foldout couch. I moved, not Reed. He said he broke it off with the other woman and wanted to go to couples counseling. My question was, why? Was there something to salvage in our relationship? At the time, I thought no. Fool me once, shame on you. Fool me twice, shame on me. Well, shame on me for staying with this man.

"Let's just go back to the condo." Another dumb mistake, buying property with your boyfriend.

Our building, called The 510, was built back in the 1920s, and, at the time, was considered the height of luxury. We drove down into the heated parking ramp where an attendant welcomed me home and parked the Mercedes. The elevator took us to our condo on the second floor. We'd gotten the place for a steal before real estate prices soared around the pandemic, and now it was valued at twice the price. But it had always been *his* place—maybe a little too special. Once inside the front condo door, I had to take off my shoes, lest the cream carpet get soiled. Reed liked abstract paintings, and nothing hanging from the walls connected to me personally or gave me any comfort. I would've preferred photography. The only photos were in the office, now my bedroom. I knew that in the breakup, he'd get the condo and the artwork—and I'd get screwed.

In the foyer was a box from my publisher, the twenty copies of my new cookbook. Fresh from the printer, the books were a reminder that the launch event was only days away. I opened the box and took one from the top. *Up North Cooking* was my first book, which made it possible to open the Up North Supper Club, the restaurant Reed and I had owned. My editor wanted a sequel, and this second book was simply titled *Up North Cooking Revisited.* The cover showed a platter of grilled and sliced ribeye steaks on a bed of arugula. Behind the platter was a view of Burntside Lake, where Reed's family owned a summer cabin. I'd taken the photo myself just a year ago.

Reed was behind me, looking over my shoulder. "I love the cover. Fantastic!"

I said nothing, but it did, in fact, look fantastic, and I was so proud of the book. My editor, designer, and everyone else at the publishing house had done a great job. And I was pleased with the new recipes, taking what was originally a book of family recipes from my times on Burntside Lake with Reed and his family and now adding to them with the more elevated American cuisine I'd perfected at the supper club.

I was tired and just wanted to take off my clothes and slip into bed. I walked down the hallway to my bedroom office. Inside, the first thing I noticed was the absence of a bed—it had been folded back into the couch.

Reed was behind me, and I said, "Don't get any ideas."

He smiled those pearly whites and replied, "Whatever do you mean?"

Burntside Lake was where we first fell in love.

We'd had a few dates. What I liked about him was that he made me laugh. A restaurant was always a tough environment: customers were demanding, food had to be prepared and served in twenty minutes or less, and the kitchen was always sauna-hot with cooks working elbow to elbow at lightning speed. Tempers could flare, and personality conflicts could ignite. Goofing, having fun, and laughing were stress relievers, and Reed could get anyone to make light of a situation.

He'd worked in as many restaurants as I had, starting in Minneapolis but also New York, Los Angeles, and Las Vegas before moving back home. I'd worked in New York and San Francisco, picking up food knowledge as I went. On our first real date at a French haute cuisine restaurant, we'd ended up back at his place, a one-bedroom apartment in Loring Park. And for a guy who'd been on the road for years, the place looked lived-in, with posters and art on the walls, a real bed with a wooden frame, and a stocked kitchen. We'd had plenty to drink on our date, enough to send us sprawling onto the bed with little warm-up chatter—enough booze to allow the self-consciousness of my burn scars to abate. Sex with Reed was ravenous—clothes nearly ripped from our bodies, deep, hungry kissing, mouths everywhere, positions swapped like Legos.

He finally did see my back, but then it was all jokey puns, like, "So hot, your skin melted." The teasing was disarming, and I was smitten.

A week later, he asked if I'd like to go up north for a couple of days. Up north always meant a lake cabin, and that was where we headed after closing the restaurant on a Sunday night. The drive in his Fiat sports car took us over three hours.

We arrived at the lake in the middle of the night. What he didn't tell me was that the lake cabin was actually on an island, far from shore. From the car, we loaded our duffel bags and groceries into a small fishing boat. The motor started and we ventured out onto the water.

The night was moonless, the sky clear, and I could see billions of iridescent stars. The Milky Way spread across the sky like a schmear of cream cheese. It was a beautiful night, but floating through the dark with no orientation was eerie. I hoped Reed knew where he was going. He finally pulled up to a dock and, with a flashlight, led the way to the cabin.

The thought crept through my mind, *What if this guy is a complete psychopath and axe murderer?* I'd only known him for a few weeks. And for a brief moment, I was truly scared. But once inside, he lit a Coleman lantern. I looked around at the pine walls, the old family photos, the shelves of books, and one stuffed panfish. I wondered why anyone would stuff a fish barely larger than a herring, and before I could ask, he said, "My first catch." Then he added, "You're my last." Funny guy.

The next day, waking up late, I finally had the chance to take a closer look around. The two-bedroom cabin, built on a point of land, was surrounded on three sides by a cedar deck, each side overlooking the lake. I could see the fishing boat we'd taken across in the middle of the night, now tied up to a dock that stretched along the rocky shore. A mist hovered over the water, and through it, I could hear the reedy sound of a loon. No other boats were on the lake, and outside of the loon call, it was silent. In all my travels, I thought I'd never been to such a beautiful place.

We recrossed the lake later that day and parked the boat in one of a dozen covered slips in a marina. Reed held my hand, and we walked up a path to Burntside Lodge. We entered a massive stone-and-log building built almost a hundred years before. The owner, Polly, immediately hugged Reed and welcomed him back to the lake. I marveled at the gleaming wood floors, massive stone fireplace, and relics of the past mining and lumber industries. At the far end of the lodge was a bar with windows overlooking a bay, and through double doors was a dining room with hand-carved furniture and tables covered with white linen. I didn't know it then, but five years later I'd have a book launch event in that lodge, celebrating the *Up North Cookbook* with recipes inspired by Burntside Lake.

That night, Reed made supper, a beef bourguignon cooked in a cast-iron Dutch oven. The French stew would later inspire my own take on the classic dish, which would grace the cover of my first cookbook.

After dinner, we drank more wine in front of the wood stove that radiated warmth. The island had no electricity, barely any cell service, but plenty of books and board games. Reed pulled out a tattered Monopoly box, and we played into the night. I was sure Reed let me win—something he never admitted to.

I fell in love with Reed that weekend. He was handsome and funny, and he could cook. He never made me feel self-conscious about the scars on my back, and the sex was fantastic. Since then, whenever we had disagreements and fought—even when he cheated on me—I thought of that Burntside weekend. There was always a place in my heart for the man who made me beef bourguignon and played Monopoly. Until there wasn't.

Lamb Ragout

This lamb recipe feels Mediterranean, and it's something you might find in Croatia. Once upon a time, lamb neckbones were used, but this recipe calls for more tender, easier-to-eat cubed leg of lamb. Spectacular when served over wide egg noodles with a sprinkling of fresh parmesan.

Serves 4

2 pounds lamb stew meat, cut from the leg of lamb (approximately 1½-inch cubes)
¼ cup all-purpose flour
1 teaspoon kosher salt
1 teaspoon ground black pepper
¼ cup extra-virgin olive oil
1½ cups canned beef consommé

⅓ cup Spanish sherry (or alternatively ¼ cup lemon juice)
1 clove garlic, crushed
2 tablespoons fresh lemon juice
1 teaspoon lemon zest
2 tablespoons chopped parsley

Preheat the oven to 350°F.

In a zip-top bag, add the lamb, flour, salt, and pepper. Seal and shake to coat each piece.

Heat the olive oil in a Dutch oven, then sauté the lamb over high heat until browned on all sides.

Add the consommé, sherry, and garlic. Cover the casserole and place it in the oven.

Bake until the lamb is tender, about 1½ hours.

Stir in lemon juice.

Garnish with lemon zest and parsley before serving.

The Perfect Salad

I was scheduled to appear on *The Jason Show* three days later. The talk show aired every day for the two hours leading up to noon. It was broadcast in a dozen other markets nationwide, and for years I'd been the Thursday Gourmet, appearing just about every week and performing some kind of demonstration. For this appearance, I'd planned The Perfect Salad based on a recipe in my upcoming cookbook.

Reed helped load up my Subaru, and then we both drove out to the station. My segment was near the end of the show, and, while Jason was interviewing a young blonde romance writer with bleached white teeth, Reed helped me set up my ingredients and tools on a table that could be wheeled in during the commercial break.

Mark, the production assistant, mic'd me up. Jeffrey, the show director, gave me the three-minute notice, and the table was whisked in. I stepped out in front of the live TV audience, waved, and then took my place in front of the table. The countdown—three, two, one—and Jason moved in next to me to make the introduction. "Welcome back to the show. Vesna, our own Thursday Gourmet, is here to show us how to make The Perfect Salad."

Dressed in my usual red apron, I waved to the camera and did a little shimmy. My show persona was something I'd come up with years ago. I likened it to a cross between Julia Child and Lucille Ball. Usually, I wasn't a loud talker, but in front of the camera, I talked loudly and laughed like, well, Lucille Ball. I always tried to ham it up for Jason. "Thanks, Jase." Like others, I called Jason "Jase."

"So, that's quite a statement, the perfect salad," he said. "I've had the perfect corn dog at the state fair, the perfect egg salad sandwich from the Monte Carlo restaurant, and the perfect kiss from my husband, Michael, but never the perfect salad."

Big laughs. Jason was gay and wasn't afraid to show it on national TV.

"Well, get ready, because you're about to have it."

"Okay, so what makes the perfect salad?"

"The perfect salad needs to have a robust lettuce that doesn't wilt under pressure. I like a combination of bibb and romaine. I always use a knife to chop the leaves—never tear, because tearing damages the leaf's cells and promotes wilting."

"No wilting under pressure!"

The audience laughed while I chopped my lettuce and placed it into a wooden salad bowl.

"Then, something with a crunch. I like apples and use a small dice, so you don't bite into big chunks that overwhelm the greens. Then pecans. Pecans have the right balance of crunch to tenderness I'm looking for. If you want to improvise here, you can use candied pecans, but today, I'm going to be a purist. Finally—and this is the secret ingredient—dried cranberries for that extra little sweet tang."

"Purist shmurist, I love candied pecans!"

The audience laughed.

I smiled and kept going. "Now, the dressing. The perfect dressing for the perfect salad will have the perfect balance between sweet and tang. Sweet tang, sweet thang. Get it?"

"I got it."

The audience laughed once more.

"I use extra-virgin olive oil. This one is from the island of Hvar in Croatia where I've just been. Then, instead of lemon or cider vinegar, we're going to use rice wine vinegar." I held the bottle up to the camera. "This has a sweetness to it and that tang I like. I add just a teaspoon of Dijon mustard, and then, for a slight creaminess, add a tablespoon of mayonnaise. I made this mayonnaise at home, but Hellman's will do just fine."

"Is that hard? Homemade mayonnaise?"

"It's simple. Egg yolks, olive oil, and lemon juice. It's one of the most basic sauces there is."

"And great with French fries."

The audience applauded.

"Yes, mayonnaise makes even the perfect fry better. But back to the salad dressing. We'll whisk all the ingredients together until the oil emulsifies and you have a dressing that won't separate."

"Wouldn't want separation." We were friends outside the studio, and Jason knew all about Reed and me—it was like him to make an inside joke. The audience laughed regardless.

I ignored the joke and moved on with the segment, the

consummate professional. "No, definitely not. Now, here's a trick. You pour your dressing into the bottom of the salad bowl before adding the greens. Then toss the salad only right before you're ready to serve. That way, the salad greens will remain fresh and crisp right up to the last moment."

"And not wilted."

"Yes, not wilted." I mixed my salad and then served two plates. I gave one to Jason.

The highlight of my segment was always when Jason gave his reaction to the food. He carefully brought the plate to his nose and sniffed the salad. Then he reached in with his fork and took a bite. He played the moment for all it was worth—rolling his eyes, chewing slowly, making facial expressions that could go either way, like it or not. Finally, his judgment: "Perfect."

The audience enthusiastically clapped.

At the end of the segment, Jason asked, "So, what's next for Vesna?"

I smiled and looked up at Jason. The question had caught me by surprise. Did I know what was next for Vesna? In my mind loomed the breakup with Reed and the eventual separation of accumulated stuff. Then my grandmother, whom I'd left behind, and the man I'd also left behind. But, of course, none of that was what Jason was looking for. The obvious hung there on the tip of my tongue: "A new cookbook coming out next week, *Up North Cookbook Revisited.*"

"And where can people find your book?"

"Well, Jase, you'll be able to find my book at your local independent bookstore. And next Wednesday, I'll be at Magers & Quinn Booksellers to sign cookbooks."

"Let's give a huge thanks to our Thursday Gourmet, Vesna."

The audience enthusiastically clapped, again.

Reed drove while I sat in the passenger seat, trying to decompress from my adrenaline-producing performance. The TV station was located in the suburb of Eden Prairie, and the way back to Minneapolis and the condo should have taken us along two major highways. Reed had other ideas. He took an off-ramp at Minnetonka Boulevard and drove east toward the lakes and Uptown.

Before I could ask, he said, "I want to show you something. It's a surprise."

I did not want any surprises from Reed. "Let's just go back to the condo."

"It'll just take a few minutes."

I doubted that but said, "Okay, fine."

He drove around Lake Bde Maka Ska, then down Lake Street. We passed empty, boarded-up stores with graffiti-covered brick facades. During the riots after the murder of George Floyd, Uptown had been ransacked. Previously, it had been a bustling hub of chic retail stores, coffee shops, and lots of restaurants. Since the riots and the pandemic, most stores and restaurants had closed. The once-bustling hub was now practically a ghost town. Reed stopped in front of a shuttered seafood restaurant.

He said, "The owners of the building are desperate to lease this space out. They've offered two hundred thousand in build-out money and free rent for a year."

"You've talked to them?" Of course, he'd talked to them.

"They reached out to me. So, you want to take a look?"

Reed found a parking spot in front of the closed restaurant.

"Why didn't you tell me about this earlier?"

"I wanted it to be a surprise. I have a key. Surprised?"

I remembered the seafood restaurant, The Port Tack. The place was huge, with two levels. On the first floor was a casual dining area opposite an oyster bar that could seat forty people shoulder to shoulder. Upstairs was more formal, with dining tables set up around a centerpiece saltwater aquarium the size of a small swimming pool. The owners had made a fortune up until the pandemic and riots. They closed the restaurant and got out before losing a single cent.

I didn't like being surprised, or rather hijacked, by Reed, but was interested to see inside and what was left. "Okay, let's take a look."

The restaurant was just how I'd remembered it. The horseshoe bar, with stations for three bartenders, was all there, including the glassware now gathering dust. The tables and chairs were still arranged and ready for service. The computerized point-of-sale management system was ready to be rebooted.

"Look at the kitchen." Reed then walked through the stainless-steel service doors. I followed. I was a chef, and my love was always the back of the house—the kitchen workspace—and this one was top-notch, twice the size of our old restaurant kitchen. The pots and pans still hung from the back wall. They had all the regular line equipment, as well as ovens and mixers for making breads and pastries. I could've parked my Subaru in the walk-in cooler. A dumbwaiter system and backstairs led to the dining room on the second floor. We climbed up.

The saltwater aquarium still dominated the room, though all the water and fish were gone. Again, the tables and chairs were still there, the glassware and tableware still in the bus stations. Almost turnkey. I wondered what Reed had in mind. I looked at him and said, "So?"

"Your first cookbook was a success. Your second will also be great. With that publicity, this restaurant could do millions."

"What's your concept?"

"The modern supper club, not unlike our first restaurant. Your books are all about casual cuisine in the Northwoods. The whole throwback supper club thing is really going strong. Just last year, a coffee table book came out showing all the old supper clubs throughout Minnesota and Wisconsin. The Burntside Lodge was featured. I'm thinking about re-creating Burntside Lodge here. Instead of tropical fish, we fill the tank with northern pike, walleye, sturgeon, and bass. We hang deer heads and old mining and lumber stuff on the walls. Fish fry on Fridays and prime rib on Saturdays. Classic martinis, old-fashioneds, and Manhattans."

I was intrigued. "So, what's the modern part?"

"Live jazz downstairs. Your modern take on classic dishes. We don't want to be too campy, too cliché."

"No deer heads."

"What?"

"No stuffed animals on the walls. Skip the old bric-à-brac and do spectacular outdoor photography. Brandenburg or David Barthel, or even Ansel Adams."

"Okay, sure. Does that mean you're in?"

I had to admit his concept was great. I could see it: the martinis around the horseshoe bar, the fish in the aquarium, and even the jazz. Everything was already there—all the dishes, equipment, and glassware. Two hundred thousand would be enough to get the place open, and then the rent-free year would provide the buffer to get the restaurant on its feet. It could be a showcase for all the recipes I'd developed in my cookbooks. It made so much sense.

Then there was Reed. I didn't want to have a relationship with him, but he was a great general manager and could run the dining room while I ran the kitchen. We'd done it in the past—before the pandemic and his cheating affair. I was sure I could work with him again. We'd sell the condo, and he could move on with whomever he wished.

But not so fast. "I'll need to think about it."

If I did decide to do the concept, it would be my second. The first had started out so great; it was a dream, really. I'd worked my way up in the kitchen hierarchy to finally become the chef at an Italian restaurant near where we were then living in Loring Park. The place was as big as the Port Tack we'd just toured, and I made good money. Reed had moved on to run a steakhouse downtown, and we were both living in his apartment. Both of us scrimped and saved with the idea of opening our own place.

Reed found the perfect location. Stan's Bar and Grill was in a tony part of the city called the North Loop. Stan's was a dark, old-timey place with few windows and the dive-bar smell of beer and greasy burgers. Stan was ready to retire. He owned the building but was willing to let someone else run the bar and grill, and to let the new operators handle the remodeling to appeal to the younger professionals buying up the newer condominiums. He was also willing to finance the remodeling.

Six months after signing the agreement with Stan, we opened the Up North Supper Club. The exterior walls had been replaced by windows that connected the restaurant to the foot traffic outside. The beer-soaked tables were replaced with booths along the wall. We left the old bar in place, an homage to the past. We kept the menu simple, just the supper club staples from my cookbook. I focused on farm-to-table ingredients, sourcing fresh produce daily from the local farmers' market, and buying our beef and other proteins from local organic producers. The only pre-packaged food we served was Heinz ketchup.

It took all our savings to get through the first six months, but slowly, we built up a steady clientele. Then, a "Best Restaurant" article came out in the *Star Tribune* newspaper, and Up North was listed in the top ten. Business boomed. The restaurant became very profitable. It was then that we moved from the one-bedroom apartment in Loring Park and bought the nearby condo at 510 Groveland. We were well-off restaurateurs—we had arrived.

How did everything go so horribly wrong?

The pandemic. It started as a rumor about people getting sick in Seattle. Then, the first incident in Minnesota. People panicked and bought up everything they could in the grocery stores. For some reason, there was a nationwide run on toilet paper. People were crazy about toilet paper and would steal rolls from our restaurant bathroom. Business dramatically slowed. We followed the latest recommendations for social distancing—each booth was walled off with plexiglass, and any free-standing tables were removed. No one was allowed at the bar. Then masking. There were none to be had, and I found a woman who would sew up cotton masks for all our staff. Every day, we lost money profoundly. Then, one of the cooks came down with the virus, and we were forced to shutter for two weeks.

Like other restaurants, we did everything possible to stay afloat—curbside takeout, sidewalk dining with any propane gizmos we could find to keep customers warm. It was all such a waste. Unlike other restaurant companies, we didn't have deep pockets, and neither a bank nor our landlord, Stan, would float us a loan. I couldn't really blame them. We had no plan to stay open profitably through the pandemic, and a vaccine still hadn't been developed. The government PPP money arrived, but it only caught us up on payroll taxes and vendor invoices.

My relationship with Reed became strained.

What are the biggest issues facing couples? Finances are number one. We had money in the bank, but there was no money coming in. Reed seemed oblivious, maybe because he'd come from money. I came from nothing, and my adoptive parents were the last people I'd go to for help. They'd already moved past the adoptions and were now fostering, often six kids at a time. They were already hand-to-mouth. The lack of money coming in caused me extreme anxiety, and maybe I took that out on Reed.

Number two on the list is intimacy. Sex had been something glorious when we'd first met, dated, and then moved in together. During the pandemic, we both worked long hours to keep the place afloat. We had no time or energy for sex. I just stopped having any interest—maybe Reed stopped also, or so I thought. Our sex had become rote, uninspired, and maybe done out of habit, up there with folding laundry.

Number three, infidelity. I came back to the restaurant one evening to check on inventory for the next day. When I opened the office door, Reed was at the desk with his pants down around his ankles. Our hostess, Dawn, was on the desktop, tits up, her legs tightly wrapped around Reed's waist. He said simply, "Oh fuck."

Fuck was right.

We closed the restaurant, and I moved into our second bedroom, Reed's study.

We tried to rekindle the relationship, but for me, the trust wasn't there. Then, we tried to rekindle the restaurant, but by the time the pandemic had abated and Up North could finally reopen, Stan had decided to demolish the building and build condos.

Without a restaurant to go to each day, I finished my second cookbook.

Now this—a chance to redeem ourselves with a restaurant three times the size of the Up North Supper Club. It was all so tempting.

Winter Salad with Squash and Beets

The perfect salad does have the proper balance of sweet, tang, firm greens, creaminess, and crunch. This one meets the challenge.

Serves 4

For the Salad

1 raw beet, cut into ½-inch squares

1 cup diced butternut squash, cut into ½-inch squares

1 (12-ounce) can chickpeas, drained

2 tablespoons extra-virgin olive oil

1 tablespoon smoked paprika

6 cups finely chopped kale

2 cups shredded Brussels sprouts

¼ cup salted sunflower seeds

¼ cup pomegranate seeds

⅓ cup goat cheese crumbles or hunks of soft goat cheese

For the dressing
2 cloves garlic, minced or grated
1 tablespoon honey
Juice and zest of 1 lemon
1 tablespoon Dijon mustard
½ tablespoon kosher salt
¼ teaspoon red pepper flakes
2 tablespoons rice vinegar
¼ cup extra-virgin olive oil

Cube your beets and squash, then spread them onto a baking tray with your chickpeas, and season generously with olive oil and paprika.

Bake at 400°F for 30 min.

Finely chop the kale and Brussels sprouts, then add them to a large salad bowl.

To make the dressing, Microplane the garlic and add it to a mason jar with kosher salt, mustard, red pepper flakes, honey, vinegar, and olive oil.

Shake vigorously until you get a creamy texture.

Toss in pomegranates, sunflower seeds, goat cheese, dressing, chickpeas, squash, and beets.

Toss everything together and serve garnished with more pomegranate seeds.

Old Bay Crab Cakes

Lisha and David Thompson, my adoptive parents, lived in an immense four-square clapboard house in the working-class neighborhood of South Minneapolis. I pulled up in my Subaru and walked to the front screen door. This was where I grew up with seven siblings.

My first memories of Lisha and David were filled with fright and apprehension. My new parents had seemed nice enough when they singled me out at the orphanage. Lisha wore a long skirt, a buttoned blouse, and her black hair in a tight bun. David wore a suit with sleeves down to his knuckles, his dusty blond hair neatly held in place with Brylcreem. They smiled as they held my hand and led me through the Zagreb and Minneapolis airports. They smiled and held my hand as we climbed the steps to a house as large as one of the orphanages where I'd stayed during the war. They spoke nicely as I met the other children and saw the bed where I would sleep for the next twelve years. They talked nicely, all smiles and softly pronounced words, but I hadn't learned the language and had no idea what they were saying.

I shared a bedroom with my adopted siblings, Anne and Esther. The adopted boys, Bobby and Hakim, shared a bedroom with Ben, the biological son. The one biological girl, Mary, had a small room to herself. She was the oldest and helped Lisha run the house.

Since that first introduction, my siblings had long ago moved out, but Mary was still there, helping with the newer foster children.

I knocked and waited. Through the window, I saw Lisha smiling, expecting the visit. She opened the door, and we embraced.

"Kika, how are you?" Lisha always called me Kika. It was my nickname from Croatia, and it had stuck with me through all those years until I finally left for college. Kika from Croatia.

"Fine."

I rarely came back to the house, but I did appreciate their mission. David was a pastor at the local Lutheran church, and both he and Lisha were deeply religious. Their calling had been to save children, simple as that. And save as many as could reasonably fit in their home. I was the fifth to be saved. Bobby and Esther had come from Haiti, Erik from Russia, and Hakim from Ethiopia. Once one left the house for college or a job— or in Erik's case, kicked out and onto the street at seventeen for drinking alcohol—they brought in another. The place was operated more like a boarding house than a home. I had no great longing to go back to a place where I'd been boarded. But then again, for those twelve years, Lisha and David were the only parents I knew, and I had respect, if not a sort of love, for them.

In the foyer were the same rows of coat hooks. The names of each child were always written on masking tape above each hook. I'd had the second one in the bottom row, which now said Terrance.

The living room was just as I remembered it—two long, threadbare couches against opposing walls where we kids sat, while Lisha, David, and Mary took the three wingback chairs at the far end. A single, tube-style television enclosed in a wheeled stand stood at the other end. We were only allowed TV on certain days and only certain shows. The show we all waited for each week was *Murder, She Wrote*. Then, on Sunday afternoons after church, we could watch a rerun of *Little House on the Prairie*. Otherwise, the room was for quiet and reading.

Lisha sat down in her chair, and I perched on the couch nearby. The conversation, as usual, was stilted.

I asked, "So, how has it been?"

"You know, children come and go. God provides. How was Croatia?"

"I found my biological grandmother."

"Oh."

Before Lisha could ask a follow-up question, a child who looked about ten walked into the room. She had woolly hair piled on her head like cotton candy. Her nose was running with caked mucus around the nostrils. The child said, "I'm hungry."

Lisha looked at the child. "Dinner will be served at five. You know that, Beatrice."

"But I'm hungry."

What I remembered about my adoptive mother was that she never lost her temper, never yelled at the kids, nor did she ever spank them. If there was a spanking to be meted out, that was saved for when David came back from the church. "You just had lunch."

The child stared at her without speaking.

Lisha turned back to me. "It's good you reconnected. It would've been nice if that happened sooner."

I knew what she meant. If my grandmother had reconnected with me after the bombing, then there would've been one less mouth to feed, one more child they could've saved.

I ignored the comment. "Turns out she worked as a cook like me. My family owned a tavern on this small island called Lastovo."

The child still stood at the entrance to the living room. Now she said, "I want a cookie."

No expression on Lisha's face. "Cookies are for good girls. Did you empty the dishwasher like I said?"

"It's Michael's turn to empty the dishwasher."

"I told you to do it. If you empty the dishwasher, I will give you one cookie."

"But it's Michael's turn."

Lisha ignored the child and turned back to me. "The ability to cook is a great thing. Cooks feed the world." She thought for a moment, then added, "Cooking and serving food is the ultimate in giving. I don't know who said that, but don't you believe it's correct?"

"Reed and I are thinking of opening another restaurant."

"Didn't you try that once? Isn't it enough to just cook nutritious food for people?"

That's what I remembered about Lisha, and what I always came back to. The woman would do God's work and save children, but she could also be crushing in her narrow-mindedness. I remembered Erik, who'd been kicked out of the house. He made the proclamation one evening that he was going to be an actor. He'd had a lead part in a school play and gotten the bug. He asked to take more acting lessons at the Children's Theater and also wanted to audition for a part in one of their productions. It was David who, like his wife, had a quote ready to go: "What is acting but lying? What is good lying but convincing lying?" I later found out it was an innocuous quote from Sir Laurence Olivier. But at the time, David just equated acting with an elevated form of lying, not worthy of his adopted or fostered children. And maybe that was the beginning of the end for Erik. A year later, he came home from senior prom with beer on his breath. The next day, he was out on the street. Erik had since gone on to perform on Broadway.

I ignored Lisha's comment about the failed restaurant. I'd learned years ago that it was better to move on rather than confront, like arguing the benefits of a computer with a stubborn Luddite. I said, "I also have a new cookbook coming out."

Beatrice was still at the entrance to the living room. "I have to go pee-pee."

"Well, go pee-pee then."

"Michael has been in the bathroom since lunchtime. He won't open the door."

Never exasperated, Lisha calmly stood. She said to me, "Michael has taken to locking himself in the bathroom for an hour at a time. I don't know what he does in there, but I should attend to this."

Growing up around teenage boys, I had a good idea what Michael did in the bathroom. "Okay, I will see you later. Love you."

"Love you."

I exited the house—the house I'd never wanted to enter.

I wondered again what my life would've been like if my biological mother had survived—those thoughts kept churning through my head. Would I have taken over the family tavern? Very likely. I could imagine going to the fish market each day to pick over what the fishermen had brought in. Then a fertile garden where we grew our own produce. I'd never grown anything more than a few herbs in a pot, and I loved the idea of my own farm-to-table loop where I could grow, harvest, clean, chop, cook everything, then collect the restaurant's organic waste to recycle back into the soil. From the local growers, I would've bought olive oil decanted into liter-sized Pepsi bottles and the Grk and Plavac Mali wine from Radić Winery. I could imagine tourists from all over the world planning a stop in Lastovo on their Croatian vacation just to eat my food. It would've been a simple, satisfying life.

Then another scenario. What if, instead of finding Marta, I miraculously discovered my mother still alive? I was sure that, unlike Lisha, she'd be proud of the cookbook I'd written and the second one just coming out. Even though my first restaurant had failed, she would be proud that I'd put myself out there and taken those risks. I thought my mother would be proud that I might try again.

I knew others my age who had close relationships with their mothers. They confided and gave advice. I would've liked to talk with my mother about Reed and how that relationship had soured. I would've liked to talk with her about Dinko. Could I tell her about the sex in the sailboat? I doubt it, but I knew other mothers and daughters confided. I would have liked to confide. But there was that reality; I'd never had a real mother.

The next day, Reed asked if I wanted to go out for dinner. I had nothing planned and thought, *Why not?* It was a beautiful afternoon in June, the kind of day Minnesotans wait for all winter. The temperature was just above 80, a passing thunderstorm had taken out most of the humidity, and the sun wouldn't set until well after 8 p.m. I suggested Sea Salt next to Minnehaha Falls. Reed said, "Great."

We drove along the Mississippi River in Reed's Mercedes with the top down. There wasn't a cloud in the sky, and all the trees and vegetation were lush green. The river road descended and paralleled the Mississippi at almost water level. Out on the river were teams of rowing scullers pulling at their oars and moving against the current. Then, in the distance, a steam paddleboat was taking tourists through the Mississippi gorge. All of this was in startling contrast to the sailboats and fishing skiffs of the Adriatic. I felt like I had a foot in both worlds.

We parked near the falls and walked the short distance to the park pavilion where the restaurant served seafood entrées along with shrimp and oyster po' boys. The line to order stretched out the door and down the sidewalk. That was just part of the fun—standing in line, drinking beer, conversing with others waiting to order. Then, watching the parade of characters with their bikes, dogs, rented surreys, and often outrageous outfits. I stood in line and Reed went to buy beers. Twenty minutes later, we ordered more than we could collectively eat: a shrimp po' boy, black beans and rice, a shrimp salad, six oysters on the half shell, and two more beers. We waited at an outdoor table under an awning of oak trees for our food to be delivered.

Reed came right to the point, "So, have you thought about that space in Uptown?"

I'd thought about the space and was torn. It seemed so perfect. The concept could be commercially enhanced by the two cookbooks—one that had already been a regional success and the other, set to be released in two days. I could picture the place just as Reed had described: martinis around the bar, elevated comfort food, the indigenous fish aquarium, and a still cozy, though more modern, cabin feel. Just like the Up North Supper Club, I'd source the food locally and run specials based on what was fresh and in season. I was convinced it would be a huge success and provide both of us with more income than we'd ever seen. We'd be the kind of restaurateurs every chef and restaurant manager dreams of.

But I also knew a restaurant of that size would take everything I had. One thing many restaurant owners learned from the pandemic was that they didn't need to be open every day of the week. They could easily close on Sundays and Mondays, giving their staff a rest. But not a restaurant with ten thousand square feet of floor space. A monster like that would need to operate seven days a week, which meant that even though we'd be rolling in dough, we'd have no time to spend it. "I've thought about it, but I'm not there yet."

"What will get you there?"

"Time to think."

Reed knew not to push it and moved on to another subject, one equally as heavy. "I want us to try again."

He sat across from me with a tight-lipped, pleading smile. His blond hair was neatly swept back, Wayfarers tipped above his forehead. Reed was handsome. Any woman would find him adorable. I said, "We've talked this to death. It's okay to move on. You could have any woman you want."

"I'm done with all that. I just want you." Pleading smile and now, pleading eyes.

"Fool me once, shame on you. Fool me twice, shame on me." I'd thought that before but now regretted saying it as soon as the words left my mouth. Those little sayings were just like Lisha and David. Little fortune cookie thoughts that didn't account for the complexities of life.

He said nothing in response but reached down beneath the table and fished something from his pants pocket. He held up his closed hand and moved it toward me. The outstretched hand opened to reveal a ring. No velvet box, just the loop of gold and a green rock, an emerald. "I'm serious. I want to re-commit."

I took the ring from his palm. I guessed it was just like Reed to do something other than the standard wedding set. The emerald was the size and shape of a Chiclet and surrounded by diamond chips. I thought it was stunning. "Reed, I don't know."

Not no, not never.

"We can book the Burntside Lodge. Invite our friends and family. I'm ready to be faithful, to commit the rest of my life to loving you."

Thankfully, the food came and filled the table with the aroma of seafood, spices, lemon, and hot sauce. For the moment, I said nothing and just stuffed my mouth with a soft bun filled with shrimp, shredded lettuce, tomato, tartar sauce, and Tabasco. I ate voraciously and looked at Reed with wide-open, smiling eyes. He said nothing more, realizing I would not immediately respond. He dug in himself, leaving the emerald ring between us like a pleading, unspoken question.

A three-piece string band had set up at the top of the pavilion steps and now began playing. The music was delightful, with a guitar strumming a rhythm, a violin playing the melody, and a cello providing the bass notes. An older couple stood and embraced as they danced, then other couples joined in. Could that be us, years from now, still in love and dancing at the pavilion? Then that thought, *Still in love.*

I reached over to pick up the emerald ring. I held out my other hand for him to take. We held hands, our arms stretched over the small table, our eyes locked. I smiled—one I thought showed sympathy but also love. My hand lightly twisted his, and then I opened his palm. I pressed the ring into the flesh of his palm and then pushed his fingers closed. I held his closed hand with both of mine and looked into his tearing eyes.

I said, "Not yet."

I was in the kitchen of the event center mixing ten pounds of lump crabmeat with mayonnaise, crushed Ritz crackers, Old Bay Seasoning, and Tabasco. The mass of ingredients filled a thirty-quart mixing bowl, and I needed both gloved hands to fold the ingredients together, careful not to pulverize the crab meat. The recipe, one from my new cookbook, had been multiplied by fifteen to feed the expected audience attending my book release event later that Saturday afternoon. I'd checked with my publicist, Samuel, about the numbers. Only fifty had pre-booked a ticket, but there would be many more who'd show up to pay at the door. So, we planned for one hundred. The ticket price of fifty dollars included a signed cookbook, a glass of champagne or non-alcoholic Catawba juice, and a crab cake appetizer. I was making enough for one hundred fifty just to be safe.

Or so I thought.

Reed was out in the center's main room, helping arrange the tables and chairs in front of a small, raised platform where I'd have to say something seemingly profound and answer questions. Reed, just two days previous, had asked me to marry him. I hadn't said anything to him the next day, and today he had to know that I might be more focused on the event. But I was only half focused.

He'd had an affair, continued to have that affair, and we'd broken up. Maybe the foolish thing was to continue living in the same condo. Maybe I should have moved out. No doubt we'd had great times together, and I loved him before our lives unraveled. Was it possible to salvage what we once had? Another question floated through my mind. Was an affair forgivable if he finally broke up with the other woman? Was it something I could put behind me? Could I learn to trust him again? I wouldn't be the first jilted lover to salvage a relationship. And the thought of opening a new restaurant, as much work as it would be, was enticing and exciting.

I wasn't going to decide now.

I worked by myself, scooping two-ounce balls of crab cake mixture onto lined baking trays, then rotating each tray through the oven. While they cooled, I mixed together the remoulade sauce: mayonnaise, capers, chopped chives, pickle juice, more Old Bay and Tabasco, and a spicy mustard. On serving trays, I placed a teaspoon of the sauce on each small crab cake, then sprinkled a pinch of chopped chives on top. The appetizer was done, the event center was filling, but I just stood there in the kitchen. I knew time was running out, but part of me was reluctant to make my appearance and face the audience.

Samuel came through the kitchen doors and silently stood before me. He was a cute young man dressed in a smart blue suit, an open-collared pastel-blue shirt, and brown oxfords. I thought he was a little new to the business and prone to getting a little too worked up.

When he couldn't get the words to spit out, I just said, "What?"

"I think you need to make more crab cakes."

"Why? There's enough here to feed a small army."

"You probably need to know—there's a large army out there."

"Like, how many?"

"There's a line out the door, down the block, around the block, and down the other side. I'm guessing three to four hundred."

"That's impossible."

Samuel reached for the paper towel dispenser, pulled the lever to produce a couple of feet, and then wiped the sweat from his face. "Maybe five hundred."

"What happened?" Only about fifty people had shown up for my first cookbook, and most were family and friends. My first book had been a success but strictly regional. Since then, I'd closed a restaurant.

"I just found out. I knew it was going to happen, but not until tomorrow."

"What?"

"*The New York Times* is featuring *Up North Cooking Revisited* as one of the best regional cookbooks to be published this year. It's going to be printed in tomorrow's Sunday edition. But it's in the online edition this morning."

"Why didn't you tell me?"

Samuel took off his jacket. The kitchen was hot—kitchens were always hot—but the wings of sweat beneath his armpits had spread out way before he entered. "I wanted it to be a surprise."

I was getting tired of surprises—the ring, the restaurant, and now this. "Fuck, fuck, fuck." Then, "What's Reed doing?"

"He's already driving to the liquor store to buy more champagne. Rachael from Magers & Quinn is going back to the bookstore to get as many copies of the cookbook as they have."

"Call Reed and tell him to swing by the condo. I have two cases of books there—that's fifty more."

"What about appetizers?"

"Not gonna happen. When they're gone, they're gone. Just pour more champagne. One more thing, tell the staff to get rid of all the tables and chairs—standing room only."

The poor boy looked stunned.

I shouted, "Go!"

The doors opened thirty minutes later. Staff members sold and took tickets as quickly as possible, poured champagne, and handed out crab cake appetizers on square napkins. I was there to sign books, taking the time to ask each person's name and spelling, which I wrote at the top of the title page. It took forty-five minutes to fill the room to capacity, two hundred and fifty people. More books and champagne had arrived, and I apologized and offered more champagne to the people who weren't able to eat.

They closed the doors, but I had Samuel go down the line of people still outside, letting them know that after I spoke, we'd do a second signing.

Then I spoke. And what I thought about while walking up

to the small stage was a simple memory of when I first put myself out there to be judged—booed or applauded. It was a simple Christmas pageant during my sixth-grade year in elementary school. I'd taken choir, and a few weeks before the pageant, the teacher asked if I would do the solo for the song "Silent Night." It was a great honor to be chosen, and I had to say yes. Being one of twenty girls and boys in the choir, standing in rows and facing the audience as a group, was one thing; stepping from the group and moving to the lone microphone was something else—both completely daunting and scary. My nerves were so rankled during the lead-up to that solo I thought my voice would crack and I'd be booed from the stage. Of course, parents never booed, but the thought was there, nonetheless. The teacher gave the cue, and I stepped forward. I didn't think but just opened my mouth, letting the words and melody flow naturally. And then I was through it, and the audience briefly and politely clapped. I'd put myself out there and made it through the performance.

Since then, I'd put myself out there many times. Becoming a chef at a well-known restaurant was one thing, and the weight of the menu and daily specials was my responsibility and reputation. There were occasions when a dish came back, and those boos were ten times the weight of any applause. But the thrill of the applause was still something surprising, and I continued to put myself out there: *The Jason Show*, the restaurant Reed and I owned, my first cookbook, and now my second.

I stood on the raised platform and thanked the audience, then thanked those who'd helped in the book's concept and production. I told a brief anecdote about one of the featured recipes—the one with its photo on the cover—a grilled ribeye on a bed of arugula with lemon, olive oil, and coarse-ground salt. Two years before, Reed had grilled that same steak for me on True North Island, and I had prepared the arugula. The anecdote was about how favorite and often simple recipes are created from inspiration and experimentation with the ones we love. Maybe not so profound, but I thought, *Touching*. The audience applauded.

That was an easy one.

Then wash, rinse, repeat—out with that audience, and in with two hundred and fifty more.

Crab Cakes with Old Bay Seasoning

This crab cake recipe is slightly different from Vesna's, with the cakes served on a bed of greens. If you want, skip the greens and whip up a spicy aioli.

Serves 4

1 large egg
1 cup mayonnaise
1 tablespoon Dijon mustard
2 tablespoons Old Bay Seasoning
1 tablespoon chopped fresh tarragon
¼ cup finely chopped onion
1 tablespoon finely chopped celery
1 tablespoon finely chopped green onion
2 cups crustless white bread, cut into small cubes
16 ounces jumbo lump crab meat, drained
2 tablespoons salted butter, at room temperature

Preheat the oven to 400°F.

In a medium-sized bowl, whisk together the eggs, mayonnaise, Dijon mustard, Old Bay Seasoning, tarragon, onion, celery, and green onion to make a dressing.

In a large bowl, toss the bread with the dressing until the dressing is absorbed, about 15 minutes.

Gently mix in the crab, being careful not to break up the bigger pieces. The mixture should hold its shape when formed into a ball with your hands.

Divide the mixture into 8 crab cakes. Place the cakes on a butter-greased sheet pan.

Bake until golden brown, about 10 to 12 minutes.

Serve warm on a platter of a variety of different spring greens dressed with lemon and olive oil.

Cold Water

The next few days were a whirlwind of activity. Radio interviews with Kerri Miller on Minnesota Public Radio and then with Lori and Julia on myTalk 107.1. I was back on *The Jason Show*, this time promoting my book. Then Samuel was able to secure a national appearance on the *Today* show via Zoom, a podcast interview with Jesse Sparks on *The One Recipe*, and a feature Sunday article in the *Star Tribune* newspaper. Congratulatory messages flooded my inbox. I'd put myself out there, and the applause continued.

My book was the number one bestseller for Midwest Cookbooks and the number two nationally behind José Andrés' latest. Samuel said my sales placed *Up North Cookbook Revisited* on *The New York Times Best Seller* list. I stood to make a lot of money.

I was off in my Subaru for previously scheduled book signings. I drove east to Madison where fans lined up down the block outside Madison Books, and then to Milwaukee for another late-afternoon book signing. I signed hundreds of books. Everyone had questions, and I was attentive to answer each one. The reality was, I was just so overwhelmed by the response and pleased with everyone and anyone who took the time to meet me and purchase the book. The next morning, it was north to a bookstore in Green Bay and then another further north in Door County. On Monday, I drove the six hours back to Minneapolis. Everywhere I went, the long lines to have me sign both my newest cookbook and the first one were surprising and welcoming. The following weekend, I'd have to go through the whole process again, this time predominantly in Minnesota.

Reed was there when I finally returned home after three days of driving. By the time I took a brief nap, he'd arranged silverware and napkins at the small dining table in our condo. Something in the kitchen smelled divine. I sat down, and he placed a Le Creuset Dutch oven in the middle of the table. Reed lifted the lid. Inside were two shanks braised in a rich sauce surrounded by diced vegetables—lamb osso buco. One of my favorites.

Over dinner, I talked about all that had transpired on the first leg of the book tour. Then, while cleaning up, Reed offered to take the next weekend off from his job at the steakhouse to drive me through northern Minnesota. We could spend one night on Burntside Lake. The help with driving would be appreciated, and I relished any chance to be on Burntside. I quickly agreed.

We left the following Friday in his Mercedes. The day was beautiful, in the 70s, and we drove with the top down. I tied my hair back in a ponytail and enjoyed the sun blanketing my skin as I relaxed all the way to Bayfield, Wisconsin. Honest Dog Books had been a big supporter of my first cookbook, and now they had a large outdoor area set up with chairs and a stage. By the time we arrived at 7 p.m., the chairs were filled, with other guests standing in the back. I walked onto the stage, and the owner introduced me. The two of us did a question-and-answer session before unleashing the crowd with *their* questions. I stayed another hour, signing books. We spent the night at The Bayfield Inn, having dinner at the rooftop restaurant overlooking the marina and Apostle Islands. We ate fresh whitefish caught that day in Lake Superior. I'd only booked one room, but it came with two full-sized beds. I insisted Reed take the bed closest to the window, and I slipped between the sheets while he brushed his teeth. There was to be no hanky-panky.

The next day, we drove to Duluth and did one signing in the early afternoon and another that evening. Afterward, we drove the two hours northwest to Burntside Lake. We parked at the lodge and then took the fishing boat across.

The sun had set, and Reed drove the boat slowly. The wind was calm, and the sky clear, revealing the planets and stars just beginning to appear. A half-moon crested the horizon and illuminated the islands as we passed between.

He asked, "Remember that first time?"

I remembered. The scary feeling of crossing the lake at night in the pitch-black darkness, the exciting raw sex. "Oh, I remember."

"Won't you miss this place if we really break up?"

I had thought of that. It was the one thing I would sincerely miss. Since we'd been together, all our summer vacations were spent on the island, often with Reed's family. For those brief days, I felt a part of a family, though I knew it wasn't my own. I was honest: "I will."

"Then maybe reconsider my proposal." Reed looked to

me for any response, but I was not about to open that can of worms.

Then the motor died.

Not even the cough or sputter of a Yugo gas tank going empty.

"What did you do?" I asked accusingly.

"Nothing." Reed turned the ignition key over and over. The starter motor was silent. "Must be electrical."

Now, we were alone and smack in the middle of a very large lake. Silence all around. Then, just the fluttering tremolo call of a loon in the distance. Laughing at us. "So, what do we do now?"

Reed stood from the driver's seat and moved to the back of the boat. In the scupper near the engine, he pulled out a canoe paddle. I sensed the presence of a smirk. He thought this was so funny, or ironic—trapped in a boat in the middle of nowhere with his distant ex-partner. He simply said, "Paddle."

"Paddle all the way to the island?"

"Sure. There's no wind, and it's a perfectly perfect night. Why don't you open that bottle of wine?"

Reed walked to the front of the boat and sat with his legs dangling over each side of the pointed bow. He started to paddle. "Put on some music."

It was a beautiful night, and I didn't need to be anywhere until early afternoon the following day. I pulled the bottle of red wine from the grocery bag, and, luckily, it had a screw top that easily twisted off. I took a sip and passed the bottle up to Reed. He did the same and placed it down behind him. He kept paddling, leisurely doing a few strokes on one side and then switching to the other.

He asked, "You know what first attracted me to you?"

I put on a James Taylor station from my phone's Spotify

app. I kept the volume low. "My boobs?" I laughed.

"When we first met, you looked beautiful even with your hair tied back, stained kitchen whites, no makeup, and yes, those perfect breasts. But it wasn't just your looks. It was your confidence. You worked the line with some very testosterone-laced guys who would've loved to walk all over a woman in their space. You would take none of their razzing, giving it back as much as you took. But it wasn't acrimonious. The confidence you projected was wrapped in a sort of self-doubt, most of the back-and-forth softened by your self-deprecating humor. I could imagine that within a week of cooking with the guys, you had them wrapped around your finger. Ultimately, working with you was just plain fun. I respected and admired you. That confidence wrapped in self-doubt, self-deprecation, self-scrutiny..." He paused, laughing at his jumble of words.

I said, "You can self-stop right there."

But he went on, "I knew you would do whatever you wanted in life, and you have. I'm so proud."

I took another sip of wine and handed it back to Reed.

I asked him then, "Why did you cheat on me?"

He took his time responding. Of course, we'd been over it many times before. He'd apologized, said he was done, but it still gnawed at me. "I don't know. I just fucked up."

I guessed we'd been all over that subject a hundred times, beating a dead horse. In the end, that was probably all he could say—I fucked up. Part of me was cynical. I knew all too well that, given the opportunity to steal, most people would take what wasn't theirs. And most men, given the opportunity to fuck, would fuck. Reed was most men. Then, I thought of Dinko back in Lastovo. I was given the opportunity to fuck on the sailboat and did not pass it up. Maybe I was no better than most men. Forgive and forget?

I leaned back in the boat seat, listening to James Taylor sing about fire and rain, and drinking more wine. I watched Reed's broad shoulders move with each paddle stroke, the boat moving imperceptibly through the water. He stopped for a moment and looked back. "How about some more of that wine?"

I handed up the bottle and then took it back after he'd taken a swig. True North Island was ahead, silhouetted in the moonlight and rising above the water like an apparition.

Reed had taken his shirt off by the time we reached the dock, his body wicking sweat. He said, "Let's take a swim."

The wine bottle was empty, and I felt good. The water was so inviting, and the temperature was still pleasant enough to be naked. I began taking off my clothes. Being naked in front of Reed was nothing new, and now he was also undressed. He dove in first, and then I followed. Cold, but refreshing. With a breaststroke, I swam further out into the lake and then floated with my arms outstretched, the stars now completely out and filling the sky with fields of crystal light. I could hear Reed nearby, slowly moving his arms, propelling his body through the water. How many times had we done this before, skinny-dipping late at night after finishing the week at one restaurant or another?

Later, sitting on the deck in our robes, we opened another bottle of wine, now too exhausted from the day to cook dinner.

We said nothing for a while, just silently drinking and watching the stars. From deep in the woods behind, I heard the hoot of an owl. A minute later, another hoot. Then, a barely audible flutter of wings as the owl flew away.

Reed turned toward me. "Let's have sex."

Sex. On Lastovo, Dinko had awakened something inside me. Before that encounter, I hadn't had sex in a long time, and maybe I thought the desire had vanished along with my naïveté.

I *did* want to try again, to see if the magic still worked. I wasn't ready to re-commit to Reed and take his engagement ring. But he was there, and the night seemed magical. I answered, "Okay."

He stood in his loose robe, holding out his hand. I took it. We walked into the cabin and then the bedroom, switching on a lamp so we could see. He untied my terrycloth belt and opened the robe. His hands traced the curves of my body, and then our mouths joined, kissing, deep and intense. We eventually moved onto the bed, entangling like seaweed, floating in and out of positions, finding the rhythm we'd lost, each remembering what fulfilled us most.

The morning sun streamed through the bedroom window and woke me early. Too early. I pulled the covers over my head, turned away from the light, and went back to sleep.

Before I woke up again, I dreamt I was back on Lastovo, at The Oleander Cottage. My grandmother was there, dressed in her dark clothing and headscarf. Then another woman, Ivana, my mother. We sat around the rough-cut dining table, playing a game of cards and drinking red wine. The game was belote. I was winning and feeling very good. My mother seemed proud of me, and she smiled with beautiful white teeth. I drank more wine. A new hand was dealt, but now I was left without trump cards or face cards. My mother doubled the stakes, and Marta redoubled. I was shocked by my change of luck. I knew I'd lost.

Then I was outside with just my grandmother. The sun had come up, the temperature was January cold, and many of the oleander leaves had turned brown. We sat at the table in our same clothes, now shivering. I reached for my glass to drink more wine, but it had turned to water. My grandmother then said, "*Tko vino večera, vodu doručkuje.*" Still dreaming, I knew instantly what it meant: "Who dines on wine has water for breakfast."

I woke, startled, with a feeling of dread. I remembered the phrase from the dream. What it meant, I didn't know. But I did know the phrase was the source of my dread.

I stood and pulled on the robe I'd worn the previous night—right before Reed had opened it up and slipped it from my shoulders. I sat back down on the bed. At that instant, I knew I'd done the wrong thing. The wine. I'd dined on wine and sex. In the moment, I'd enjoyed both, but my resolve to move on from Reed had now been broken.

I waited for the water part.

Reed was already up and out of the bedroom. I knew he'd be down on the dock with coffee and a book. I went into the bathroom, brushed my teeth, and then tied my hair back with a rubber band. I scrubbed my face.

The robe bothered me—a reminder of the night before. I went back into the bedroom, took it off, and tossed it carelessly into a corner. I dressed in a shirt and jeans. My cell phone was on the nightstand, and I checked for any important new messages. None that I'd have to deal with that morning. I shoved the phone into my back pocket. In the small kitchen, I poured myself a cup of the coffee Reed had made.

Then I saw it. On the kitchen dining table was the ring he'd revealed days before, the emerald and diamonds I hadn't taken. The ring was on a stack of papers bound with a metal clip. Before I could sit at the table, Reed opened the outside door and walked in. I had the feeling he'd been waiting for me.

Right away, he said, "I think we can do it again."

I looked up. He hadn't changed out of his robe, no doubt still lost in the revelry of the previous night. "A do-over?"

He smiled. "Sure. I love you, Vesna. I want to spend the rest of my life with you."

I said nothing.

His smile weakened. He moved on. "We can marry and then fulfill our dream of the new restaurant. You and me."

"Maybe just *your* dream."

"No, our dream."

I sat down before the ring and stack of papers. I saw the word "LEASE" on the cover page. No doubt these were the documents to secure the new restaurant space. Ten thousand square feet, an almost-new kitchen, a spectacular bar, and a fish aquarium to rival a suburban swimming pool. The thought of running a place like that was daunting but also exciting. I loved a challenge and knew I could do it.

Then there was Reed. He'd always been the love of my life ever since first seeing him at the restaurant where he started work as the new manager. Could I move on from all that had happened since? Make a fresh start?

From somewhere, Reed produced an expensive Montblanc fountain pen. He unscrewed the top and handed it to me.

I took it.

I pushed the ring aside and began reading the papers. The build-out money was there, along with rent waived for the first twelve months. The rent after that was reasonable based on the square footage. The restaurant would need to be successful to cover the rent, but in the business, that was always a given. If it was successful, we stood to make not only a lot of money but also a name for ourselves in the restaurant community. My cookbook was now a bestseller, and the sensation of that alone would help make the restaurant the talk of the town. The last page of the lease was for signatures. Reed's was already there, along with the signature of the building owner. My name was printed below, with an empty line. Everything seemed to be falling into place.

Then my phone rang, just a distracting vibration in my back pocket. I instinctively pulled it out. Long distance from Croatia.

I answered, "Hello."

"Yes?" The voice on the other end was clear.

"Sara?"

"Your grandmother is very sick. I think you need to come soon."

Water for breakfast.

Osso Buco

Once upon a time, osso buco was exclusively made with veal, but that seems to have gone the way of fur coats and aerosol hairspray. Lamb works just as well, and if you have any hunter friends, have them bring you a pair of venison shanks. Fantastic!

Serves 2

¼ large onion, chopped
1 small carrot, chopped
1 celery stalk with leaves, diced
2 cloves garlic, sliced
2 tablespoons all-purpose flour
1 slice veal or 2 beef shanks (about 1 pound)
1 cup white wine
½ cup crushed tomatoes
1 sprig rosemary
1 sprig fresh thyme
3 cups beef stock

Preheat the oven to 325°F.

Preheat a Dutch oven over high heat, then add 1-2 tablespoons of oil. Pat the meat dry with paper towels, then season generously on both sides with salt and pepper.

Brown the meat in the Dutch oven. It usually takes 6 minutes per side to achieve a nice, deep brown.

Remove the shank and place it aside. Reduce the heat and add the onion, carrot, celery, and garlic to the Dutch oven. Sprinkle with 2 tablespoons of flour and cook until softened, about 6 minutes.

Deglaze the pot with the wine, being sure to scrape up all the brown bits with a wooden spoon. Reduce until about half the wine is left, about 2 minutes.

Add the tomatoes, herbs, and the shank back to the pot. Submerge the shanks in the beef stock and cover the pot with a layer of tin foil to seal in the juices. Add the lid to the pot and bake in the oven until tender and fall-off-the-bone, about 2 hours.

Serve over mashed potatoes, egg noodles, or polenta.

PART THREE
The Moon Tavern

Bean Soup

I could see Sara standing by her BMW as the ferry pulled into the dock in Lastovo.

I'd stayed on the deck of the boat throughout the trip, nervous about being inside where I might get seasick again. I hadn't brought a sandwich along and drank only water. The wind had been up, and swells rocked the ferry, but I did not repeat my first embarrassing voyage.

The summer weather had arrived, and now the temperatures floated in the eighties during the day. Sara still drove with the top down, maniac-fast, with the blast of air keeping us comfortable. She wore another Hermès scarf, this one vintage with an intricate design of floating skeleton keys, and a tight-fitting sleeveless dress the color of ripe olives. As usual, she made me look like a vagrant in comparison with my knee-split jeans and coffee-stained shirt that I'd worn for over thirty hours of traveling. I'd had little sleep on the succession of planes and was jet-lagged.

Sara had told me over the phone that my grandmother was ill with terminal breast cancer, but that was all I knew. Now I asked the questions that had been looming in my fogged mind. "How long has she known?"

Sara replied, "I had asked her, 'When did you last see your doctor? Why are you not in treatment?' She said the last doctor was in August at hospital in Split. That was ten months ago. 'This is not right,' I said. Then she said to me that doctor wanted to cut off her breasts. She refused. Then they wanted to do the chemotherapy, but she would need to live in Split for six months. She also refused that, saying she was too old to handle all that business. She would rather die without the cutting, needles, and poison. Said she already suffered enough and looking ahead to what was next."

"What's next?"

"In her mind, Heaven, I guess. Marta is no communist."

"Is anyone around to help her?"

"A nurse from Split comes out to the island every month. Provides Marta with pills for the pain."

"Why do you think she kept it from me when I was last here?"

"Old ladies do not want their children to make fuss or be upset. I think she wants to tell you her story and your mother's story before death. I think she has possibly more to say now."

"You think so?"

"I don't know for certain. But I think if she did not have more to say, she would just die in peace and not require you to come this far to see suffering. She would not have called me."

We drove past Radić Winery with its "no tourists" sign, which kept outsiders away and him and Mia in their cloistered bubble. I could see workers in the rows of grape vines pruning the new shoots. I couldn't see the Land Rover or any sign of Dinko. We kept driving through the hills until the old town of Lastovo opened up before us in the deep valley. We passed the many vacant and crumbling ruins before pulling up near my grandmother's home behind the old tavern and deserted town square. We walked the rest of the way.

I knocked on the door, Sara behind me. I heard a muffled "*Uđi.*" Come in. The door was unlocked.

Marta was in the living room, sitting on the couch with Goto in her lap. The rooster looked at the two of us and then jumped down to menacingly circle the room. Marta didn't get up from the couch. She sat with the hem of her nightshirt poking out beneath a dark brown quilted robe. It'd been only three weeks since I last saw her, but the change was striking. The woman sat slumped to the side, her head propped up by a hand, her elbow leaning against the couch armrest. The weight loss was evident in her thin neck and gaunt face. Her hair was uncharacteristically uncovered, and I could see patches of bare white scalp, like a peeled orange. Despite her appearance, Marta's face was welcoming with a genuine smile.

She said, "Vesna."

I walked carefully past Goto, who made a feckless attempt to peck at my ankles. I softly kissed my grandmother on each cheek. "*Tako mi je drago što te vidim.*" So good to see you. The words came to me without thought.

From behind, Sara said, "Neighbors come by and deliver meals and make sure she is okay."

I sat down on the couch next to Marta and took her hand. "*Jesi li dobro?*" Are you okay?

"*Ja umirem.*"

I didn't know the words and looked up at Sara.

"She says she is dying."

"We should get you to see a doctor. We can take you to Split," I said. Sara continued to translate.

"No more doctors."

"Then what can I do?"

"Make your food. Listen. I have more to tell."

Sara left and I was alone with my grandmother. I had no place to stay and was dead tired from my travels. Marta could see that and stood up to show me where I could sleep. I walked behind and followed her into a room with a sewing machine set up on a table next to a small single bed. "*Spavaj*," she said. Sleep.

The door closed. I put down my backpack and sat on the edge of the bed. I slowly undressed and then slipped under the covers. But then I couldn't sleep, my eyes sweeping the room for each detail. Above the bed hung a simple wooden cross, two sticks joined by a peg. A watercolor hung on the opposite wall, a picture of a blue sea with a single island in the distance—possibly Zaklopatica, where I'd bought seafood from the fishmonger woman, and where I'd gotten on the sailboat with Dinko. It occurred to me that the bedroom was the same one my own mother had slept in, and that she likely painted the watercolor, and that each night she went to sleep looking at the image of the sea. If we had made it through the war, this bedroom might have been where I slept. I would've grown up next to the sea, taking in the warmth of the sun during the summer months. I would've known Sara and Dinko as classmates in school.

How would my life have turned out? Simpler, I guessed.

Would you know paradise if you'd never seen anything else? I might have gone to the university in Zagreb, learned something of the rest of the world, and then possibly made my way back to the idyllic island. I would've known that living on Lastovo and running the family tavern was all I needed. Then, I'd have a family of my own.

I finally drifted off to sleep.

I slept for twelve hours.

I woke and walked into the living room. My grandmother was on the couch, again with Goto pressed in her lap. Dinko sat across from her, both having coffee. He stood when I entered.

I asked, "How did you know I was here?"

Dinko was dressed in tan shorts that fell long to the tops of his knees. A pink cotton shirt was open to the second button, the sleeves rolled up to his elbows. His wavy black hair hung into his eyes, and he brushed it back with his fingers, tucking the loose strands behind an ear. I'd seen him do the endearing gesture countless times. "It's a small island. Everyone knows."

I presumed Sara was something like the town crier. "Well, it's great to see you."

He stepped forward to touch my shoulders and kiss me on each cheek in greeting. But it was more than just a Cro greeting. His hands remained on my shoulders, and his lips lingered a split second longer on each cheek. Then he looked into my eyes. "I've missed you."

"I've also missed you." I said this instinctively but had mixed emotions. It seemed just yesterday I'd been up on Burntside Lake with Reed, the ring and restaurant lease between us, a chance to start a new chapter in my life. Or maybe a redo of the old. I wasn't sure. Now Dinko was before me like a dream in a Minnesota slumber.

He excused himself quickly. "I must go, but I will be back for dinner tonight. Marta invited me. But she says that you will do the cooking. Of course, I will provide translation services. I am anxious to know more of your grandmother's story."

Then he was gone.

I walked to the only other market on the island, which was up the winding alleyways to the ridge of the valley. I'd noticed that my grandmother ate little, and her cupboards were bare of any groceries that could be salvaged into a meal. What I had in mind was a hearty, warm soup. I bought cans of cannellini and pinto beans, a smoked sausage link, pancetta, onions, garlic, and a tube of tomato paste. Though I always preferred to make my own, I bought a liter of chicken stock. Across the street was a café with fresh pastries and bread. I chose a firm, round boule.

My grandmother had a small galley kitchen, but I chose to cook in the old tavern that was once my family's. I walked down the pathway with my groceries, past the overgrown garden and the dilapidated chicken coop. At the front entrance, I opened the heavy wooden door with the skeleton key Marta had given me. I switched on the lights. I could just barely make out the scent of the mussels Marta had made weeks ago, the smell of seafood, wine, and garlic.

In the kitchen, I reached up to lift a two-liter saucepan from the ceiling rack and lay it on the old gas stove. The chef's knife I chose from a wooden rack had been hand-forged many years ago and was stained black from disuse. I scrubbed the knife in the sink until I could see shining steel, then used a honing block to get a good edge.

I chopped onions and garlic and slid them into the saucepan. I lit the gas stove with a wooden kitchen match and turned the flame to its lowest setting. I added olive oil and then let the onion and garlic sweat until translucent. I added diced pancetta and sausage slices. Just then, I remembered that all the spices were back in my grandmother's kitchen.

Marta looked up at me from the couch when I walked back into the house. I used the word "*začini*." Spices. Where the Cro word came from, I had no idea, but the language was now starting to emerge in my subconscious mind.

Marta took it as a question and slowly stood.

I put up my hands, "*Ne, ne,*" but was ignored. Marta stood with Goto still perched in her lap. The rooster fell to the floor in a flutter of wings.

She followed me into the kitchen. I said what I needed, "Paprika, salt, pepper."

My grandmother slowly pushed through random jars and found the spices. She placed all three on the counter.

Against more objections, Marta followed me down the path to the tavern and then sat in a chair near the stove. She watched as I added the beans, stock, and tomato paste. I put in two tablespoons of paprika, then added salt and pepper to taste.

Marta, my grandmother—my *baka*—stood and moved toward the stove. She said, "*Grah.*"

"*Što?*"

"*Grah.*" She picked a bean from the saucepan. "*Grah i varivo.*"

"Bean soup. *Da.*" I smiled.

Later, I tasted the soup—rich, full of flavor, the beans

adding hardiness. It was good but needed to simmer to let the flavors blend and develop.

I let my grandmother taste the soup. Marta blew across the hot liquid held in the spoon, then took a sip. She smiled and nodded. "*Dobro*," then added another pinch of salt. I was not offended.

Marta then opened a drawer beneath one of the counters. She pulled out an old wooden box the size of a shoebox. She lifted the hinged top and sorted through a collection of brown cards. She pulled one out. She said again, "*Grah*," and then handed me the card with its pencil-written notes. It was a recipe with the *Grah i varivo* title at the top. I read down the list of ingredients: the beans, sausage, onions, garlic, paprika, pancetta—everything I'd just used for my soup.

Marta handed the box to me. "*Tvoje*." Yours.

I looked through the recipes. All were written on the same cut-out squares of brown pasteboard cards, the backs showing the printing of food brands. All were dog-eared from years of use. There had to be well over a hundred.

These were truly special.

Dinko drove up to the house a few hours later, after I'd changed into a summer dress with a pattern of sunflowers. He'd also changed and now wore light linen pants with a matching cream shirt. His hair was neatly combed back from his forehead. In each hand was a bottle of wine, a white Grk and a red Plavac Mali. He smiled and said, "*Dobra večer*."

Dinko helped Marta back down to the restaurant, and we sat at the same table in the dining room where we'd eaten the mussels weeks before.

We ate the *grah i varivo* with the crusty boule, and it wasn't long before Marta launched into her story.

A month after I arrived back in Lastovo, after learning of your mother's death, I received a letter addressed to her. The postal service delivered mail erratically during the war years, but often, if someone was traveling, you could give your letter to that person. That person would then pass it along to someone else. So, you see, I received the letter addressed simply to Ivana Ivelja in Lastovo. The letter found me. It said that you were alive and at a hospital in Dubrovnik.

Again, I traveled. This time, a fisherman took me in his boat to Vela Luka. From there, I traveled by bus to Korčula and then another boat to Orebić. I found someone in that small fishing village who was going all the way to Dubrovnik. So, after traveling for three days, I reached the hospital. You were still there.

You had been burned very badly. They had you lying on your stomach. The burns on your back were exposed to the air, and I could see where your skin was missing and other areas where blisters still clung to your body. A tube traveled through your nose and into your stomach to deliver food. You were not awake and could not talk. They said that your pain would be too much if you were awake, so they kept you sedated with drugs. I tell you this because you will understand that I could not take you back to the island.

I stayed with you for the next two weeks until you were able to eat on your own and speak. You were just a little girl, three years old. They still gave you very many drugs for the pain, and I am not sure you knew who I was. But then, how could you? I had only seen you a few times and mostly when you were just a baby. You asked for your mother. I told the truth. Your mother was no longer with us on Earth but in Heaven with God. You were so sad, but you could not cry out through the pain and drugs. Your eyes teared.

I had to leave. The war was still going on, and I had no money left for a place to stay or to buy food. I walked down to the docks and waited until I found a boat going to Korčula. From there, I made it back to Lastovo.

Now, I want you to know that your grandfather, Ivan, was a good man. He was a soldier in the war, and later worked hard at the restaurant to make a living for us. He loved your mother. But he could also be a hard man. He made Ivana move away to have her child, and when she refused to give you up for adoption, he did not want you or Ivana back in our house. A month after I had returned from seeing you, Ivan came back to Lastovo on leave. I told him you were alive but in the hospital with grave burns. I pleaded with him to travel to Dubrovnik to bring you back and raise you in our family—to have a family again. He said no. I pleaded more, but he continued to refuse. Ivan went back to fight the Serbs, and I did nothing.

Times were different then.

I am very sorry. I abandoned you when you needed family the most. Of course, I knew you would go to an orphanage, and I hoped you would go to a nice family in a country where there were no bombs. This all happened, and I am so happy that you were able to go to America. The war in Croatia continued for another four years. For years after that, few people came back to summer on the island. Our life was very difficult.

We had no bodies to bury, but I convinced the priest to place a grave marker in the church cemetery. It was war, and many bodies were not returned. I lied to the priest about your death.

I demanded from Ivan that we bury Ivana with her child, who was now also dead to us. You had to be dead to me. That was the only way I could live with myself.

Marta bent over and laid her face in her hands. She wept softly, and I moved to hold her. I now knew I'd been abandoned. The information was all too new and raw; I knew the story wouldn't sink in until much later. Then, I didn't know if I'd feel anger or resentment.

What I did know was that my grandmother had lived with the trauma and grief for all this time. That I had returned after thirty years might have provided some relief, but it also brought the trauma and grief back to the surface.

The *grah* was left unfinished. Dinko and I helped Marta back up the steps to her house. In her bedroom, I helped her undress and slip beneath the sheets.

Before he drove off, Dinko held me for a long time, and I cried on his shoulder.

Creamy Kale, Sausage, and Potato Soup

This recipe uses the Slovenian smoked Polish sausages from Zup's, the local grocery store in Ely, Minnesota, but you can use your own favorite smoked sausage.

Serves 8

2 tablespoons extra-virgin olive oil
1 medium yellow onion, chopped
4 cloves garlic, minced or grated
1½ pounds Yukon Gold potatoes, quartered and cut into ¼- to ½-inch chunks
4 cups finely chopped kale
8 cups (2 quarts) chicken broth
1 teaspoon smoked paprika
4 smoked Polish sausages, cut into ¼-inch slices

1 (15-ounce) can cannellini (white) beans, drained

⅓ cup heavy cream

2 teaspoons kosher salt

Freshly cracked black pepper, to taste

Zest of 1 lemon

¼ cup fresh lemon juice

Place a large pot or Dutch oven over medium heat. Add the oil, onion, and garlic, and cook, stirring for 3 minutes.

Add the potatoes, kale, broth, and paprika to the pot. Bring to a boil, then lower the heat and bring to a simmer. Cover and cook for 20 minutes to soften the potatoes and kale.

Stir in the sliced sausage, beans, and heavy cream. Simmer for 5 more minutes.

Stir in the salt, pepper, lemon zest, and lemon juice, and serve.

Ajvar and Pogača

I woke up early to the startling sound of Goto crowing outside.
I looked at my cell phone, just after 6 a.m. I tried to get back
to sleep, but Goto kept crowing, and now the scorching
sunlight filtered through the thin drapes, and the combination
of rooster shriek and lid-piercing light made it impossible. I
stood from the narrow single bed and dressed, slipping on
shorts and the Trampled by Turtles T-shirt Mia had come to
know me by.

My grandmother was up but dozing on the couch, her
shoulders slumped against the backrest. She was dressed in her
nightshirt and quilted robe. On the side table was a bottle of
pills. I quietly walked over in bare feet to read the label.
Oksikodon. Phonetically, it was the same as in English,
oxycodone. There had to be over fifty pills still in the container.

I made coffee and then sat outside at the one small table

overlooking the street, reading emails. From my editor, I learned that the cookbook was quickly going into a second printing. I responded, *Fantastic!* Samuel, my publicist, wanted to know if he could set up Zoom interviews while I was in Croatia. *Sure.* Then, further down, past the dozens of spam emails, was a message from Reed. *Asked the building owner if he would give us a few more weeks to decide on the lease. Said that he'd give us two. When do you think you'll be home? Miss you. Love you. Reed.*

I didn't know. How long does it take for someone to die? And just that thought made me feel callous and self-serving. I'd launched the book and did as much publicity as needed to sell copies, and I could do more remotely from the island. The restaurant was still an exciting idea, and I knew in my heart and bones it would be a success. I thought Reed might be able to turn his life around and become monogamous. Might. And if he couldn't, I was sure we could work together professionally with little animosity. Then it occurred to me that Reed might care more about the restaurant than about our relationship. Regardless, he'd bought us two more weeks to decide. I wrote back, *Grandmother is very sick. Can't leave now, so not sure when I'll be home. Love, Ves.*

And for some reason, I locked onto the thought of two more weeks in Lastovo. I would stay with Marta in the house and see her through to the end—even if it took longer. And if I were staying that long, I needed a car. The Yugo would do.

I texted Sara. We made a plan to meet the next day at The Oleander Cottage.

I waited until my grandmother was awake before I left. Once up, she moved slowly but walked without help to the bathroom and then to her bedroom to change. She came out half an hour later, dressed in a floor-length black skirt and a large brown shirt that might have been Ivan's from years past. Her hair was covered with a dark scarf wrapped like a turban. I reheated the coffee, and the two of us sat in the living room making stilted conversation—as best we could with the language barrier. Marta did not take more oxycodone, but I felt she was waiting for me to leave before she did.

I left midmorning and walked the three miles down through the old town, past the school, to The Oleander Cottage. Stjepan was in the garden, the Yugo nearby like a faithful dog, and Sara's BMW was parked on the road. The place now had a "For Sale" sign out front, written in both Croatian and English.

The door of the cottage opened, and Sara stepped out, looking uncharacteristically casual in denim overalls. Her long copper hair was pulled back in a thick braid. She greeted me with two kisses, "*Ćao!*"

"*Ćao!*"

"The Yugo is yours. I talked to Stjepan. He said it is yours for two hundred fifty euros." Sara yelled something in Cro to Stjepan, who stood in the garden and repeated, "*Da, da, da.*"

Sara turned back to me. "He agrees that the car is in fine working condition. The starter has been fixed, and he says that the tank is full of gas. But I would not believe him on that. You should go immediately to the petrol station and have it filled."

"I just need to rent it for two weeks."

"Stjepan does not want to rent. He wants to sell. This is good bargain. If you do leave once more, I am positive you will be back. When this happens, the Yugo will be waiting for you like long-lost boyfriend." Sara laughed at her own small joke.

I paid two hundred and fifty euros to rent the car for the two weeks I'd stayed at The Oleander Cottage. Now, to buy it seemed a no-brainer. I counted out the euros to Sara, who then walked the money over to Stjepan. He held up the paper money and yelled, "*Hvala.*"

I asked Sara, "Do I get a title or something?"

"Maybe sometime. It is not important. Now sit and have coffee with me. I need to tell you about my last trip to Hvar. Then I need to sell you this cottage."

We sat outside at the table where, weeks ago, I'd served octopus *ispod peke* to Dinko and my grandmother. Behind the cottage, I could see the *roštilj*, the dome still on the brick shelf where I'd left it. I remembered that my grandmother's recipe box had one for octopus—*hobotnica ispod peke*—and another for goat, *jarac*.

Sara started in without any prompting. "So, last Friday, I went to Hvar, you know, to get sex. I do not know if I have said, but there is only one other lesbian on Lastovo, and she is a most terrifying hag. I will not bore you with details, but just to say we have met and do not have same interests.

"I arrived on last ferry that got into Hvar at seven. I took hotel room where I enjoy to stay, which is up the hill from the *pjaca*—a place named The Incidental. I do not know where this English name came from, but I think they were trying for *Usputan*. A better name, I think, would have been The Casual. If you go to Hvar, you should stay there. Very laid back, casual. After registration, I had a nice meal by myself and then went to the disco.

"I have been to this disco before. It is mostly straight people there, but I have met other women. Some are lesbians like me but also indifferent lesbians who very much flip-flop based on whim or whimsy. What is it? Whim or whimsy? I do not know the distinction."

I thought. "Whim is like impulse, you know, impulsive. Whimsy is like fantasy. I think you could use either or both."

"Okay, whim and whimsy. Impulse and fantasy. Yes, that would describe these people. So, I go to this disco called Club Oh! Like, 'Oh Baby!' It is close to midnight, and the place is full, and everyone is dancing like crazy. I find a seat at the bar and order a Cosmo, Cosmopolitan, and I am looking around. You know. Then I see this woman sitting across the bar, looking at me. She is with this boy who is talking in her ear, but I can tell she is not interested. She is looking at me and giving me, you know, that look. I give her back a wicked smile. Like, you know what I know. We are attracted to each other.

"Finally, she gets away from boy talking to her, walks around the bar, and stands beside me. She asks if I want to dance, and of course I say yes. Then we dance.

"You know how those discos do it. One song lasts forever and then blends into another so that you never know when to sit down. It was like that, and we danced and danced, sweating all over the place, then doing some stroking with hands. I think the boys around us were very excited. Then we are thirsty and go back to the bar.

"Her name is Sofia, and she is Italian, so we both speak in English. She is very beautiful, with long black hair, very fit, as you Americans say, and with a lengthy and interesting nose, a nose like a raven's beak. I like this nose. I do not know why, but this is true. We are standing at the bar, now drinking cold Ožujsko beer. She asks me, 'Want to get high?' and I say, 'Sure,' and she hands me a pill. I know what this is. I think you call it ecstasy or molly. I take the pill with a swallow of cold beer.

"We dance like crazy until the disco stops playing music

at three in the morning. We are still very high from drug. I do not know if you have taken this drug, but it can be very enjoyable. You can party all night, and everyone is best friend. Then, with someone like Sofia, you are best friends and whimsy lovers. We cannot keep our hands off each other. The disco empties, and we follow everyone across the town to a park above the beach. In the park, there is more music. I think you call it a rave. Now we are outside with many people dancing, and we are dancing like crazy. It was very fun, Ves. You cannot believe.

"Then the sun starts to rise like balloon. The music ends, and now we want to make love. This Sofia is so crazy. She is worker on one of many private yachts tied up at the quay. She pulls my hand and takes me there. She says the owners are gone and that we can have the whole yacht to ourselves. This is very fantastic.

"She takes me to owner's luxury bedroom, and we proceeded to make the sex. It was very dynamic. Then we are tired and fall asleep. We sleep very late into the afternoon. This was mistake because the owners are now back on the yacht and find us in their bed. This is very bad for Sofia.

"I give her my phone number and leave. She calls me after I have arrived back in Lastovo. She said she was fired and now alone in Hvar with no place to go. Of course, I tell her to come to Lastovo. So, she is coming tomorrow."

"That's great, Sara."

"Yes, I think I like Sofia, and maybe it will be fun. I am hoping you will meet her."

"Sure. I would like that."

"Now, let us talk about you."

"Yes?"

"What about you and Dinko?"

"What about Dinko?"

"I think he is very nice catch. He is very rich, and his wine is the best. I think he is a man who would not beat you."

I wasn't sure how to reply to Sara's comments. A man who would not beat a woman was fine, but a very low bar. He was a nice catch for someone, but maybe not me. I didn't know. And then there was Reed. "That's certainly a prerequisite for a good catch—someone who would not beat me." I laughed.

She moved on. "So, how much do you think this very special Oleander Cottage is valued at? I can give you a very special price. You will always then have a place to come back to."

"Was your plan to make me buy the car so that I'd possibly stay and buy the cottage?"

"It was something that I thought of, yes. I have yet to witness if it will work or not."

Then, as though Dinko knew we'd been talking about him, a message came up on my phone. *Will you join us for lunch tomorrow?*

I didn't have to think, or maybe didn't want to, and quickly responded, *Yes.*

He texted back, *Bring a bathing suit and shoes to hike in.*

I reheated the bean soup from the night before and sat with my grandmother at the small dining table. She ate the lunch slowly, each spoonful of beans and broth an effort. I encouraged her, "*Jedi, jedi.*" Eat, eat.

But then Marta stopped and shook her head. "*Ne mogu*

više." No more. She stood from the table and then went back to the couch where she sat facing the window, watching anything that might move on the street. Goto jumped on her lap, and she carefully petted his feathers.

The rooster made a soothing, clucking noise.

In the afternoon, the nurse came by for her monthly visit. She spoke English well and introduced herself as Petra Nović. She carried a backpack that, when unzipped, revealed a blood pressure cuff, stethoscope, files, scissors, forceps, and boxes with labels I couldn't decipher. Petra looked to be in her mid-forties with blonde hair cut in a bob and clothes with scores of Velcroed pockets. Goto lightly pecked at the nurse's hand as she took Marta's blood pressure and listened to her heart. Petra then picked up the bottle of oxycodone and approximated how many were left. She placed it back on the side table.

She spoke Cro to Marta, I assumed asking how many she was taking per day. My grandmother responded, *"Pet ili šest."* Five or six.

I asked, "How many should she be taking?"

"As much as she needs to control the pain. Most likely, the cancer has spread to her bones, and that is the cause of the pain. I do not know for sure because your grandmother refuses to seek any hospital care or treatment. Without any treatment, the pain will continue until it is debilitating. This could go on for a month or more."

"What would you do if she were in a hospital?"

Petra had been watching Marta while speaking and now turned to look at me. "We could have done something eight months ago when she was in the hospital in Split. She could have completed chemotherapy and perhaps radiation. Then, there are drugs to slow the spread. But she refused treatment. The only thing we can do now in the hospital is keep her comfortable, perhaps provide a morphine drip."

She then added, "I'm pleased you are here. I do not think your grandmother has anyone else."

"No."

Before leaving, Petra gave me another container of oxycodone, one hundred pills. "I think your *baka* is taking more than five or six each day. That is not a bad thing. She should be taking what is needed to stay ahead of the pain. This will last her until I visit next month, assuming she is still with us."

After the nurse had left, I sat with my grandmother as she listened to a Croatian talk show on the radio. I could pick up small pieces of the dialogue but was mostly clueless as to what they were saying. Instead, I went back through the box of old recipes. One was for a condiment I'd heard of called *ajvar*.

I showed the recipe to my grandmother, who smiled and nodded. She said, "*S kruhom.*" With bread.

I walked to the market and picked up the ingredients needed: eggplant, sweet red bell peppers, garlic, chili peppers, and vinegar. I found a loaf of soft, dense *pogača* bread that would pair well with the *ajvar.* Once back, I showed my grandmother what I'd bought. Marta nodded with a thin-lipped smile.

I took the groceries and walked the path to the old tavern. There, in the large kitchen, I followed the recipe, first roasting the eggplant and peppers over a stovetop flame until they blackened. I let them cool, then peeled off the skins. I scooped the creamy flesh from inside the eggplant. With a large mortar and pestle, I ground the eggplant, red bell peppers, chili peppers, and garlic. To that, I added heated olive oil, salt, pepper, and a few tablespoons of red wine vinegar.

We sat at the small dining table in the house, ate the *pogača* bread slathered with spicy *ajvar*, and drank a bottle of Radić Plavac Mali. My grandmother seemed pleased and was able to eat two slices. Goto pecked at his own dinner in the corner of the room, his feed scattered in what looked like a dog bowl.

Again, our talk was stilted and uncomfortable with the language barrier, and Marta became frustrated with the effort. I knew she wanted to talk, to tell me more, but it was impossible. Finally, she said, "Dinko." I knew what that meant—get Dinko back so she could finish her story.

Though I protested, my grandmother washed the dishes and set them out to dry in the side wire rack. She went to her bedroom early.

Later, I sat outside in the cooling night air, drinking one more glass of wine.

I thought about what to do. I now knew more about her illness and prognosis. There wasn't much time. Only a month ago, I'd discovered the one person connected to who I once was. My grandmother had told her stories, but she could tell me so much more. And for sure, she might know others in Lastovo or elsewhere who knew my mother and father and would have their stories.

My grandmother would die soon. That was a certainty. And she'd only recently reconnected with me, her lost granddaughter. The woman had gone through so much—a war, a lost child, the grandchild she'd abandoned, a town that had become deserted, and a husband long passed. Was it joy that my grandmother felt when I showed up on the island, or was it deep regret and more sadness?

I would never ask and would never know. But I guessed it was mixed—joy, grief, and regret—all spread throughout, like the cancer she was dying from.

Eggplant Cilantro Dip

A personal favorite appetizer is an eggplant dip. This recipe is super flexible. Try roasting a head of garlic alongside the eggplant for deeper flavor, add smoked paprika or chipotle for a smoky kick, blend in roasted red peppers for a sweet twist, or add a splash of your favorite hot sauce.

Serves 4 to 6

1 large globe eggplant
2 tablespoons extra-virgin olive oil (reserve 1 tablespoon)
1 clove garlic, minced or grated
Small pinch of red pepper flakes
2 tablespoons lemon juice
1 tablespoon lemon zest
1 teaspoon kosher salt
½ cup chopped cilantro

Preheat the oven to 400°F.

Poke the eggplant all over with a fork.

Cut it in half lengthwise, then brush with the reserved 1 tablespoon olive oil.

Bake on a roasting pan, cut side down, for 40 minutes.

Cool the eggplant to room temperature and then scoop the flesh into the bowl of a food processor.

Add olive oil, garlic, red pepper, lemon juice, salt, lemon zest, and cilantro to the food processor and blend until smooth.

Serve with warm pita, seeded crackers, or even fresh veggie sticks like cucumber and carrot.

Roast Chicken and Potato Salad

I drove the Yugo up the long driveway, past the "no tourists" sign, to the turnaround in front of the two-story stone house. Mia stood waiting in the doorway. Her chestnut-brown hair was, as usual, tied up in adorable pigtails. She ran to the door of the Yugo and was there to give me a hug when I stepped from behind the wheel.

"I've missed you," I said.

"We didn't think you would ever return, and now, see, you're here again to be with us. I am sorry, though, that it was the unhappy situation of your grandmother that brought you back."

Mia didn't wait for me to respond but took my hand and led me through the house. "We have a picnic planned at a special place not far from here."

Dinko stood in the kitchen making our lunch with an older woman—I assumed the aunt Mia had talked about. She looked striking with her dark hair streaked through with gray. She wore glasses with chunky black frames and a robin's-egg-blue dress with sleeves that covered her arms.

Dinko said, "Welcome," then introduced his aunt: "Ves, this is Dijana. Dijana, this is the Vesna I've told you much about."

The aunt stepped from around the center kitchen island and held me by my shoulders, smiled, and kissed each cheek. She spoke English: "I am very pleased to finally meet you. Dinko has never brought home any female friends."

Dinko, behind her, looked embarrassed. He mockingly said, "Yes, all my secret woman friends that I've never introduced to you." We all laughed.

Dinko and Dijana packed a picnic lunch in an antique backpack made of woven grape vines, no doubt used years before during harvest times. Dinko put his arms through the oiled leather straps and then donned an olive-green felt hat with a floppy brim. He wore hiking boots and shorts, like a regular Boy Scout. I smiled.

Mia led the way through a back door. The aunt waved to us through the kitchen window.

We passed rows of grapevines with buds ready to burst into fruit. Dinko talked about the vineyard as we walked—the process of managing the soil with the cover crops of mustard and vetch to supply nutrients, trimming the vines, and finally harvesting the grapes at their peak balance of sugar and acidity.

Past the vineyard, the three of us followed a path that climbed into the hills. The sun was high overhead and hot.

"Where are we going?" I asked.

Mia replied, "A secret swimming hole."

With the sun's heat, swimming sounded spectacular.

Dinko, with his wicker backpack, continued to lead the

way, pointing out vegetation along the path. "Wild fennel." He stopped in front of tall, wispy stalks with their yellow flowers and seed pods.

"Can you eat them?"

"Yes, of course, everything. Seeds can be dried and used as a spice. The root bulbs are much different from what you know. They are smaller but just as edible. Very good with fish."

We walked on, and Dinko pointed out wild sage and then rosemary. He pulled a sprig, crushed it between his palms, and held it up. I lowered my face to his open hands and smelled the oils, the burst of rosemary fragrance. "We also have wild garlic that can be eaten in the winter and *rujnica* mushrooms that grow behind logs of rotting cedars. With wild boar, the mushrooms are very enjoyable."

The path crested through a notch between hills, and in the distance, I could hear water cascading through rock. Mia said, "We're almost there."

I followed as Mia and Dinko moved carefully down an incline, the path little more than trampled foliage. The stream was somewhere to their right. The sound of the water was now a loud, gushing torrent.

Mia said, "That's the waterfall. The pool is just beneath."

At the bottom of the incline, the cedar and pine forest opened up to a clearing. Then, a pergola built of slender pine trunks that held up a cover of stripped branches. On one sun-drenched side of the arbor hung a muslin sheet that gently moved with the wind.

I knew Mia and Dinko must have spent hours constructing this for our one lunch.

Next to the pergola was a shallow pool of blue-green water. The rocks beneath shimmered with waves of moss that moved to an invisible current. I was overwhelmed by the beauty. "This is so incredible."

"Mia's idea. I just helped with the wood structure."

All of us were hot and sweaty from the hike and in a hurry to see who could change first and enter the pool. Mia and I changed behind the muslin sheet, and she was first in the water, her bathing suit already on beneath her clothes. Dinko was next, standing at the edge of the pool in tight swimming shorts, his muscled arms out wide, ready to dive. He dove in and came up next to Mia, both now treading water and telling me to hurry up.

I stood at the edge of the pool in my one-piece bathing suit that concealed my burn scars. "Is it cold?"

Mia yelled back, "Of course! Refreshing."

Then I dove. Beneath the water, I opened my eyes to see the other two with their legs kicking. I came up beside them, giddy and laughing. I followed as Dinko and Mia swam to the other side where a rock the size of my Yugo gently sloped from the pool. We crawled up to its flat surface and then lay dripping wet under the hot sun.

Later, we ate, still in our bathing suits. Dinko's aunt had packed a whole roast chicken, potato salad, cheese, a homemade jar of pickles, ripe cherries, and a baguette. Really, enough to feed a family of ten. Mia made a chicken sandwich of sorts, while Dinko and I grazed on the assortment. The roast chicken was flavored with the same kind of fragrant wild rosemary Dinko had crushed between his palms. I could also taste a hint of wine vinegar and olives. The potato salad was a tart mixture of boiled potatoes, thinly sliced onions, and arugula, with more of the wine vinegar, olive oil, and seasoning. The cheese was *paški,* from the island of Pag—soft white and firm with a nutty, grassy flavor. We ate a few pickles plucked right from the jar and finished with handfuls of cherries that stained our lips a clownish purple-red. Mia sipped from a bottle of Coca-Cola, while Dinko and I drank his white Grk. By the end, I was quite stuffed and possibly a little tipsy.

Mia stood right after she'd finished her lunch. "I've forgotten. I said I'd meet my friend, Adrijana. I must go now." She pulled her pants over her bathing suit, slipped on her tennis shoes, and, with her shirt in hand, added, "I'm so sorry I forgot."

To me, it was a little obvious. Mia had put so much time into helping build the pergola, setting up the muslin sheet, and orchestrating the picnic. There was no way she would've planned something else with a friend. The whole picnic was a setup.

Dinko played along, maybe—or maybe not—oblivious to his daughter's motives. "Are you okay getting back by yourself?"

She rolled her eyes, looking at him as though he were the silliest man on Earth. "Is the sky blue? Is water wet? Does a one-legged duck swim in circles?"

Then Mia was gone, laughing as she scrambled up the slope to the path that would take her home.

I said, "That Mia is a very clever girl. You must be so proud."

"Something like that." He laughed.

We swam again, both diving into the pool at the same time and then swimming the length to the far rock. We lay on the sun-drenched rock, near each other but not quite touching. I couldn't help but remember the time on the sailboat, Dinko leaning over to give that first kiss. I shivered with the thought. He was right next to me now, and I could feel the heat that radiated from his body.

Mia had set us up to be alone, and I didn't want to

disappoint the girl. I sat up and leaned over on my elbow, looking at Dinko's eyes, which were shut from the sun's glare. I stared at the man, his dripping curly black hair, his delicate eyelids, his soft lips. I bent down and gently kissed those lips. His eyes stayed closed, and he accepted my kiss.

He opened his lips wider to feel my tongue that searched the edges of his mouth.

Then we heard rustling. We stopped. It could've been a deer or a small squirrel, but it could also have been Mia somewhere above us, watching. Without talking, we both understood. I was the first to stand and splash back into the pool. Dinko leaned forward to cover his embarrassing tent-pole erection and then crab-walked into the cold water.

As we walked back, Dinko said, "Your grandmother. I am so sorry. It was a terrible time then, during the war. People have stopped remembering and stopped talking about it. They would rather not dwell on the cruelty that took place. You and I were only babies, but my father talked about the war. Hated all Serbs. They bombed Dubrovnik and many other towns and cities. They killed indiscriminately. Many parents were killed and their children abandoned. I'm sorry that you were abandoned. That must feel so unfair, so unloving."

Unloving, unloved. That's how it did feel. Was my grandmother a bad person? I didn't think so. An unwanted pregnancy with my mother, a child whom Marta and Ivan would have to raise, and the stigma of the illegitimate child in a small community with deep religious values. But still, I knew Marta carried the heavy burden of guilt. And maybe, like a penitent in the confessional, my grandmother could now speak about her sins before she died. I believed in my being there to listen. I could offer solace.

Then I remembered that Mia had also been abandoned. She and I had that in common. "Mia must feel the same way. Unloved."

"I've tried to shelter her and provide the love that she did not receive."

"You've sheltered her by not bringing another woman into your house."

"Yes."

"It seems she doesn't want the shelter anymore. And she wants you to be happy."

"Yes, it seems."

I didn't know what that implied or meant for me. I could see myself loving this man. But my life was complicated. I was somehow still entwined with Reed, who I knew desperately wanted to marry and start over. I couldn't bring that mess into Mia's life or Dinko's. At least not until I resolved it myself.

I let the conversation end there.

Dinko conveniently changed the subject. "How is your grandmother today?"

I remembered. "She wants you to come to dinner tomorrow. She has more to tell."

Roasted Chicken with Olives, Rosemary, and Tomatoes

This simple, delicious roasted chicken thigh recipe is best served with hearty polenta. Marta would have loved this.

Serves 4

1 tablespoon extra-virgin olive oil
2½ pounds skin-on, bone-in chicken thighs
Kosher salt and ground black pepper
1 medium yellow onion, diced
4 tablespoons capers
⅓ cup Worcestershire sauce
1 (28-ounce) can crushed tomatoes
1 tablespoon brown sugar
1 cup pitted black olives
1 tablespoon red pepper flakes

1 lemon (zest and juice)
4 sprigs rosemary (reserve 2 for garnish)
1 tablespoon chopped fresh parsley

Preheat the oven to 425°F. Pat the chicken dry with paper towels, then season with salt and pepper.

In a medium sauté pan, heat the olive oil and cook the chicken thighs skin-side down until browned. Remove from the pan and set aside.

Remove the excess fat from the pan, leaving about 1 teaspoon behind.

Reduce the heat to medium, then add the onion and garlic, and sauté until browned.

Add the capers, Worcestershire sauce, crushed tomatoes, brown sugar, olives, red pepper flakes, lemon zest, and rosemary sprigs to the pan with the chicken.

Bake for 25 minutes without a lid.

Finish by squeezing the lemon juice over the chicken dish and garnishing with fresh rosemary and chopped parsley.

Serve with polenta, couscous, or mashed potatoes.

Croatian Brodet

Marta slept in the next morning. I took the time to walk down to the old tavern and scrub the ancient brick barbecue grill, the *roštilj*. The inside walls were thick with black soot and caked-on grease. I used old newspaper to line the bottom and then clawed at the soot and grease with a wire brush. The bricks beneath emerged. The deck of the fireplace was stained with decades of grease rendered from cooked meat that had baked into the stone. Nothing would clean the stains. In the end, it was just as well—it added a rustic patina, like weather-worn copper.

I found the spits that would hold and roast an entire young pig, a deer, or skewers of fowl. Chunks of wood were still stored beneath the *roštilj*, ready to be burned down into cooking embers. I was tempted, but what I had in mind for that night's dinner was a traditional Croatian seafood stew called *brodet*. I'd found the heavily dog-eared recipe the day before, and Marta had approved.

For the *brodet*, I needed fresh seafood. After coffee with Marta, I drove the twisting roads down to Zaklopatica, now confident in my ability to shift and drive the Yugo.

At the fish market, I tried to explain what I needed as best I could in my limited Cro. The fishmonger woman stood patiently. The reality was, I only needed the one word: "*Brodet*."

"*Ajme, brodet!*" The woman walked around the cooler of crushed ice and fresh seafood. "*Grdobina?*" She held up an ugly, flattened monster I knew to be monkfish—a huge mouth with rows of sharp, tiny teeth and skin that reminded me of the burn scars on my back. Ugly—but I knew the delicious meat tasted like lobster.

"*Da.*"

Then, "*Škarpina?*" She held up a large fish similar to a grouper.

I said, "*Manja.*" Smaller.

The woman produced a thin fillet knife, quickly cut off the head, and then filleted the meat from the bones, offering what looked like seven or eight ounces.

"*Da.*"

She held up the spine and bones. "*Temeljac?*"

I assumed *temeljac* meant stock or broth, which was what I'd used fish bones for in the past. "*Da.*"

The woman wrapped the bones in brown paper and put them aside. She then held up an eel the size of a fat garter snake.

I'd never cleaned an eel and didn't intend to start now. "*Ne.*"

Finally, a handful of mussels and six large prawns.

The woman wrapped all the seafood separately and then

placed the packets in a recycled plastic grocery bag.

On my way back to the house, I stopped at the food market and bought more garlic, parsley, tomatoes, onions, and polenta.

I spent the rest of the afternoon cooking in the tavern kitchen, which was now starting to feel like my own. Marta was also there, propped in a chair and holding Goto, whose head twitched and spun whenever he heard the clang of a baking pan, the sputter of olive oil, or the chop of the knife.

I started with the fish stock, covering the bones with two liters of water. I added onion skins, celery, a chopped carrot, salt, and pepper. I covered the pan and let it simmer on the stove. I cleaned the ugly monkfish next, deboning and carving the meat into bite-sized portions. I threw those bones in with the stock. I cut up the *škarpina*. I set aside the chunks of fresh seafood to be added to the *brodet* right before serving.

I had another hour before Dinko would arrive and took the time to clean the dinnerware and set the one table we'd been using for each meal. My grandmother moved from her chair and helped fold napkins into squares that she placed atop each plate. She rearranged the placement of knife, fork, and soup spoon just so. I was sure this was how she'd done it over the years, and maybe also the generations before.

While we worked and moved throughout the tavern, Marta was uncharacteristically quiet. I wondered how much pain she was in, and how much oxycodone she'd taken. Maybe not enough.

I asked, "*Jesi li dobro?*" Are you okay?

"*Jesam, dobro sam.*" Yes, I'm fine.

That was all she had to say, and I imagined my grandmother was preoccupied, thinking through the unfinished story she wanted to tell that night. After leaving me at the hospital in Dubrovnik and going back to Lastovo, her life might have resumed—running the tavern and waiting for the war to end. But I wasn't sure. If the previous dinner was any indication, I expected a bombshell.

When it was time to finish the *brodet*, I poured olive oil into a saucepan and began adding thinly sliced garlic, chopped onion, tomatoes, and parsley. I cooked the vegetables slowly on low heat. While they cooked, I strained the fish bones and vegetables from the stock. I added white wine to the saucepan, then the clear stock. Lastly, I added the fish.

Marta found a ceramic soup terrine, one with images of chasing fish above waves of seagrass. She handed it to me with a smile, maybe remembering the times she'd used the dish to feed the families once brought together in this shared gathering place.

Dinko arrived with two bottles of his white Grk wine. We all sat at the table, the terrine with the Croatian *brodet* between us, giving off an aroma of rich fish stock. I ladled three bowls, and Dinko sliced the bread. He gave a small Croatian toast: "*Živjeli!*"

The equivalent toast in America might have been simply "Cheers," but I knew the literal translation was "Let's live." Marta forced a smile and slowly lifted her wine glass. This was a woman who knew she would die soon. We all knew.

We started in on the *brodet*.

Marta spoke.

By 1992, the war was over for us. The Serbs were no longer in Dubrovnik or on the coast. Ivan was back for good. He had been

wounded from shrapnel that left him with a pronounced limp. We opened the restaurant, but transportation to the islands was still not good, and the food supplies were scarce. We relied on what we could grow on land and harvest from the sea, and that was good enough. But the summer families from Zagreb and elsewhere had not returned. The war was still going on in the southern and eastern regions of the country around Okučani and Pakrac. Of course, all of the foreign tourists were scared to visit us. I do not blame them.

Without the summer people, the locals had little money to spend on eating in restaurants. We mostly served coffee and drinks. Of course, the men still wanted to socialize and drink.

We ran the tavern together. I worked in the kitchen, and Ivan served the few people who came in. We did not have family or babies to care for—other mouths to feed—so we did okay.

The war ended in 1995—this was four years after the bombing in Dubrovnik that killed Ivana. Young men who had entered the war were now coming back. Some, like Ivan, had been injured with scars of battle. Some had died in the war, their sacrifice commemorated on plaques and monuments.

Then, a young man showed up at our tavern. He walked with crutches, one leg amputated above the knee. He wore a green army uniform and carried a duffel bag over his shoulder. I did not recognize him at first. His hair had grown long and covered his ears. He had a growth of beard on his face from traveling. But what I noticed was the neck of the tamburica that stuck out from the top of his duffel bag. This was Josip. Your father.

What I have told you was true. We thought he had died in the battle at Slano. This is what others on the island had told us. What happened is that Josip was hit in the abdomen by a rifle bullet. He went to a hospital, gravely wounded. He was there for a year and very sick. No one believed he would live, so that is what others thought. But he survived and was sent back to the war. He was then wounded again in one of the final battles near the town of Bihać in Bosnia. A shell landed near him, destroying his leg.

Now, he was here in Lastovo. He knew that Ivana had gone to Dubrovnik to have her baby. He had visited her when he could take a leave from the war. I told him a lie then. Maybe for his sake, because he would never know his child, and maybe for my sake, because the truth was too painful. I had lived with the guilt of your abandonment for four years. I told him that both Ivana and the child had died. I told him both had died in the bakery when a shell exploded and created a great fire from the ovens. Of course, he was stunned.

Ivan was there and said nothing.

I took Josip to the church cemetery. There were few automobiles and petrol was scarce, so we walked. Josip walked the four kilometers with his one leg and crutches, but he had already been walking with crutches for many months and was not fatigued. We walked in silence.

The markers were there, Ivana's and yours. This was proof to Josip that both of you had died and received a proper burial. He sat down on the cut grass of the cemetery and touched the stone of the graves, tracing the deep grooves of the names and dates with his fingers. He wept.

I am so ashamed.

Josip stayed with us in our house for three months. He slept in the room where Ivana had slept and where you sleep now. He helped in the tavern, serving drinks and cleaning up. Then, on some nights, he played the tamburica like he had as a boy before the war, when he fell in love with your mother. Now he was much better—not so much quick-fingered, but more that he played with strong emotion and sensitivity. He played mostly the old folk songs we all knew. The men would sing along—some moved to tears. They would put coins in his camouflage army cap. While he stayed with us, business was better.

But one morning, he packed his duffel bag and tamburica. He said goodbye and left us. We had become very close to him during this time, and now we were sad to see him leave. He did not tell us why and did not tell us where he was going. I am thinking he must have gone back to Ston where he grew up, and some of his people, the Duževićs, still lived. I am not sure.

I tell you all this because I want you to know. It has been so long, and I have lived with my lies and guilt for all this time. Now you know that you have a father who survived the war. It has been over twenty-five years since he was here in Lastovo, so I do not know where he is now and if he is still alive. This is the information I give you.

There, it is done.

My father was alive.

Seafood Chowder with Bacon

My own mother passed down her recipe box along with a copy of *Joy of Cooking*, a hardcover edition from 1973. Of course, the availability of fresh seafood was limited in the Midwest, so the only fish stew recipe in the box was a seafood chowder made with Atlantic cod.

Serves 4 to 6

4 slices bacon, chopped
2 tablespoons salted butter
1 cup diced yellow onion
1 cup diced celery
2 tablespoons minced garlic
¼ cup all-purpose flour
3 cups clam juice
1 pound Yukon gold potatoes, cut into ½-inch pieces
1 tablespoon fresh thyme leaves

2 tablespoons Old Bay Seasoning
1 dried bay leaf
2 cups heavy cream
1 tablespoon kosher salt
1 teaspoon ground black pepper
1 tablespoon Louisiana hot sauce
1 tablespoon Worcestershire sauce
20-24 ounces fresh cod, cut into 1-inch chunks
Juice of ½ lemon
Chopped parsley, for garnish

In a large Dutch oven, cook the bacon until crispy. Transfer the bacon to a paper towel-lined plate, leaving 1-2 tablespoons of bacon fat in the pan.

Add the butter to the bacon fat and melt over medium heat. Add the onions, celery, and garlic. Cook on low heat, covered, for 5-7 minutes, until softened.

Add the flour and cook, stirring constantly for about 2 minutes to cook off the flour taste.

Add the clam juice, making sure to scrape any brown bits off the bottom of the pan.

Add diced potatoes, thyme, Old Bay Seasoning, and bay leaf. Bring the mixture to a boil, then reduce the heat to medium-low and simmer for 15 minutes.

Add the cream, salt, pepper, hot sauce, and Worcestershire sauce. Return the pot to a simmer and add the chunks of cod. Simmer for about 7 minutes more, until the cod is cooked through. Stir in the lemon juice and bacon.

Garnish with chopped parsley.

General Gotovina's Chicken Soup

Marta slept in again the next day. From the kitchen, Goto crowed incessantly from his cage, threatening to wake her. I assumed he was hungry for his breakfast. The plastic bucket of chicken feed was beneath the sink, and just the sight of the opened cabinet door quieted the rooster. Then I unlatched the cage and carefully reached in to retrieve the food bowl. Goto stepped forward. I was sure he'd attack my hand, so I braced for the contact. Then it happened—his beak poking at the flesh on my wrist. I was startled at first, but the pecks were slight, almost like sharp little kisses.

When Marta finally emerged from her bedroom, she was dressed in the now familiar dark attire: a long black skirt, a brown blouse, and a black headscarf tied beneath her chin. We had coffee together, but then she left the house. Marta said, "*Idem posjetiti prijateljicu.*" I knew *prijateljica*, friend, and assumed she was going to visit a neighbor.

I checked my emails. My editor wrote that the next reprint of the cookbook would be twenty thousand copies. The cookbook sold for thirty-six dollars, so that would amount to three-quarters of a million in revenue. My contract gave me roughly twelve percent of net sales, so on top of the initial printing, I was looking at a potential income of almost a hundred thousand. I would thankfully have no immediate money worries.

Then, an email from Reed. He'd tried to call the night before, right after I'd learned about my father. I hadn't wanted to speak with him then. I was still processing the new discovery, wondering what it meant and what I would do next. But I knew I had to find my father. Reed left a voice message: "Just checking in to see how you're doing. Love you." Now the email, still cagey about what he wanted, *How are you? How is your grandmother?* I knew what he wanted—for me to sign the lease. I responded, *Fine. The weather is gorgeous. Grandmother is hanging in there. Love, Ves.* Equally cagey.

Then, an email from Sara. *Will pick you up for lunch tomorrow. I will show you my home.*

I responded. *Okay. Noon.* Life went on in Lastovo.

Marta was back a few hours later, and that night, we had a dinner of leftover *brodet.*

We ate in silence. No one was there to translate, my Croatian was still evolving, and my translation app was slow and clumsy. But then, toward the end of the meal, she said, "*Držimo svoje grijehe blizu.*"

It took me time to understand. *Držimo,* to hold or keep. *Grijehe,* sins. *Blizu,* near. Keep our sins near. Or keep our sins close. We keep our sins close. My grandmother had held on to her sins for all this time, telling no one, not even her priest.

Not until now. Maybe there was some absolution in finally telling the story of Josip. I didn't know. I had no illusions that I barely knew my grandmother.

I took a walk early the next morning before Marta woke and after confidently feeding Goto in his cage. Past the market was a footpath I'd seen with the sign, "ZAKLOPATICA." I followed the path as it veered from the road and led me downhill through pines and cedars, which provided shade from the hot sun. I entered an olive grove. The trees were in spaced rows among a ground cover of grasses and weeds, but they looked tended, with small piles of pruning scattered throughout. Against the trunk of one tree lay a wooden ladder with dowel rungs bored into the side rails. Further on, an old man holding pruning shears stood on another ladder.

I called out, "*Dobro jutro.*"

He looked over from his perch and nodded. "*Dobro jutro.*"

I guessed the man was as old as my grandmother and had lived here just as long. And I wondered what he knew. Did he go to the same school and church? Did he spend time at Konoba Mjesec? Did he ever meet Ivana and Josip, or hear about their deaths? Was he in the war? Did he have sins held close? The man smiled but said nothing more.

I heard a car pass nearby. Eventually, the path led to the road that descended into the village of Zaklopatica.

Dinko's sailboat was tied up against the quay, rocking with the small swells that penetrated the protected cove. It brought back stirring memories.

The fishermen were just past the sailboat, the ones who'd helped me weeks before when the Yugo's starter motor had failed.

One yelled out, "*Ćao, američka lady! Dobro došla nazad!*" Welcome back.

Another asked, *"Gdje je Stjepanovo komunističko smeće?"* I presumed it meant, "Where is Stjepan's communist piece of junk?"

I smiled and waved. I quickly used my phone to translate. I said, *"To je sad moje komunističko smeće!"* It is now my communist junk.

They all laughed, one shouting in reply, *"Jao! Joj! Au!"*

I waved again and then walked back the way I'd come.

The old man was still in his perch, pruning the olive trees, removing dead or diseased branches to encourage the new growth. Life went on in Lastovo.

At the house, Marta was gone again, no doubt visiting the same neighbor from the day before.

Sara picked me up at noon, and we drove off in her BMW with the top down, my hair blowing and swirling in a hurricane mess. Just past the school where I'd seen Mia playing tennis, Sara turned east. We passed the church and cemetery where my mother was buried next to a headstone with her daughter's name on it—my name.

Marta had said she did it because she couldn't live with the shame and regret of abandoning me in Dubrovnik after the bombing. But she'd lived with that shame and regret, regardless. I realized then that the headstone was a lie. Marta wanted the islanders to believe I had died alongside Ivana— that the abandonment never happened. And if Josip were alive and in Lastovo searching for Ivana and his child, he would search no further.

Sara drove through the hills at a terrifying speed, all the

while talking. "Sofia is coming next week to stay for some time. I am very excited."

"I'm looking forward to meeting her."

"She is very beautiful."

"Yes, you told me."

From the top of the next hill, I could see the deep blue waters of the Adriatic and the smaller islands Dinko had sailed past weeks before. Further out, I could just barely see a lighthouse above a tiny island entirely devoid of any vegetation. I pointed it out to Sara.

She spoke loudly over the sound of wind and engine: "Glavat Lighthouse. There is a dumb story. Greek gods could not decide on what island was more beautiful: Mljet, which you see in the distance, Korčula over those hills, or Lastovo. Of course, Lastovo, but one god argued for Mljet, another for Korčula, and another for Lastovo. Zeus then sent an emissary to Glavat where he could see all the islands at once and make decision. He stood on Glavat for some time but could not decide. This made Zeus angry, so he turned poor emissary into stone. He became the bare island you see, now with lighthouse sticking up like emissary's middle finger." She laughed at her joke and then added, "My house is near shore, down this road."

She turned off the pitted blacktop. Ahead, I could see the witch's hat chimney that rose from the terracotta roof, then the two-story stone house built on the rocky slope of the hill. The BMW came to a stop.

We walked down steps of carved stone to a wide veranda that overlooked the islands in the distance. Inside the ancient stone house, the furnishings were anything but old: a modern kitchen with marble countertops, heavy velvet drapes the color of red wine, and two plush love seats facing a coffee table of glass set on a pedestal made from a slice of fluted marble column.

Sara took a platter of meats and cheeses from her refrigerator, then poured us both a glass of white wine. We sat out on the veranda to enjoy the cloudless sky and deep blue sea.

Sara told me the story of the house. "It has been in our family for three generations. My grandfather purchased house in 1968 when communist Marshal Tito was dictator. Croatia then allowed private ownership that was forbidden in other communist countries. My grandfather was from Belgrade but moved his family to Zagreb to become postmaster there— important job in those times. People with money in Zagreb would spend summer months on the coast or islands. Lastovo was secret military base, but as government official, my grandfather was able to visit. I grew up spending my summers at this house.

"The end of Tito and the war were not good for my family. Croatia is Roman Catholic. Belgrade, where my family is from, is in Serbia and Orthodox Catholic. One uses Latin alphabet and other uses Cyrillic. Big deal, right? Well, both hate the other. During the War, my grandfather was removed from his job because he was Orthodox, even though he had lived in Zagreb for over ten years. My father was then successful lawyer, but many people would not consider to use his firm.

"Times were bad. My family left Zagreb before they became deported, which is term used when taking family into the woods, shooting them in back, and burying in shallow grave to be dug up by foxes and crows. I grew up in Berlin. I learned English there and also German. My grandparents are dead, but my mother, father, and two sisters are still there.

"I must tell you, my parents never accepted my lifestyle, so they were not unhappy when I chose to move from them.

We still had deed to this Lastovo house, and I was fortunate to reclaim it. That is how I came to live here.”

I listened intently. I knew of the war, of course, and knew of the ethnic cleansing, but to hear it firsthand was something else. “How do they know who is Orthodox and who is Roman Catholic? It seems so arbitrary.”

Sara shrugged. “Yes, that is the word, arbitrary. We did not attend church, and my friends did not care who was Orthodox or Roman. Not until the war. Then it was all about your surname. From name, people understood your religion and nationality, like you know Jones could be Church of England, while a Müller could be Lutheran. So, your name is Ivelja. You would have been deported if you lived in Serbia. As the war continued, many atrocities were committed on both sides. The Serbs had General Mladić. Croats had their General Gotovina. Both were convicted at The Hague for war crimes.”

“My grandmother named her rooster General Gotovina, Goto.”

“Yes, the namesake of your grandmother’s rooster. This is funny, maybe ironic, maybe not. Some Croats believe he is big hero, and that he should not have been convicted. He was for sure hero in winning the war and making Croatia independent.”

I held my breath. The war had disrupted the life of Sara and her family. The war had shattered my grandmother’s life and forced me to a place far away from where I might have been—where I should have been. “My birth mother was killed during the bombing of Dubrovnik. Serbs killed her.”

Sara raised her hand in a flippant gesture. “So, that General Gotovina deported and buried a few Orthodox Christians—Serbs—may mean nothing to her. Now, I do not know your grandmother, but I have seen her in town. This is small island. Have you noticed she is always in dark clothes and headscarf?"

"Yes, I just thought it was an old custom. Maybe because she's a widow."

"It is custom for widows to wear dark clothing and black, but only for one year. Some women experiencing tragedy may wear dark clothing for longer. Then some women never come out of mourning for remainder of their lives. This is your *baka*."

"She has been telling me the story of my parents. She knew I was alive after the bombing, but because I was an illegitimate child, she abandoned me in the hospital. I spent two years after that in orphanages before an American family adopted me. Then, just last night, she told me that my birth father may still be alive. She let him think I had died with my mother."

"I think she has been in mourning ever since. You are her—how you say—replacement—no, surrogate... You are surrogate priest, and now Marta has told her story and confessed her sins."

"She said something odd, '*Držimo svoje grijehe blizu.*'"

"Yes, we keep our sins close. This is to say she has never told anyone about what happened. She has kept sins to herself. But now she has confessed to the one person who matters. Maybe now she dies in peace."

My grandmother was not in the house, possibly visiting a neighbor again. Goto was also gone.

I thought maybe I should call Reed; I'd been avoiding him

for days. It was past three in the afternoon, and with the seven-hour difference, he might be just waking up. Or if he'd worked the night before, still in bed. I put off the call.

Then I thought of Dinko and what we'd shared over the last few days. He'd translated Marta's stories and now knew so much about me and what I'd gone through. He knew more than Reed. In some ways, I felt closer to Dinko than any other man I'd been with.

I wanted to see him again.

An hour later, my grandmother had still not come home. I worried. The woman was weak and shouldn't have left the house. And I felt guilty that I'd gone out for lunch with Sara. I resolved to stay closer and keep a better watch on my new *baka*.

Then something occurred to me. It didn't make sense for Marta to bring Goto along when visiting neighbors. It wasn't as though the bird was a friendly Labrador retriever you could pet. But the rooster was definitely gone. Something told me to look elsewhere. The tavern.

I walked down the path between the overgrown vegetable garden and the dilapidated chicken coop. The back door to the tavern was unlocked, and I walked into the kitchen. The lights were on. A pot still simmered on the stove with some sort of broth. It smelled delicious. Marta must have been cooking this whole time.

I called out, "Baka?"

No response.

Next to the pot lay one of the old recipe cards from the wooden box. *Pileća juha*. My grandmother had crossed out *Pileća* and written below it, in a barely decipherable script, *Gotovinina*.

To myself, I cried, "Oh no."

I knew then that my grandmother had butchered the rooster.

I called out again, "Baka?"

No answer.

I walked into the front of the tavern. My grandmother was there, slumped over the table we'd eaten at the night before. In front of her was a bowl of the soup next to a clean spoon. I touched her on the shoulder. "Baka?" I touched my grandmother's hand. It was cold. "Baka, Baka."

Then I saw the empty bottle of oxycodone.

I sat down next to her. I held my hand in front of my grandmother's open mouth, checking for any sign of a breath.

Nothing.

She was dead.

I stared ahead, not wanting to look again at the woman beside me. I stared ahead with my jaw stiff against the emotion welling inside. What Sara had said now seemed prophetic: "Maybe now she dies in peace."

The emotion crashed outward, and I sobbed uncontrollably.

I called Sara—she would know what to do.

Then I called Dinko.

Lemony Chicken and Rice Soup

It seems morbid at this point to offer a chicken soup recipe, but that's what the story calls for. And an old spent hen or rangy rooster will do just fine.

Serves 6

2 tablespoons extra-virgin olive oil
2 medium leeks, thinly sliced, white and light green parts only
1 medium zucchini, chopped into a ¼-inch dice
2 cups thinly sliced lacinato kale
1 cup Jasmine rice
1 tablespoon kosher salt
1 teaspoon ground black pepper
6 cups chicken stock
2 large eggs, yolks separated from the whites

⅓ cup lemon juice

2 cups cooked shredded chicken

3 tablespoons chopped fresh dill

2 tablespoons chopped fresh parsley

Additional lemon wedges and herbs for garnish, if desired

Heat olive oil in a large saucepan over medium heat. Add the leeks and zucchini and cook for 2-3 minutes, until the leeks are translucent. Add the chopped kale and the rice and cook for 1 minute more. Season with salt and pepper.

Add 5 cups of chicken stock and simmer for 15 minutes, until the rice softens.

In a 2-cup or larger glass measuring cup, whisk together the remaining cup of chicken stock, egg yolks, and lemon juice.

Gradually mix the yolk-lemon-stock mixture back into your soup pot, then cook on medium heat for 5 more minutes.

Add the chicken to the soup pot and continue cooking until the chicken is warmed through and the rice is cooked. Approximately 30 minutes.

Add the fresh dill and parsley.

Garnish each bowl with a squeeze of fresh lemon juice and additional fresh herbs before serving.

Black Risotto with Cuttlefish

My grandmother's funeral had been held just two days after she died. Between Sara and Dinko, they'd taken care of everything. Dinko had a carpenter at his vineyard build a plain pine box. Sara contacted one of the two policemen who lived and worked on Lastovo, and that man came to examine the body and arrange for a death certificate to be issued. Refrigeration was limited on the island, and there was no morgue. Dinko worked with the priest to get the body in the ground as soon as possible.

When the pine casket was delivered the day after her death, Sara and I cleaned and dressed the emaciated body that had never left Konoba Mjesec, the Moon Tavern. In a cedar chest, I'd found the only clothes Marta owned that weren't a mourning shade of black, gray, or dark brown. The blouse was Adriatic bright blue, with sleeves tied at the wrists with narrow bands of red ribbon. The white skirt was long and full. I remembered the description of the Easter Carnival outfit she'd worn to the dance sixty years before, when she first met my grandfather. It had to be the same one. I also found the red scarf—the one my grandfather had used to find her. The Cinderella story.

The dress looked strange in comparison to what I'd known her to wear. But then, Marta's period of mourning could now be over.

Sara, Dinko, and I lifted the body into the pine box while the carpenter looked on. Before the lid was lowered and screws driven to close it, I placed sealed jars of the General Gotovina chicken soup next to my grandmother's body. They would rest together.

A few congregants came to the church service. Outside of Sara, Mia, Dinko, and his aunt Dijana, I knew only the fishmonger woman and Stjepan. No one else. Many came up after the service and, through Dinko, expressed their condolences. Marta had remained remote to these people, alone in her grief and shame, and none had a personal story or recalled a memorable encounter. The pine casket was put into the ground immediately after the service.

Dinko rented out a *konoba* in the cove of Zaklopatica, and we had a farewell dinner of sorts with Dinko's family, Sara, and now Sofia, who'd arrived the day before. Over courses of cheese and Dalmatian ham, fresh oysters, and a whole-roasted *škarpina* with *blitva*, I told what I knew of my grandmother and what she might have wanted with an intact family in a less cruel world. Of course, this was my fantasy.

We drank lots of wine. Sara looked happy next to the woman she'd only just spent one wild night with in Hvar. Sofia was beautiful, with long, silky black hair, dark eyes, and what

Sara had called her raven's nose. She looked pleased to be around people who had grown close in a very short time.

Over those two days, I stayed in the house amongst my grandmother's things. I felt lonely in the small rooms and called Reed to tell him what had happened. He did the right thing and listened. I called him again the next day to ask what was happening in Minneapolis. He talked about his work at the steakhouse and the opportunity to start fresh with a restaurant we would own. He wanted me to fly home as quickly as I could. I found myself wanting to do just that. In my mind—*go home.*

But I had unfinished business.

It was Dinko at the end of the farewell dinner who said, "We should find your father."

We sailed from Lastovo early in the morning, heading for Ston. Dinko had me sit in front of the steering wheel while he maneuvered the boat safely out of the protected cove. He said he'd help find my father, and the quickest and easiest way to Ston was by boat.

Once free of the bay, Dinko had me steer. I drove the boat into the oncoming waves and wind, while he pulled the ropes that unfurled the sails. He was dressed in the swimming shorts he'd worn that day at the picnic up in the hills. A white V-neck T-shirt outlined his muscled shoulders, and he moved effortlessly with the ropes and winches. The sight made me remember his dive into the swimming hole, and that kiss.

We sailed past Glavat, the remote island of white rock with the lonely lighthouse. I remembered Sara telling the story about the emissary of the god Zeus. And like the emissary, I looked back at Lastovo, then Korčula in the distance, and in front of us, Mljet. They all looked beautiful against the azure waters of the Adriatic. Like the emissary, I couldn't decide which was the most beautiful. Zeus would have turned me to stone.

We skirted past the island of Mljet. Ahead was a ferry taking tourists to see the national park, with its brackish-water lake and the fifteenth-century storybook monastery that rose from a small island like a mirage. I'd only seen the photos but would go there one day. The ferry sent up a wake that rocked the sailboat like a bathtub toy.

Dinko adjusted the sails and then steered west toward the mainland.

We sailed through a tight channel between the mainland and a small island, and then Dinko started the diesel engine. Again, he had me steer the boat into the wind, while he took down both sails. He then had me point the boat north through a channel that gradually narrowed. Dinko relaxed in the cockpit and watched me at the wheel. He smiled and then took a photo with his phone. He said, "You're a natural, for sure."

The channel was now no more than a river, and ahead I could see a high modern bridge that passed above, cars like insects crawling both ways. Dinko took over the wheel and slowed the engine. "We can't go much further. Very shallow near Ston. We can use the dock at a restaurant, Konoba Mandrač. I know the owner there, Silvijo, who buys much wine from me. He is also a talented chef. Tomorrow, he can drive us into Ston."

Dinko turned the boat away from the restaurant dock and then proceeded to back it in. A teenage boy stood waiting. Dinko yelled out, "Marko, *kako si?*"

The kid yelled back, "Dinko, *šta hoćeš?*" then laughed. I

knew this was considered a rude greeting that meant: "What do you want?" But, of course, it was given in jest.

Dinko laughed and threw a rope to the boy. Minutes later, we were tied up, and both Dinko and I stepped to the dock across a narrow plank.

He greeted the boy with a hug. Then, to me: "Silvijo's son, Marko. Marko, this is Vesna from America."

Marko smiled and then, with a quick bow, said, "Welcome, Miss."

Right away, I could see the pens of live seafood that lay submerged right off the dock. One held oysters, one mussels. A larger pen held fish, another with octopus and what looked like squid. I asked Dinko, who said, "*Sipa*. Cuttlefish."

Silvijo welcomed me with a kiss on each cheek and Dinko with a firm handshake. He looked to be in his forties with thick dark hair streaked with gray.

The restaurant behind him was much larger than the small taverns out on Lastovo. Two rows of tables lined an outside patio. The tables were ready for dinner service with white napkins, tableware, and wine glasses. Behind and inside were more tables and chairs. Silvijo led us through the restaurant to a chef's table at the edge of the open kitchen. The stoves, cutting tables, and service window were all clustered near the centerpiece of a brick-and-stone *roštilj* grill—huge, like the one at my family's *konoba*. Six *peka* domes were inside the *roštilj* and covered with glowing coals.

Silvijo poured us glasses of the Plavac Mali from Dinko's vineyard. "This is nearly the last. I trust you brought more?"

"Of course. Six cases in the boat. I will bring them in later. I have six of Grk, also."

"No worry, I will have Marko get them."

Then, to my embarrassment, Dinko said, "Vesna is also a chef and a very famous cookbook author."

Silvijo turned to me, interest in his eyes. "So, a chef and writer? A critic also, no doubt?"

"A tourist with an interest in fine food."

"Then you must have our famous black risotto with cuttlefish—*crni rižoto od sipe*. Come now. I will show you. But you must never publish this recipe."

"I promise."

While Dinko sipped his wine, I watched Silvijo prepare the risotto. He started by disassembling the cuttlefish. I knew what they were and had eaten black cuttlefish risotto before, but I'd never worked with one or seen it cleaned. The fish itself was a prehistoric-looking squid with a hard, bony body, dark catlike eyes, and two white horror-movie tentacles. Silvijo first cut off the tentacles, adding, "Good bait for traps." Next, with his fingers, he gently tore through the skin surrounding the body and pulled out the white meat beneath. Using a sharp fillet knife, he cut the meat from the bone—a disk of soft calcium the shape of a child's slipper. Beneath the meat was the ink sac that he carefully pulled away from the organs. He squeezed the sac like a toothpaste tube, pushing the ink into a small bowl. He offered me a taste. I dipped a pinky in the black liquid and held it to my lips. It tasted of the sea—salty, briny— but with a richness like umami. Finally, he cut the meat into strips.

Then, "Now you do one."

And I did. Though working with the horror-movie creature was strange, I enjoyed being in the commercial kitchen and learning something new—a technique I would never attempt back in Minneapolis.

The risotto itself was uncomplicated, like most foods in Croatia. Shallots and garlic were slowly sautéed in a saucepan. The cuttlefish and rice were added, then parsley, stirring until the rice kernels were roasted and translucent. Silvijo deglazed the pan with white wine, added the ink, then peeled and chopped tomatoes. He slowly poured in hot fish stock until the risotto was slightly chewy and the stock creamy with the starch of the rice. He let the pan rest for a few minutes, then added more parsley, salt, and pepper.

"Simple, elegant. The secret is actually in the stock." He offered a soup spoon of stock, and I tasted the rich broth.

"Oh, that's good. What do you use?"

"Secret. I would have to kill you then." Silvijo laughed and gave me a shoulder bump. I bumped him right back.

Dinko sat across from me, both of us sipping our wine and watching Silvijo prepare his kitchen for the evening.

I asked him, "How will you find my father?"

"Ston is very small, maybe only a hundred people whose families have lived there for many decades. They will all know each other. I will ask about Josip Duževic, a man with just one leg. They will know the family, and there will be someone who knows Josip."

Silvijo laid down a plate with fresh filleted anchovies marinated in a simple brine of vinegar, pepperoncini, olive oil, salt, and pepper. He briefly described the appetizer and then hurried back to prepare for service. Dinko ate with his fingers, pinching an anchovy fillet along with a slice of pepper, then popping them into his mouth like a strand of pasta. I did the same. Something about eating with your fingers gave food another dimension, almost indescribable, but maybe atavistic, like a caveman picking over a freshly killed deer.

Then, the cuttlefish risotto that stood up to the original portrayal as "famous." Rich, creamy, with all the flavors of the sea. We sat at the chef's table just outside the hustle of the evening's service, and I watched Silvijo with his staff as he controlled the flow of food to the customers, never once raising his voice, always calm, always in command. In my best moments, that was how I liked to work.

Dinko must have been reading my mind. "What is it like working in a kitchen? Do you enjoy it?"

"It can be exciting, calling out the orders, preparing great plates of food, and working with a few close friends. Then, when everything clicks, the mood changes—it becomes relaxing in its own way. There's a flow, and you lose your thoughts in it. Hours go by like minutes."

Dinko smiled. I'd hit a nerve of recognition. "Yes, with the vineyard also. I've worked with the same people for years. We enjoy tending to the vines, all of them our children to be nurtured. Time goes by like a steady breeze, and there is a feeling that we are just another part of the vine, like the sail that is one with the wind. Some of us sing to the plants and thank them when they give up their fruit."

"What is it you sing?"

"You know, traditional songs. One is '*Na malenom brijegu.*' It translates to 'On a Small Hill.' There is a woman with your same name, Vesna Luketić, who is famous for this song. Here, I will sing just a little for you."

And he sang, just a few Croatian words in a soft, clear

voice—beautiful, just like his daughter, Mia.

He finished and then said, "In English, this means, 'On a small hill, in the middle of a vineyard, while picking grapes, a young man and a girl meet.' This is a very sentimental song about two people who meet in the vineyard, fall in love, and live together for the rest of their lives. The grapes—they grow like crazy when they hear it.

"I once listened to this other Vesna sing at a small *konoba* on the island of Zlarin, which is not too far from here. I know a secluded cove there with water like a looking glass where you can see to the bottom—eight, ten meters down—the fish swimming beneath like birds in the sky."

"I'd love to go there with you sometime."

"I will take you. We will sail there, and you can prepare a meal."

I could imagine it—sailing, then pulling into a remote cove with no one around, swimming off the boat, baking under the Mediterranean sun, eating something fresh, like oysters plucked right from the sea. I could imagine having sex with this man who sang to his grapes.

I asked, "You love sailing?"

"Of course. I grew up on an island. I have been sailing for as long as I can remember. My father sailed, and his father sailed. I sail now with Mia, and she knows everything about the boat. She can sail it by herself, I am sure. Many times, I go out by myself. I have sailed all over the islands. That is how I found the cove at Zlarin. Sailing is the time I can think."

"What do you think about?"

"I let my mind wander. I think about Mia, and my mother and father when they were still with me. I think about the vineyard and how to make better wine. All the time, I think about how to make the best wine."

"Do you think about love?"

"As you know, I have been very careful with Mia and with bringing other women into our home. But yes, I think about love. I think I've met someone I'd like to love." He looked at me with a knowing smile.

The comment was unexpected, startling. I thought then that I could love this man—a man who sailed the Adriatic, made incredible wine, and sang to his grapes.

A lock of hair drifted across his eye, and I reached over to gently stroke it, wrapping it back behind an ear. He touched my hand then and brought my fingers to his lips. He kissed my fingers gently and then let go. My hand hovered in the space between us and then fled back beneath the table. At that moment, I desperately wanted him.

But I had my life back in Minneapolis. Why that thought just crept in at that special moment, I had no idea. I guess it was always there in the back of my mind, looming like an impossible debt that had to be paid.

Then, stupidly, I said it. "I'll be leaving soon."

"Why?"

It was a simple question. The obvious answer—Reed was waiting for me. We'd had a life he now wanted to renew. I had history in Minneapolis, a career, and the restaurant lease Reed wanted me to sign. But now, thinking of it, the reasons felt contrived and remote. Another planet.

I didn't answer.

"Your grandmother will have left you a house and a restaurant."

It hadn't occurred to me, but what he said was true. Marta had told me I'd inherit the property. A small village *konoba*. A box of my birth family's cherished recipes. A sixteenth-century family house. It seemed so... I tried to find the right word. Part of me thought, *Simple*—a simple life. Another part of me knew I could do so much more in America, in a city the size of Minneapolis. No, the word was "escapist." I would be escaping my life and entering the fantasy world of a small Mediterranean island.

"A life here seems like a fantasy."

He just smiled at the comment, no doubt thinking, *What is wrong with a fantasy? What is wrong with living a fantasy life?*

At the end of our meal, Silvijo poured us homemade *rakija*, two small cordial glasses filled with the amber liquid distilled from apricots—the Cro version of grappa. We toasted his food and drank the potent liquor.

Later, in the sailboat, Dinko showed me my private cabin, the bed already made with clean sheets. He stood behind me as I paused in the doorway. I could feel the heat from the man's body and his presence. I could feel that very real tremor of desire wash over me.

I succumbed, reaching back with my hand that touched his tight stomach. He closed his hand over mine. I turned and kissed him on the neck, kissed him on the edge of his jaw, and then found his lips.

I pulled him inside the cabin. We stood beside the bed, now kissing deeply. I unbuttoned his shirt, sliding my hands inside the light cotton, touching his chest and then his abdomen. He wore no belt, and I unbuttoned the top of his shorts that fell to the floor. He wore no underwear.

Dinko undressed me slowly, kissing my neck and then the soft tissue around my sensitive nipple. He took my nipple in his mouth gently. I leaned back on the bed. With my eyes closed, I felt him kiss my stomach and then move further down. I reached an orgasm seemingly in minutes, and then another after he'd entered me and moved his hips slowly to the motion of my pelvis.

I had undressed unselfconsciously. I must have revealed my burn scars, but they were something unacknowledged, and in the passion of our lovemaking, about as important as a random menu typo.

In the middle of the night, we made love again. Then again in the morning, when, from outside, we could hear the cicadas starting their high, pulsating drone with the ascent of the new sun.

Instant Pot Lobster Risotto

Ves and Dinko were served black risotto with cuttlefish, a delicacy on the coast and islands of Croatia. Cuttlefish can be challenging to find in landlocked Minnesota, so I'll offer up an alternative that uses the time-saving device of an Instant Pot. (Okay, don't be a foodie snob.)

Serves 6

2-6 ounces frozen lobster tails
2½ cups chicken broth
1 tablespoon salted butter
1 medium yellow onion, finely chopped
3 cloves garlic, minced
1 cup arborio rice
¼ cup dry white wine
1 tablespoon Old Bay Seasoning

3 tablespoons butter
¾ cup freshly grated parmesan cheese
1 teaspoon fresh lemon juice
Kosher salt
Freshly ground black pepper
Lemon zest, for garnish

Thaw the lobster tails for 20-30 minutes. Just enough so you can use kitchen shears or a knife to cut the tail in half vertically, with a line cut down the top of the shell. Spread open the tail and set it aside.

Set the Instant Pot to its Sauté function and melt 2 tablespoons of butter. Add the onion and cook for 3 minutes, then add the garlic and cook 1 minute more, stirring continually. Add the rice and stir until toasted, 2 minutes. Deglaze the pot with the wine. Cook until most of the wine is absorbed, then turn the Sauté function off.

Add the broth to the pot. Set the trivet on top of the rice mixture in the pot. Lay a piece of tin foil over the trivet. Place the lobster tails on top of the tin foil on the trivet (this makes it easier to lift the tails out of the pot).

Sprinkle the lobster tails with 1 teaspoon of Old Bay Seasoning. Add ½ teaspoon of butter (roughly 2 thin pats) to each lobster tail.

Place the lid on the Instant Pot, then lock the cover and turn the vent to sealing. Press the Manual button and set to 5 minutes (it takes time to warm up, and the timer will say "On" during heating and count down from 5 once heated).

Once the 5 minutes have elapsed, turn the valve to Venting to quickly release the steam. Steer clear of the vent, as the steam will be hot. Once the steam has fully released, remove the lid and lift the lobster out (the juices from the lobster can flow into the rice).

Stir in the parmesan and lemon juice, then add salt and pepper to taste. Place the lid back on the pot to keep the rice warm.

Lift the meat out of the shell. Chop it into ½-inch rough-cut sections. Mix it back into the Instant Pot rice with any accumulated juices.

Serve the rice, garnished with a few meaty lobster chunks and lemon zest on top.

Oysters with Lemon

Silvijo's son, Marko, drove us from the *konoba* through the hills and then past fields of salt ponds, like rice paddies or the cranberry bogs back in Wisconsin. Some of the ponds looked flooded, and others dry with a coating of crystallized saltwater that sparkled like fields of diamonds.

Marko undoubtedly had driven many others to Ston and was an excellent tour guide. His English was good. "The saltworks date to Roman times, two thousand years before Christ. They called the place Stagnum, which means stagnant, because the water here is very still and shallow. The salinity of the stagnant water is such that the Romans could harvest the salt in great quantities. Salt in ancient times was important commodity and valued as highly as gold. This is true. Over the years, the saltworks changed hands many, many times. Slavs, Bulgarians, Byzantines, Hungarians, Serbs, Bosnians, you name it. Today, it is owned by a stingy man, and, as you will see, it needs many improvements. We are all hoping that it will change hands again soon."

In the distance, I could see the wheeled bins on a system of railroad tracks that traversed the dikes rising up between the ponds. The bins were made of iron, and all were completely coated in rust from salt exposure. The buildings, with their missing or broken windows, looked to be in ruins.

Marko continued, "The original castle and town were severely damaged during an earthquake in the year 1252. The new castle and town that you see before you was built after that time. A sister castle and town, Mali Ston, which means little Ston, was also built. Between the two is the Walls of Ston, which is second in length only to the Great Wall of China. It is one thousand, two hundred meters long, almost an American mile. This was to protect the saltworks and the peninsula of Pelješac from invaders. There was once a great church in the old town of Ston, but that was demolished by American bombs during World War II. So, you can see, the wall was of little consequence over time." He looked over to me and gave a smile and knowing wink.

I said, "On behalf of my country, I officially apologize."

Marko laughed. He came to a stop just outside the Ston castle. "Enjoy your day. Please call me when ready to return."

Inside, the old town spread out in a labyrinth of narrow streets lined with shops, restaurants, and apartments. Unlike the abandonment and decay of Lastovo, Ston felt lively with refurbished centuries-old buildings.

We sat at a table outside a café and ordered espresso from a young woman. She spoke English, and Dinko asked if she lived nearby. She said yes and that she lived right there in the old town. He asked her about the name Duževió. He explained that I was from America and looking for relatives. The woman said she'd heard the name and that maybe there were Duževićs still living in Mali Ston.

After espressos, Dinko led the way through the winding medieval streets to the Walls of Ston. Long, strenuous flights of steps took us high into the surrounding hills. From the crest, now covered in perspiration, I looked down at the castle and town of Ston and the salt ponds in the distance. I could see the narrow channel of still water that led out to where Dinko's sailboat was docked. The view was stunning.

The wall meandered through hills with little shade, the sun seemingly getting hotter by the minute. Then I could see the castle and town of Mali Ston, all downhill.

Off the town square was the quay, and past that were shallow bays dotted with floats. Dinko said, "Oyster and mussel beds. Each float is a line that drops to the bottom. The oysters and mussels grow on the lines. It takes two to three years for the oysters to mature, mussels a year or less."

The wall descended to the second castle and the square that fronted the quay. Dinko led the way to a small tavern just off the square with a sign that read "Konoba Kamenica." Beneath that hung a sign in English, "Fresh Oysters." We walked inside. I was sure they also sold cold beer.

We sat at an unfinished butcher block counter. A man behind it, dressed in a denim apron, greeted us, *"Dobar dan."* He looked to be in his fifties, with graying hair, deep lines through his face, and a smile that showed one missing incisor.

I responded, *"Dobar dan."*

The man, sensing my flawed accent, switched to English. "What can I get for you?"

There was no menu, and as far as I could determine, they served only oysters and beer. And maybe to let the man know he was local, Dinko responded in Cro, "*Dvanaest kamenica.*" A dozen oysters. Then, "*Dva Osječka. Ledena.*" Two Osječko beers. Ice cold.

The man poured the cold drafts of beer, the thick glass mugs forming condensation that dripped onto the porous wood counter. After the hot, mile-long walk across the wall, the beer tasted superb.

While Dinko spoke, I watched the man quickly shuck the dozen oysters, which he then placed in the kind of shallow pan used for *peka*, now filled with crushed ice.

Dinko asked about the family of Dužević, still in Cro but translating the man's response. The man said that he did know the family, but they had all moved away after the war when there were no tourists and no jobs to be had.

Dinko asked about Josip, a war veteran with only one leg.

Yes, the man had known of war veteran Josip Dužević. He stayed for a few years after his family had left.

I asked in English, "Did you know him?"

The man looked at me and slowly shook his head. He responded in English, "No. Josip did not like much to be around people. Without a leg, he could not find work. To feed himself, he played the *tamburica* in front of the restaurants. Tourists, when a few finally returned, put coins into his old field cap from the war."

"Where did he go?"

"I would think Dubrovnik. Why is it you ask?"

"He was my father. I was adopted into an American family during the war. My mother died. I thought he had also died. But maybe he's still alive."

The man took an order from another customer and, while shucking more oysters, said, "I will make a call."

The oysters were served with slices of lemon—no cocktail

sauce, mignonette, or even hot sauce. Simple, and they tasted of their natural briny liquor. While we ate and drank beer, the man went into a back room to make the call.

Minutes later, he returned. "Yes, my friend knew him. He said Josip Duževć went to Dubrovnik where he might play the *tamburica* and make more money. My friend said this was fifteen years ago. He has not heard anything since that time."

Dinko finished an oyster and took a swallow of beer.

"Okay, tomorrow we go to Dubrovnik."

The taxi dropped us at the north Buža Gate to Dubrovnik's old town. No cars were permitted inside the seventh-century walls.

Dinko pointed to the bluffs high above the city. "Mount Srđ. You can just barely see the old fort, built during the Napoleonic Wars. It's called Fort Imperial. In 1991, when you were here, the Serbs occupied the entire bluff, all except for the fort. They shelled the city for seven months, targeting the old town as well as everything else. The Serbs never overcame the small garrison that held the fort. It is now a museum."

I looked up, and somehow I remembered the bluff that shadowed the city. Maybe I remembered the sound of the shells as they arced through the air and descended. The explosions always seemed to be far away, until they weren't.

We walked through the gate, an arched tunnel beneath a thirty-foot-tall gray stone wall. Inside, the narrow pedestrian alleyways funneled downhill to the town's center. We kept walking, now passing small boutique hotels, restaurants, and the apartments of those who lived there. I knew my mother and I had lived in one of the apartments. I had no idea which one.

We entered the town square. At one end was a church with a medieval clock tower. Then, spread out over the square were patio restaurants, each one abutting the other in what looked like turf battles, the color of tablecloths denoting loyalty. If Josip had moved to Dubrovnik, he'd be here with the tourists.

Dinko asked around with waiters, shopkeepers, and policemen—a man with one leg who played the *tamburica* on the street for coins—a beggar. No one remembered a man with that description.

We walked past an octagonal structure with a domed roof, like a king's mausoleum. Each of the eight walls was adorned with the sculpted face of strange creatures, some human. One looked like a little devil, an imp. Next to that was a god-man with an ear-to-ear mustache and pointed beard. Another was a more ordinary monk with his tonsure haircut. Then a horned calf and a monkey. All had bronze fountain spouts that protruded from their mouths. I thought I remembered the funny imp and the smiling god Neptune. The walls of the immense fountain were peppered with the marks of shrapnel bursts. The water no longer flowed.

We walked toward the west Pile Gate. We passed a beggar woman who lay flat on the ground, face down, arms outstretched in full prostration. She was dressed in long black skirts and a dark headscarf, like my own grandmother. In front of her was a small plastic cup for coins. Dinko dropped a coin into the cup and then asked her about a man who played the *tamburica*, a war veteran with only one leg.

The woman didn't look up but responded in Cro. Dinko translated.

She told him that her husband was a war veteran with only one leg. But he had died three years ago.

"*Je li svirao tamburicu?*" Did he play the *tamburica*?

"*Svirao je na svoju bocu rakije.*"

Dinko translated, "He played only on his bottle of *rakija*." He laughed at that and placed another coin into her cup.

"*Neka je Bog s tobom.*" God be with you.

Then, strangely, I knew where I was.

I took Dinko's hand. "*Prati me.*"

I walked down a narrow alleyway, pulling Dinko behind. Ahead was a monastery. I remembered that inside the monastery's chapel were rows of simple pews. I'd gone there with my mother and sat in the back row because we were not congregants. I remembered that behind the altar hung an oil painting of Jesus on the cross. His eyes were closed, and he looked down with a sad face. The sad face made me sad, and because of that, I did not like the place.

I passed by the monastery and then took a left. At the end of that alley, a small square opened up with a dozen or so shops. I remembered that the bakery my mother worked at was part of a market with other food merchants: butcher, cheesemonger, greengrocer, fishmonger, and a small general store that advertised cold Karlovačko beer and cigarettes. That store, now with a counter opened to the street, sold gelato to tourists.

In the far corner of the square was the bakery, left as it had been after the bombing.

The bakery was now a historical ruin. The roof was gone, and broken terracotta tiles lay in the center of the building among broken stone, shards of glass, and a rusting hulk that might have been a stove. One wall was still intact, with an entrance and wooden door. I remembered the door.

The ruins were surrounded by waist-high stanchions linked with chain. A plaque in front told the story in both Croatian and English.

It showed the date of the bombing, December 7, 1991. It told of the Yugoslav People's Army—the Serbs—on the bluffs with its artillery aimed at the old town. The bakery was destroyed in the bombing, and three people were killed. Their names were printed: Monika Nović, Nino Kovačević, and Ivana Ivelja.

Dinko held my hand while I read—and while I quietly wept.

I looked up again at the door—simple, with an unadorned frame and flat panels. It was now cracked and sun-faded, but I still remembered. I remembered my mother opening the door, leading me through, and closing it behind me. The door squeaked every time it moved.

I remembered my mother had the same caramel-blonde hair as mine, the same button nose, and full lips. At the bakery, her hair was always tucked beneath a white toque. I remembered that Monika was young like my mother and worked the counter, speaking with the men who came by in the mornings for their coffee and jam-filled *krafna* or glazed *slanci*. Nino was the owner—a short, middle-aged man with an enormous belly. He would order the girls around like his personal slaves and did not like me spending my days in the bakery. He scared me with his rolling pin the size of a fireplace log.

I now remembered the bombing. The sirens had gone off, and we were all expected to go to the nearest bomb shelter, which was in the catacombs beneath the monastery. But we never went to the shelter. The Serbs hadn't yet bombed the town, and no one thought they would. Dubrovnik's old town was a Yugoslavian treasure, a UNESCO World Heritage Site. My mother kept baking and Monika kept selling. And then a bomb hit nearby, and then another. It was too late to run to the shelter, so we all huddled near the modern gas ovens that seemed impervious. A bomb hit nearby. My mother panicked and ran. I was in her arms. Then another bomb struck the back of the ovens. The blow threw us to the ground. I remembered the heat from the fire and the weight of my mother on my back. She was so heavy, and I squirmed to get out from under her. I ran. Then another explosion as I ran through the bakery door. That was what I remembered—nothing else until I woke up in the hospital.

Dinko was holding me now. I was shaking and sobbing uncontrollably. All the memories that had been trapped in my mind were now there—a raw, open wound. I buried my face in his chest, and he pulled me close.

Through my tears, I spoke in halting Croatian, "*Čula sam eksploziju. Moja majka je bila nada mnom. Izmigoljila sam se da se oslobodim. Pobjegla sam iz pekare. Ostavila sam majku. Nisam znala je li živa.*" I heard the explosion. My mother was on top of me. I squirmed to get loose. I ran from the bakery. I left my mother behind. I did not know if she was alive.

My Croatian, which had been returning piecemeal, now came flooding back to me like the memory of that day.

Dinko responded in Cro, "*Imala si samo tri godine. Nisi mogla ništa učiniti da je spasiš.*" You were only three years old. You could have done nothing to save her.

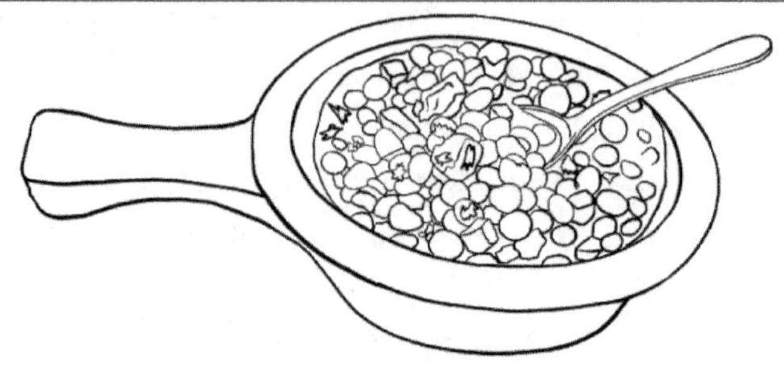

Lentil Stew with Sausage

This recipe for a stew of sausage and lentils is one Marta might have made in the *konoba*. It's a hearty stew, best saved for the colder months.

Serves 6

⅓ pound bacon (about 5 thick slices), cut into 1-inch by ¼-inch strips
1 medium to large yellow onion, chopped
⅔ cup carrots, diced
⅔ cup celery, diced
1 teaspoon ground cumin
2 cloves garlic, minced
1 pound dried brown or green lentils
3 cups water
3 cups chicken stock
½ teaspoon dried thyme
1 dried bay leaf
½ pound pork sausage, one with lots of paprika if you can find it (about 2 to 3 links)
¼ cup chopped fresh parsley, with a little extra for garnish

Heat a large, thick-bottomed pot (6 to 8 quarts) over medium heat. Add the bacon and cook until much of the fat has rendered out and the bacon is browned and cooked through, about 5-10 minutes.

Use a slotted spoon to remove the bacon to a dish and set aside.

Remove all but 2 tablespoons of bacon fat from the pan.

Turn the heat to medium-high and add the carrots, onions, celery, and cumin. Stir frequently, scraping up the browned bits at the bottom of the pan, and cook until softened, about 5-7 minutes.

Add the garlic and cook 1 minute more, until fragrant.

Add the lentils, cooked bacon, stock, water, thyme, and bay leaf.

Bring to a boil, then reduce to a simmer. Cook partially covered until the lentils are tender, about 40 minutes.

While the lentils are cooking, heat a frying pan over medium heat. Add the sausage links. Gently cook, browning on all sides, until just cooked through, roughly 10 minutes. Remove from the pan and let them cool long enough to handle. Cut into pieces of your desired length (1 to 2 inches, or you can just keep them whole) and add to the stew for the last 10 minutes of cooking.

Stir in parsley, then add salt and pepper to taste.

American Tuna Salad

We set out early the next day to sail back to Lastovo.

The wind was out of the northwest, the direction we were headed. Dinko motored until we rounded the island of Šipan near the channel entrance to Ston. He turned toward Mljet, raised sail, and then cut the engine. The gentle wind was now off our right, starboard side, and the sound of the bow breaking through the waves was comforting and meditative. For the next hour, I sat with my back against the bulkhead of the boat's cabin, feeling the sun on my skin and thinking about all that had transpired. The language had come back to me like out of a dream, and I woke up to the knowledge that the life I'd had before the explosion was real, with real people I interacted with and spoke to in the language that was no longer foreign. Dinko had been there and was as surprised and shocked as me. Under his breath, he muttered, "Crazy."

Near Mljet, Dinko switched directions and moved the sails. We now headed directly toward Lastovo, which loomed in the distance like the shadow of a cloud.

In the small galley kitchen below, I made a simple lunch. At the marina, we'd quickly shopped for groceries in a market with little selection. What they had was mostly canned, dried, or otherwise preserved food designed to survive a cross-ocean voyage. I bought canned tuna in oil, a jar of green olives, an actual onion, a squeeze bottle of mayonnaise, and, surprisingly, a fresh-that-day loaf of *pogača* bread. I made an American tuna salad, substituting the diced pickles with olives, and instead of dill, I found dried thyme in the galley cupboards.

I brought up lunch on a teak tray. Dinko put the sailboat on autopilot and then sat down to eat.

We spoke in Cro—mine still halting and unsure, while his slow and clear so that I could more easily understand.

"How do we find him now?" I asked.

"I don't know. There are people who specialize in these sorts of things."

"Private investigators?"

"Yes, they can track down tax records, places where he lived, people who knew him."

"What if he's homeless? The man in Mali Ston said he played his *tamburica* on the streets for coins. He might be living on the streets."

"Yes, I think this is a possibility. We can keep looking. Maybe Korčula, Split, or Hvar. We ask around. If he's been there, people will know a man with one leg who plays the *tamburica*."

The father I never knew. My adoptive father had been remote, unapproachable, and stern in his Bible teachings. I was baptized at the age of eight; no one knew if I'd been baptized before. I was confirmed at the age of twelve and went to church services at least once a week. But, in a way, it never took. My adoptive father's church seemed as remote as him, the two linked in my mind like my burn scars and lost language.

I knew other kids with fathers who seemed to be part of their lives—supportive mentors and friends.

I asked Dinko, "What was your father like?"

He began in Cro but switched to English as the complicated string of words became difficult for me to follow. "He was in the war for three years, so, early on, he was not there. My mother took care of the vineyard with the few older men left behind. I was six when he left and almost ten when he returned. I grew up quickly. I was expected to work in the fields with the men, help in the kitchen with my mother, and not complain. When he returned, I think I resented that he could now simply step back into his role and run the vineyard. I hadn't gone to school during those war years, and now he sent me back as though I was still a child. I didn't think of myself that way. But he was right, and eventually, we formed a relationship. In college, I studied horticulture to improve the vineyard, but also literature. My mother had a love of literature and especially poetry, and we had that in common. I lived in two worlds.

"One time, my father and I took a sailing trip together. He had the same boat that my grandfather originally purchased. This one. We could now travel all over the Adriatic because Croatia was no longer communist. We went to many of the islands. My father said that when he was younger, he wanted to be something other than a field hand. He loved sailing and wanted to sail around the world. He said that he tried, but the Yugoslav Navy caught him just as he left Lastovo. He was lucky he wasn't put in prison. Anyway, this is what he told me.

And then he said that I could do anything I wanted. I did not have to be a farmer if I wanted something else for myself."

"What did you want?"

"I didn't know."

"And then your parents died."

"Yes. That is when I decided to sail around the world. My father had been the inspiration. Funny, I only made it to Italy. I mostly drank and played. I guess I was in mourning, and that's how I processed their death. But, if you want to know what my father then meant to me—his absence? I realized I had lived my life up to that point looking for his approval, and when I did get it, the approval was validating. Without him, I had no one to look up to for that approval, no one to confess the options and aspirations for my life. So, you see, I was rudderless."

We finished our lunch. Dinko stood and took the sailboat off autopilot. He turned the wheel that moved the rudder. The boat came about, switching direction and catching the wind at a different angle. He smiled. "You see? Rudderless, wandering, catching whatever breeze that happens to cross my bow."

I looked up at Dinko. I said the obvious, "I didn't have that connection to a father."

"And you never will. Like me, you grew up, internalized your own aspirations, and became your own father. In novels, it's called coming of age. You will have no need for him now."

"Then why do I still want to find him?"

"Blood is blood. We want to know where we came from so we can better understand where we want to go. I know where my father came from and where his father came from. I ultimately decided that I wanted to be part of my family's legacy and run the vineyard."

"You love running the vineyard? No more sailing around

the world?"

"The world is all here. I have traveled. What there is to see, I can also see in the vineyard soil cupped in my hands. The world is infinitely big, but it is also infinitely small. I think you can find more in life if you just stand still and truly look around and within. That is what I think."

I did not feel rooted. I had a life back in America, but it was starting to feel otherworldly. A best-selling book, though I did not feel like a best-selling author. Reed with his plans for marriage and a restaurant. Maybe Konoba Mjesec was a legacy like Dinko's vineyard. But it was a simple tavern with barely fifty seats, when I could be running a supper club in Minneapolis with five hundred.

Dinko stood behind the wheel of his family's sailboat. He looked steadfast, controlling the boat with the touch of his fingers, the sails with winches and pulleys. He looked ahead, knowing how to move with the wind and waves to his destination. I longed for that kind of clarity.

I needed to find that clarity—find it within myself, find it by myself.

Near the entrance to the cove at Zaklopatica, Dinko started the diesel engine and then took down the two sails. We glided through the channel, and then Dinko moved to set up the ropes and bumpers to back into his spot at the quay.

I saw her then—Sara, standing at the quay, looking in our direction. She smoked a cigarette, her elbow up, the filter tip never leaving her lips by more than an inch.

Dinko stepped from the stern of the boat and onto the quay with a dock line. Sara, looking at me, barely moved to get out of his way.

"You are in big trouble," she said to me.

"What?"

She put the cigarette to her lips, inhaled, and then exhaled the smoke through her nose like some terrifying dragon. "Your boyfriend is here on the island—has been staying at Nautilus Hotel since yesterday. He is asking questions. I think you are in big trouble now."

There had been little cell phone service while sailing, and then I'd barely looked at my phone over the past few days. I did now and saw the missed calls and texts.

Fuck!

I texted him. *Just arrived back. Meet you for dinner at your hotel.*

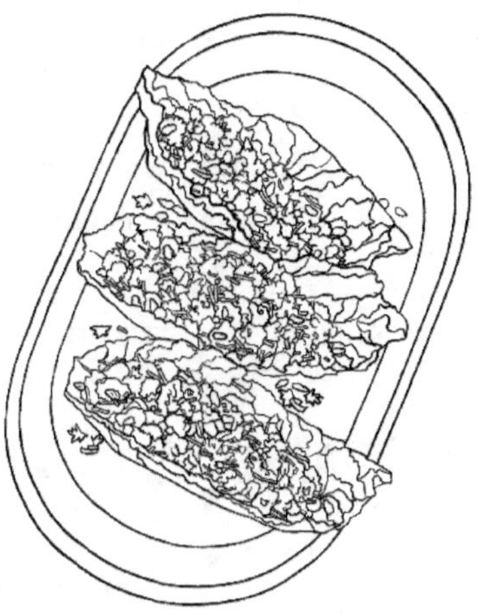

Spicy Asian Tuna Salad

Here's a spicy take on tuna salad. In the story, tuna packed in oil was used. This is correct. Don't get suckered into that spring water-packed variety; all the flavors will be washed away.

Serves 4

1 cup mayonnaise
¼ cup Sambal Oelek
¼ cup sesame oil
2 teaspoons soy sauce
2 teaspoons honey
1 teaspoon lime juice
2 teaspoons ginger powder
1½ teaspoons kosher salt
2 teaspoons sesame seeds (white or black)

½ cup craisins
½ cup chopped cilantro
½ cup shredded carrots
½ cup finely chopped green onions (green and white parts)
2 (5-ounce) cans white albacore tuna packed in oil

With a spatula, carefully mix all ingredients in a medium-sized bowl.
Serve as is, with crackers, or wrapped in large lettuce leaves.

Celeriac Salad

I drove with Sara through the hills to my grandmother's house in the early-afternoon heat with the top down, the speed frightening. I was nervous about my suddenly discovered language and reluctant just then to speak with Sara about what had happened—reluctant to speak in Cro.

She said, "I was relaxing on terrace with Sofia. I then saw Dinko's boat coming from direction of Mljet. I knew you were with him. Everyone on island knows. So, I rushed to tell you about your husband. He arrived on ferry two days ago, asking around where you live. The taxi driver, Miša, knew you lived with your grandmother, so he took him there. Miša called me because he knows we are friends."

I held on to the door handle as Sara sped through the turns. "So, everyone knows everyone's business?"

"It is small island. So, I drove over to meet your Reed. He

is very handsome, no?"

"Yes, I guess."

"Well, he is. This Reed waited for you outside the front door, sitting on stoop with his suitcase. I said I was Vesna's friend and then found spare key under flowerpot—very obvious. I let him inside. I lied and said you had gone to Vela Luka to shop."

"Thank you."

"This is no problem. You will do the same for me if need arises, I am sure. I tell him you will not be back for another day, maybe two. Reed looks around the house. It is hot inside with all the windows closed. It is also very creepy. No offense to you or your deceased grandmother, but it is like old lady house with a smell similar to perfume you buy at Pazar in Split—like soap and wet carpet."

"No offense." I wanted to laugh, but the reality of Reed in Lastovo was anything but funny.

"He asks if there is air conditioning. I say no. I don't tell him, but it is well understood in Croatia that air conditioning creates draft that is bad for health. He asks about a hotel. I tell him the best hotel on island is in Pasadur, The Nautilus. The Nautilus has air conditioning for tourists who have no concern for health."

The Yugo wouldn't start. I turned the key again but knew better than to overstrain the starter motor or drain the battery. I sat in the car and pensively waited. For what, I was uncertain. I should've known Reed would do something like that. I knew him well enough. He would've been back in Minneapolis, not knowing what I was doing so far away in Croatia. He'd be dwelling on that restaurant lease, which might determine both our fates, anxious that the opportunity might pass him by. He was an impatient man who couldn't be still. He might also think I was with another man.

Of course, there *was* another man. Dinko knew the trouble I was in, and we'd parted on the quay without an embrace or goodbye. We'd been together for three days. We had sex. But now this complication. When I left the boat, he simply said, "*Sretno ti bilo.*" Good luck to you.

I pumped the accelerator—something I remembered Dinko doing when he'd helped with the gas. I pumped it five times. I knew there was something called "flooding an engine," giving it too much gas, so I stopped at five. I crossed my fingers, holding them up to show the world I truly wanted to believe in the manufacturing capabilities of old Yugoslavia. And yet there was something else. Part of me hoped it wouldn't start, allowing me to postpone the reunion with Reed for another hour or two. I kept my fingers crossed; I knew nothing good ever came from avoidance. I turned the key once more. The starter motor engaged. The car sputtered to life.

I put the car in gear and let out the clutch before it could change its mind, or I changed mine. I drove off through the hills, chasing the sun that was making its way toward the horizon, blinding me at times.

I felt guilty. Back in Minneapolis, I'd left my relationship with Reed wide open. I did once love him, and part of me wanted to love him again—have my old life back. I knew the restaurant idea was solid, and we could make it successful. I could see myself taking the emerald ring and exchanging vows, maybe up north at the Burntside Lodge.

I was well aware of the source of that guilt. I'd had sex

with Dinko. Maybe more than that, part of me—the other part—thought I might be in love. He was gentle and honest. He knew who he was and what he wanted. And what he wanted was all there in the vineyards and in his home. Would he make room in his life to let me in? I wasn't sure. But I also knew that any decisions made about Dinko or Reed or the envisioned supper club in Minneapolis would not come from any man's dreams or assurances. The next step in my life had to come from within me.

But then, who was I? There was a time I thought I knew. Cooking, Reed, that first restaurant we owned, Burntside Lake, a successful cookbook. Now, miraculously, I'd discovered a grandmother. I found what my life might've been like if I'd never lost my mother in the explosion. Memories had come back. I recovered my lost language. I wasn't sure who I was anymore.

The night before, after the trauma of Dubrovnik, I was not in a place where I could resume the passion of the night in Ston. I was sure Dinko sensed it, and we slept apart. After finally falling asleep, after replaying the incidents of the day over and over, I had a dream. I dreamt in Cro. My mother was still alive. I was three again. I had a toy plush donkey held tight to my face. My mother said, *"Da možeš poželjeti bilo što na svijetu, što bi to bilo?"* If you could wish for anything in the world, what would that be? I replied, *"Htjela bih biti blizu."* I would want to be close.

I woke up in my cabin with those words and tried to understand what they meant. Close to whom? Close to what? I dressed and climbed the stairs to the boat's cockpit. The sun was just coming up. Dinko was still asleep, and I walked alone through the marina. I saw two people—a couple on another sailboat—moving dock lines and getting ready to motor out into the Adriatic. The man pulled in the gangplank and the woman started the diesel engine. He then went to the bow of the boat and uncleated a line. She put the boat into gear, and they slid easily away from the dock. The couple never spoke a word.

They were close.

I drove the Yugo past Radić Winery. The aunt would be preparing dinner with Mia. Dinko would be washing up after working in the vineyard. I thought they'd grill lamb with wild rosemary picked from the surrounding hills, make *blitva* with new potatoes from their kitchen garden, then maybe a pastry stuffed with a jam of wild blackberries. There'd be a closeness in their kitchen, with little spoken before they sat down to eat. I thought maybe I could be part of that family's closeness. Or, who knew, maybe find a closeness with someone I had yet to meet.

I'd come to Lastovo to find family. To be close.

The decision was there, as though I'd finally stepped into myself.

I would not go back to Minneapolis. Not now.

I had seen the newer Nautilus but never stepped inside. The hotel had been refurbished with modern double-paned windows, no doubt to hold in the AC that many American tourists insisted upon. An extended veranda was built, with a louvered roof that could be closed against rain or cold wind. Out front, additional slips were added to their private dock to accommodate the larger boats of the very rich. Two boats were there now: a sailboat slightly larger than Dinko's and the other a motor yacht with a crew member who slowly mopped its deck. All of this was right up Reed's alley.

I found him on the veranda at a table set for two. He stood when he saw me, a wide smile plastered on his face, handsome in his tight Lululemon shorts and white Polo shirt. "Surprise!"

Somehow, I expected a Croatian kiss on each cheek, but he went right for the full-mouth greeting. He tasted of wine and something else. Oysters maybe.

I almost said, "*Dobra večer.*" But what came out was, "Hey, yeah, surprise! Welcome to Lastovo."

Reed pulled out the chair for me—a real departure from the norm. I braced for whatever he had in mind, or whatever I had coming.

He said, "I understand now why you wanted to come back. I've been here since yesterday, and this place is amazing. So spectacular."

"I came back because my grandmother was ill. And then she died."

"Of course. I'm so sorry. And you'd just rediscovered each other. What a tragedy."

He reached out and put a hand over mine. I looked at the two hands on the tabletop. My own felt disconnected, as if it were a stranger's.

The waiter stopped at the table—a young man I'd never seen. Reed had a half-full glass of wine in front of him, and I ordered a glass of the house white. The waiter returned moments later with an opened bottle of Radić Grk. He poured a sample. I breathed in the familiar aroma, then took a sip. "*Vrlo dobro.*" He filled the glass and then left.

"You speak Croatian?"

"Some. It came back to me." I didn't want to explain what had happened or how the language had returned. It seemed too personal. And then I didn't want to start down a conversation path that might lead to who I was with at the time.

But then he said, "I thought you'd be on the ferry that came back from Vela Luka. I waited as everyone descended." An innocent smile on his face.

"I was actually in Dubrovnik. I sailed there." Then, maybe to deflect the next question, I said, "You should have told me you were coming."

"I think you would've told me not to, but I still want to be your husband, and I wanted to be here with you."

The waiter was back, a pad of paper and pencil in hand. He looked down at us and spoke in English, "Are you ready to order?"

I quickly scanned the menu. Listed were tourist steaks and hamburgers I knew would be close to inedible. Other items were local and possibly fresh. I chose a celeriac salad that looked promising, then the sea bass, grilled Dalmatian-style with olive oil and a hint of rosemary. I figured the sea bass, locally called *lubin*, would be fresh.

Reed knew better than to order beef and simply said, "I'll have what she's having."

We were alone again, watching each other, trying to understand motives. I knew what he wanted and figured the emerald ring and the restaurant lease were somewhere in his luggage. Then the word came to me: "manipulative." I thought, *Keep it civil, get through the evening so I can go back to the house and think.* It would not be easy.

"So, who did you sail to Dubrovnik with?"

I wasn't going to lie. "A man I've met here. I was searching for my biological father. I was told he might be in Ston. We found out that he'd once lived there but had possibly moved to Dubrovnik. It took us another day to sail down the coast. We didn't find him in Dubrovnik either."

"A friend?"

"He's a friend. His name is Dinko Radić. He offered to help. I didn't speak Croatian well, so he helped ask questions and translate."

Reed's lips curled into a forced smile. "His name is Dinko?"

I knew the name Dinko or dink had other amusing connotations in English—nitwit, jerk, nerd, or dual-income-no-kids—but I wasn't going to play into that. "Yes."

He let it drop. "Okay."

The salads came out unusually fast, a sign they weren't made to order but scooped from a large vat. It did look good, though, and I took a bite. The celeriac was cut into uneven strips but had a nice crunch. The dressing was made of mayonnaise, Dijon mustard, capers, and chopped parsley. It wasn't bad, but I could think of something better, and right then, maybe to ignore the uncomfortable conversation we were having, I walked through the recipe in my mind. The celeriac sliced into thin strips, julienned, then coated with an aioli made of olive oil, lemon, and a pinch of hot red chilis. Finally, sliced gherkins, capers, and chopped parsley.

We ate in silence for a moment.

Reed then talked about the new supper club. He'd lined up vendors for locally sourced beef and produce. He found an antique dealer to acquire much of the bric-a-brac that would go with the supper club theme. He talked to a few nature photographers who would supply the photos I wanted. All comfortable chitchat for Reed. I said little, just enough to sound engaged.

The sea bass came—one whole fish for the two of us—

on a platter surrounded by sautéed zucchini and *blitva*. I then had a thought to elevate the native dish. I'd boil the potatoes but give them a loose, chunky mash, then sauté the chopped chard with garlic, heavy cream, salt, and pepper. The combination of the chunky mash and cream would smooth out the rough dish and give it a rich texture. It then occurred to me that my *blitva* wasn't new or original but had been written on a card in my grandmother's recipe box—the box of recipes that had now been handed down to me.

I said it then, "I'm not going back with you."

He looked stunned. "Is it this guy Dinko? Are you in love?"

"I might be. He might be. I don't know. But it's more than that."

"What? I don't understand why you'd want to toss away everything you've accomplished and have yet to accomplish. You really want to stay on this isolated island?"

He wouldn't understand; Reed was driven. I was driven also, but maybe that was the problem. I'd worked my ass off in restaurants, opening my own with Reed, only to see it shuttered. And for what? My passion was food. I loved to create new dishes for myself and for those who cared. Once you crossed some imaginary line and served heaps of mass-produced food to strangers, that passion for food became something else. I guessed a passion for making money. Of course, I needed money, but the cookbook was doing well, and I had some savings. I would do something in Lastovo but on my own terms.

And then Dinko. There was something special between us. What had he said? "I think I've met someone I'd like to love."

I said to Reed, "I'm sorry. I need to figure out who I am,

and I can't do that in Minneapolis."

"I thought you wanted to be together with me again—those days just weeks ago on Burntside Lake."

"There'll always be a part of me that still loves you. But that part is not who I am anymore. What happened on Burntside was a mistake—my mistake. Now I need to stay here and explore this new life I've discovered. You can go ahead without me. Go do the restaurant. Sign the lease on your own. Use my name and cookbook to promote the place. You can do this all by yourself. You might even find someone who shares your vision."

Whatever optimism or enthusiasm he had was now gone from his face. He wiped a tear from his cheek. The platter with the cooked sea bass—dead fish with its head and cloudy eye—lay between us, barely touched. The *blitva* looked like a tired, half-cooked casserole, and the zucchini sat in a puddle of olive oil, wilted and translucent.

He said, "I'll always love you."

I stood up then and reached over to touch his shoulder. He stood, and we embraced. What else was there to say?

"Goodbye."

Reed tightened his embrace. One last time. "Goodbye. I love you."

I left then and didn't look back. I felt his eyes track my movement, maybe wondering what had happened and gone wrong. In the end, it wasn't him; it was me. Later, for sure, he'd spin it that way. Whatever was needed to get through each day.

The door of the Yugo creaked when pulled open. I sat in the driver's seat, trying to calm myself.

But then panic set in. If the car wouldn't start, I'd be back in the hotel and restaurant, trying to find a taxi. I'd be back at the table with Reed. I pumped the accelerator exactly five times. I held up my left hand, fingers crossed, then turned the ignition. The car came to life.

I quickly put the car into gear and released the clutch before the Yugo could change its mind.

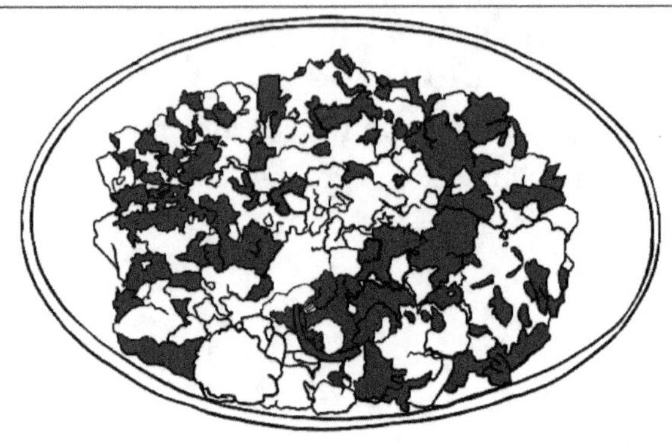

Špinat with Cream

Blitva is ubiquitous in Croatia, and its ingredients, Swiss chard and potatoes, are grown in back gardens everywhere. Although Croats seem to never tire of the dish, some might. This recipe, using spinach (*špinat*), is loosely based on Vesna's grandmother's. It's a winner and one that you might never get sick of.

Serves 4 to 6

2 pounds red potatoes
24 ounces spinach, washed, drained, stems removed
½ cup salted butter
2 tablespoons all-purpose flour (sifted)
1 cup cream
Kosher salt and pepper
2 (or more) cloves garlic, crushed

Peel and quarter the red potatoes. Boil for 15 minutes, or until tender. Drain. Mash lightly with a fork. They should still be in pea-sized chunks after mashing.

Clean the spinach and boil it in a separate pot of water until the leaves are limp. Drain.

Make the sauce. Melt the butter in a saucepan over low heat. Add the flour and stir to combine. Do not let the butter or flour turn brown.

Add the cooked spinach and stir to combine.

Combine the potatoes and spinach mixture, then gradually add the cream.

Add the crushed garlic cloves, then add salt and pepper to taste.

Roasted Pag Lamb

From The Oleander Cottage, I walked the mile or so to the church cemetery. I picked wildflowers along the way—the ones that grew in the tall grass beside the road. The weather was August hot, and I wore a floppy woven hat against the rising sun. I passed the tennis courts where I'd run into Mia that second time. Only one of the courts was being used—a couple I had yet to meet who owned a house nearby and spent every summer on the island. I'd heard they were from England but, like me, had roots in Croatia from before the war. I would meet them someday.

At the graves, I emptied the three earthenware vases of the flowers I'd put there the week before. I refilled them with the wildflowers in my hand. A watering can was always left near the church building, and I filled it from an outside spigot, then filled the vases.

All three stones were identical gray marble, with names

and dates written in a serif font. A few memories of my mother had come back to me since that day when I found the bakery's ruins, remembered the explosion, and recovered the language that had been lost for over thirty years. One memory was simple. I was walking through the streets of Dubrovnik's old town. I held onto my mother's hand. We passed the fountain with the funny faces and took drinks from the water that gushed from the sculpted lips. It was hot, and the water was cool and refreshing. We walked on to the Pile Gate.

Then, beneath the high-arched entrance that penetrated the walls, we met a man. He crouched there in his camouflage uniform and cap, smiling with his arms wide. He said my name, "Vesna," and I knew I was supposed to run and hug him. But I did not know the man and stood behind my mother's skirts, wary. Later, all three of us walked through the town to a shop that sold sweets. He bought me a small dish of raspberry gelato. I sat on a low stone wall and ate my gelato while they talked. Afterward, we all walked back to the gate, but this time, I walked between them, holding each of my parents' hands. Of course, the man was my father, whom I thought I'd never met.

My own grave. That person had died and come back to life. I thought that if the parish priest knew, he'd have the gravestone removed. For a while, I thought it should be removed. But now I liked the idea that I'd been given a new life and that it was okay to mourn the life I had before the explosion. I could mourn the life I was denied. And in a way, I could also mourn the life I'd left in America. I felt like a new person, and what I once had in Minnesota now seemed like a dream.

I kept walking, now up through the Lastovo old town with its empty homes and crumbling walls. There were some signs of life, and not just the feral cats that inhabited the ruins. Sara, who finally sold me The Oleander Cottage, had been working to locate some of the actual deedholders and convince them to sell. Now, her real estate signs seemed to be on every alleyway. One sign was in front of my grandmother's house. I could never have lived there in the small rooms sheltering the secrets and ghosts of my past.

I opened the back door to the *konoba* and began to prepare a dinner for Sara, Sofia, Dinko, Mia, and Dijana. I'd been going through my family's recipes, making changes that would make them my own, and preparing the dishes. I'd called my editor and suggested the book. "What do you think about Croatian food?"

"We don't care if it's dog food. Write anything—it will sell."

We had a good laugh at that. I went on to tell her about the family tavern, the recipe box, my grandmother, and how I ended up in America and then back in Croatia.

My editor said, "Write that."

"The story?"

"Yes, write the story, write the recipes, write all of it."

It made so much sense. My readers would want to know why I went from writing about Midwestern food to writing about Croatian food. My readers would want to know my story.

I'd been writing for a month now and testing the recipes on my friends. It had become a regular Thursday night party with the Thursday Gourmet. Tonight, I would make roasted Pag lamb, *paška janjetina*. A switch from seafood.

The Pag lamb I'd ordered came from a wholesaler in Split, who'd dutifully put it on a ferry. Pag lamb was considered the finest in the Mediterranean, and I was anxious to see what the fuss was all about. The cut was a whole leg that I planned to put on a spit and roast over an olivewood fire in the restaurant's stone *roštilj*. I slathered the leg with a blended mixture of olive oil, garlic, rosemary, Ston salt, and coarse-ground pepper. I would pair the meat with the *blitva* recipe that included cream—the one taken directly from the family's recipe card. As a starter, I'd serve roasted fresh anchovies, simply cooked with olive oil and salt over the same fire. I'd sauté zucchini with tomatoes and onions, all from The Oleander Cottage garden—the garden that Stjepan continued to work, with me by his side. I loved that I could now grow much of the produce I ate. It seemed a cyclical connection that appealed to my new sense of belonging.

That evening, we all sat at a table outside. Dinko had brought his white Grk to serve with the anchovies and then the red Plavac Mali for the lamb. Sara wore a light cotton sundress, while Sofia looked alluring in tight knee-length yoga pants and a white tank top. They looked happy together, exchanging looks and casually touching. Dinko sat between his aunt Dijana and Mia. He wore a jaunty straw fedora like something Frank Sinatra would have worn, his aunt looked sophisticated in a black cocktail dress, and Mia just looked cute in her pigtails.

All the adults were drinking the white wine when I came to the table with the anchovies. I took photos of the food before allowing them to dig in. While they talked amongst themselves, I was back inside turning the spit that held the leg of lamb. I used a thermometer to check its doneness. Perfect. I had Dinko help me remove the spit and had him carve, while I finished preparing the *blitva* and vegetables. I served the main course on a wood platter that, with its scuffs, nicks, scratches, and baked-in fats, had been in the tavern for over a hundred years. Again, I took photos before letting them serve themselves. Family style.

Toward the end of the meal, Sara said, "It is a shame you do not open the restaurant to the public. Such good food, you would make a good living." She spoke in English for the sake of Sofia, who had not yet learned Cro.

A good living was what I already had. Also, I'd received a fifty-thousand-dollar advance for the Croatian novel/cookbook. "I like cooking for you guys. Restaurants are so much work. Though I do miss the excitement."

"Maybe just part-time?"

A part-time restaurant. Was there such a thing?

It was Sofia who then spoke, her Italian accent turning the rough English into a lyrical language. "You know, there is a place in the Caribbean on the island of Tortola. I have been there many times, working on the private yachts. The place is called Trellis Bay. It is very beautiful. The bay is shallow, maybe five meters, and you can see the sea turtles and rays swimming below. There is only one restaurant on the beach, and it is only open one day a month, and only on the night of a full moon. They cook a whole pig on the beach, then a seafood boil, and, you know, rice and beans. People make reservations months in advance just to be part of this dinner. But it is also a celebration. In ancient times, women used to ovulate on the full moon. This is proven history. It has to do with the moon, the only source of light at night. It is so much better sex when you can see. No?"

I didn't know how to respond, no or yes. But it was true. Now, when I had sex with Dinko, I wanted to see his body. I wanted to see my body intermingle with his. Daytime sex was the best. I said, "No," and then, "Yes." The others laughed.

Sofia continued, "So, here is what I am saying. This place is already Konoba Mjesec, Moon Tavern. Now, you open only every full moon. This is the time for sex and fertility. Yes?"

We looked at each other, letting Sofia's idea sink in. It was a fantastic idea. I could do my cookbook and continue writing, catch up on all the lost time I'd spent working fourteen to sixteen hours each day in kitchens, but still get the joy and excitement that came from serving a community of people who loved good food.

Sara looked at Sofia, so proud of her thoughts and creativity. They all knew the idea was a good one.

Dinko was the first to say it, and he said it in Cro, "*Dobra ideja.*"

Mia said, "I will be your hostess."

Sofia said, "I will wait on the tables. This is what I did on a luxury yacht."

Dinko said, "We'll serve my wines, of course."

I was captivated by the idea. Once a month, I'd open the doors and serve the food I would write about. Maybe on the full moon in Lastovo, there could be a whole celebration. It could start with the winery. "Only if Dinko opens his doors on that day and allows guests to see his vineyard and experience his wines."

Dijana, who'd been quiet up to that point, spoke up: "*Bilo je i vrijeme.*"

Sara translated for Sofia. "It's about time."

The days started to cool by September. Dinko would be working long hours to harvest the grapes and begin to make that year's wine. He still had some free time, and on a warm Saturday, he and Mia drove to The Oleander Cottage, parked, and together we began our walk to the beach and the *konoba* that served the famous lobster pasta. The same folk band would be there, and the owners of the *konoba*—the brothers— wanted Mia to sing "Marijana" again.

I walked easily, now used to long hikes through the hills. It was what I liked to do—walk to the restaurant I owned, walk sometimes all the way to Zaklopatica where I could now order fresh fish in advance, the fisherman coming back with what I wanted, the fishmonger woman setting it aside and giving me a call.

On August 18, I'd had the first full-moon dinner where I served grilled whole *škarpina*, my celeriac salad, *blitva*, roasted vegetables, and wild boar from a ranch on the island of Hvar. The boar came skinned and cleaned, and, while it roasted on the spit in the ample stone *roštilj*, I basted it with olive oil infused with the rosemary and sage that grew wild everywhere on the island.

The advertising for the first full moon dinner was only word of mouth, but Sara had connections with some of the tourist groups, and all the reservations were taken. Dinko had done as promised and opened the vineyard for the guests where they tasted his best Plavac Mali and Grk. From there, a chartered bus ferried them to Konoba Mjesec for dinner. The dinner had gone well, with Dijana helping in the kitchen, Mia seating guests, Dinko presiding over the wine, and Sofia and Sara serving the food. Moreover, I had enjoyed working in the old family kitchen. I found cooking for others less of a drill and more of an exciting experience that reminded me of why I had initially loved working in restaurants.

We'd had the first rains since the dry months of summer, and now the hills were alive with verdant wild herbs, pines, cedars, and olive trees bursting with fruit. For a time, Mia walked between us, holding hands with both her *tata* and me. Then she led the way as the path turned steep. She wanted to see the bunker again, so we veered off the path and hiked up through dense foliage to the concrete structure. Like the time before, Mia warned us about black widow spiders. Then, inside, once our eyes adjusted to the dim light, I could see the same cannon and the rusted bunk frame below the painting of the woman. It seemed some of the paint had chipped away from the concrete wall, but the image was still there. Mia had said before that the painting was of her mother. It was Dinko who knew the real origin. He spoke in Cro.

"The soldier's name was Goran. He had once worked for my father before being drafted into Tito's Yugoslav army. He was stationed on the island and spent two years living in the barracks and taking his guard duty here in the bunker where he looked out over the Adriatic for the Western invasion that never came. He met a girl from Zagreb during her summer vacation. Her name was Lucija. Her father was a general in the army. Even though it was not allowed, she would come up to the bunker and talk with Goran. They fell in love. He painted that picture to remind him of the love he felt for the girl.

"Lucija had a boyfriend back in Zagreb who was a colonel. The colonel was a protégé of the general, so when Lucija revealed her love for Goran to her father, there was hell to pay. Soon after, Goran was transferred to someplace remote in what is now Montenegro. That was all before the war. As you can see, she was very beautiful."

Mia did not bring up that she once thought the painting was of her mother. She asked, "So what happened to Goran and Lucija?"

"The colonel died in the war. Goran came back and again worked in my father's vineyard. I worked with him for years until I went to college. He never found another woman to love. He'd always only loved Lucija. And Lucija had always loved Goran, and she never found another man. It was many years later that she took a vacation to the island she had once visited every summer. And it was a miracle that one day she hiked up to see the painting, and Goran was there, sitting below her image. He had waited all that time, grieving his lost love. But then love came back to find him.

"They are still here today. Mia, you have met her. Lucija once served the food at Konoba Amfora. Goran has his own farm now where he grows vegetables. They lived happily ever after."

Mia took her father's hand and then mine. She joined our two hands together. She said, "Like the two of you."

I smiled. "Perhaps."

Mia quipped, "No *perhaps*. Definitely."

We walked on to the beach.

At the *konoba*, all three of us were greeted like family by one brother, Karlo, with a shoulder embrace and a kiss on each cheek. He remembered me from before. He said in English, "The famous chef and cookbook writer from America." I blushed at the compliment. The other brother, Arlo, came out from the kitchen, and the embraces and kisses continued.

Mia, Dinko, and I were seated at a table near the stage where the instruments were set up. I remembered that Vanja played the pear-shaped *lijerica*, and Barba, whose name meant "uncle," played the mandoline-like *tamburica*. Of course, we ordered the lobster pasta, the brothers' specialty.

The *konoba* was filled with thirty or more people, all crowded at the few tables, all ordering wine and pasta. The brothers worked furiously to keep up, and steaming platters of lobster pasta crossed the kitchen window and were delivered to the waiting customers. The atmosphere was lively, and I just took in the hustle and bustle of the thriving tavern.

Then, applause as the two musicians came on stage. Vanja stepped up to the microphone, while Barba, with a slight limp, walked to a chair, sat, and picked up the *tamburica*. Vanja said nothing but just drew her bow slowly along the neck of the *lijerica*, creating the moody tone I recognized from before. She then stamped her foot three times, and the two moved into a flurry of notes that made a wall of sound that rivaled an entire orchestra. I almost jumped up to dance.

Toward the end of their first set, Vanja brought Mia on stage. She nervously smiled as she looked out over the crowd, who waited apprehensively for what would happen next. Vanja moved the microphone down to Mia's height and then stepped to the side. Mia stepped up and brushed a wisp of hair from her face. Then Vanja and the man played.

Mia sang "Marijana." Her voice was high-pitched, soft, and clear. The audience remained captivated as she sang. I now knew the meaning of all the words and thought they were simple and beautiful—an ode to a small girl and the love she shared. The way it was sung brought me almost to tears. I looked at Dinko, a proud father, who I could tell was also near tears.

Mia sang one last song, a more upbeat Croatian folk song that snapped the audience out of their pensive mood. She bowed at the end, and the audience stood to clap and shout for more. Vanja leaned over to the microphone and said, *"Nakon pauze."* After the break.

Mia walked quickly back to the table, avoiding eye contact with the audience, who were still clapping.

Vanja and Barba left the small stage.

It was then I saw something in the *tamburica* musician's

face that felt familiar. It was the way his lips moved as he looked at the audience and smiled—a slight lift on one side of his mouth, teeth just barely showing. Then, the eyes, the color of amber or gold. I'd seen the same smile and eyes before. In my dream. In the mirror.

He limped as he walked away from his stool. I could see the ankle of the one bad leg, a sock stretched around something thin, mechanical. A prosthesis.

I asked, loud enough for the whole restaurant to hear, "Josip?"

The man turned.

Stephanie Hansen & Kurt Johnson
Burntside Lake, Ely, Minnesota

Recipe Index

ABOUT THE AUTHORS

Stephanie and Kurt have sailed the islands off the Croatian coast many times. Their favorite island is Lastovo, with its sixteenth-century town, quaint taverns, and turquoise waters. *The Moon Tavern* is a collaboration that draws on the married couple's shared experiences there and elsewhere. Stephanie is now a best-selling cookbook writer and host of her own national network cooking show, *Taste Buds with Stephanie*. Kurt is the author of four novels, including the Minnesota Book Award winner, *The Barrens*. Together, they teamed up to write the first in a continuing series of culinary love stories set in exotic locations.

www.ingramcontent.com/pod-product-compliance
Lightning Source LLC
Chambersburg PA
CBHW071448140726
47997CB00005B/1631